SOUL SEEKING

R. MICHAEL CARD

Gryphon's Gate Publishing

Soul Seeking

Copyright © 2018 R. Michael Card

Published by Gryphon's Gate Publishing

Cover Art by Darko Tomic

Gryphon's Gate Publishing

550 King St. N.

PO Box 42088 Conestoga

Waterloo, ON

N2L 6K5

Ebook ISBN 978-1-988115-60-3

Print ISBN 978-1-988115-59-7

It was high summer, and yesterday Beremus—the weeklong Feast of Berem, god of celebrations, drink, and dreams—had begun.

The common room of the Ox and Axe was crammed with boisterous revelers toasting the festive god. The three serving girls had their hands full with the large and rowdy crowd, yet they still managed to slide through the throng with ease, as well as somehow understand the shouted requests thrown at them. The three large hearths were all roaring, roasting ox and venison and stewing root vegetables in a thick gravy. The scent of the food was nearly overwhelmed, however, by the stench of sweat from the mass of people, even with all of the windows thrown open to let in light and whatever meager breeze might dispel the oppressive heat within the single room. Overall, it was an assault on the senses.

Jais was glad to leave the noise and heat of the common room and step outdoors once again. His family's small wagon sat just outside the rear door of the Ox and Axe laden with fresh stag: cleaned, skinned, and ready for cooking. His uncle's hunting would help to feed the village today, and Jais had one carcass left to deliver.

He hefted it from the wagon bed and reentered the tavern to hand it over to the beefy tavern keeper, a man named Rolm. Rolm accepted the meat and handed Jais the full payment for the load, two silver coins, allowing him to escape the inn for good this time. The tavern keeper would easily make that money back by the end of the day, but it wasn't an unfair price. The exchange had been worked out long ago by Rolm and Jais' uncle. Which was good because Jais didn't want to stick around. Having lived secluded from the rest of the village most of his life, he wasn't fond of large crowds. He didn't mind the people so much as the noise and close quarters. It wasn't how he preferred to meet with others. So he was halfway to freedom when a large form staggered over toward him shouting his name.

"Jais! There you are. Stay and help me win a bet." Ale-infused breath washed over him as Erid, a large young man, grabbed him by the shoulder.

"Not today, Erid," Jais said pulling away. He turned and was nearly out the door when another voice stopped him.

"Oh, Jais, you have to prove him wrong. He's a big lout, and he knows he can't beat you. He keeps saying he can finally best you at grip-wrestling." The voice was one he knew well, Alnia, the miller's daughter. His heart constricted in a very familiar way as it did every time he talked to her. He turned back and couldn't help but smile when he saw her. She was flushed with drink, like everyone else, but on her it only served to accentuate her beauty. Auburn hair tumbled in waves to frame a round-cheeked face with sparkling green eyes and full lips, and the dress she wore had a tie around her torso under her bosom, accentuating the curves. Jais' heart quickened.

He would stay for her. Just long enough to prove Erid wrong. Then he'd return home to his chores.

"Of course I will," he said and joined them, pressing through the crowd to their table.

The village of Klasten's Green was not large, and there were only a handful of others around Jais' age. They were all crowded around one small table. Ulf, a farmer's son and the youngest of their troop. Kina and Lisa, sisters, only a couple years apart in age and daughters of the single merchant in town. Danz, Alnia's older brother who stood to inherit the mill in a few years. Hansa and Rom, sister and brother and farmers as well, then Erid, the smith's son, and of course, Alnia and himself.

Yana and Esrine were present as well, two of the three tavern keeper's daughters, but they were far too busy to join the group today, and most other days as well.

Erid pushed Danz out of a chair and sat, putting his elbow on the table, hand raised. Jais sat opposite him and did the same with his arm, clasping the other man's sweaty palm. Grip-wrestling was not a new activity for him and Erid, and it was far better than the brawling they'd done as kids. Erid was the largest boy in town standing a full head and shoulders above Jais and built thick and strong from hours a day in the smithy. Jais was not a tall man, but as broad as Erid across the shoulders just on a more compact frame, and he'd always been stronger.

Alnia called out, "Begin!" and the two began to struggle against each other, trying to push the other's hand down to the table. Erid had grown stronger with each passing year, but still Jais knew how this fight was going to end. Already their arms were tilting in Jais' favor, and with a little more effort he finished the contest, touching Erid's knuckles to the wood.

Erid huffed, red in the face, open-mouthed, eyes alight with a kindling rage. The man had always had a short temper. It was one of the reasons Jais wasn't fond of him.

He thought to try to diminish the man's anger with some advice. "Don't drink so much next time," Jais said. "It only weakens you."

Erid shot to his feet. "How can you best me every time? No one else in the village, not even my father, can beat me!" Spittle flew from the young man's lips. There was murder in his eyes. He wasn't accustomed to losing... to anyone else.

Well, his attempt at advice hadn't done much.

Jais stood, relaxed and composed, ready for a fight, knowing he'd beaten Erid, in every encounter for the last eight years. "I'm leaving. If you want me to put you on your back outdoors, join me." He shrugged. "I work as hard as you, and I don't drink half as much. Maybe that's why."

Erid sputtered and fumed, but didn't approach or follow Jais as he left. These grip-wrestling matches had been their sole contest ever since the third time Jais had laid Erid down in a brawl. The other man knew he wouldn't win. Jais was quicker and stronger, at least now he was, but he'd taken a fair share of beatings as a boy before he'd gotten to that stage.

He was out at his wagon when he heard the steps behind him. He turned expecting Erid, but found Alnia instead. She ran to him, a great grin on her face. Throwing herself into his embrace, she wrapped her arms around his neck, her ale-soaked lips finding his. The rest of her body pressed against him as well, stunning him. This was the most forward she'd ever been. Usually she was much more reserved. Perhaps the ale had incited this.

She dropped away from her tiptoes and stepped back. Her eyes were gleaming, a surprised grin on her face. Perhaps the act had shocked even her. After a moment, she pursed her lips, seeming uncertain. Then she spoke softly, "Erid will cool down eventually. He knows he can't beat you. He just can't stop himself from trying."

Jais nodded, uncertain what to say and a little caught up in the previous moment.

"Will you be back to town soon?" she asked with a bite of her bottom lip. "Tonight? For... the revels?"

The revels...

There would be a big bonfire in the village square, and all of the unmarried men and women in the small village would show up to dally and explore their options.

A part of Jais wanted to return, a large part, but he knew his aunt and uncle would not approve.

"I'll see if I can slip away," he said and meant it.

"Good." Her grin widened as she bobbed on her feet then turned and ran back into the tavern.

Jais caught his breath, swallowed hard, and hoped, by all the graces of Asavi, he'd be with Alnia tonight.

JAIS GUIDED THE SMALL WAGON UP INTO THE HILLS, AWAY FROM Klasten's Green. His home wasn't so much on the edge of the village as well away from it.

Aunt Sarelle always said their distance from the village was for two good reasons. The first was to be closer to the forest, which provided their livelihood. The second was that they were not truly accepted in the village. This was due to aunt Sarelle being a healer, a very good one, perhaps too good. Her work was looked at with an awkward mix of fear and gratitude. The villagers liked having someone who could treat wounds and diseases, especially as effectively as she did, but they still thought it too close to magic for their liking. It didn't help that the woman was almost fifty years old but didn't look a day past thirty, still in the bloom of life and beauty. They tolerated her because of her ability, as much as they feared her for the same reason.

As a child, Jais hadn't liked being so far away from any potential playmates. He'd snuck away now and then to find friends, but that had had mixed results. Yes, he'd found friends: Alnia, Kina & Lisa, Hansa and Rom. But he'd also found... rivals. Ulf, Danz, and Erid had had their own little group and didn't much like him showing up. They'd teased him, called his aunt a witch, said she and his uncle did all manner of things with demons out in the woods. That had led to fights. He didn't win at first, but he'd learned quickly what worked and what didn't. By the time he was twelve he could knock down all three of those boys. At first they teased him about that too—from a distance—but a few more bruises and the boys eventually dropped their taunts. By the time he was fifteen, they were all—some more than others—friends, the fights dismissed as childish tomfoolery.

The cabin he shared with his aunt and uncle was on the highest of a series of hills to the east of the village, next to a vast forest. The trail from the village up to his home followed a burbling stream, which ran out of the forest near their cabin.

As he crested the last of those hills and his home came in sight, Jais stopped the wagon and looked back. The only sound was the nearby brook and the wash of wind in the long grasses. He could see the village nestled on the plains below and another set of hills rolling off to the south-west. To the north and west the land stretched away, mostly flat, dotted with farms. The Eresvan River, wide and flat, curved around the western side of the village. It ran out of the mountains to the north—fed by several tributaries, like the stream he stood next to—past Klasten's Green, and south to the capital of their small kingdom, Erestin. From there the river emptied into some distant sea, the name of which Jais didn't know.

He sighed.

There was so much of this world he knew nothing about. His aunt and uncle occasionally talked of faraway places. They'd traveled a lot in their youth before... before his parents had died and he'd come to be with them. Not long after that, they'd settled here, in the distant north, far from anything interesting. Erestin wasn't even a large or important kingdom from what he'd gleaned, overhearing his foster parent's conversations. It was a small, quiet land in the vast northern expanse, one of several small northern kingdoms or city-states.

His gaze drifted back to the village.

His hope to be back after the sun had set grew stronger. He'd been fond of Alnia for years now. She was the prettiest girl in town, at least in his opinion. She could marry any man she wanted. These last few years she'd flirted with him a little, but today she'd been so... open. He had to meet up with her tonight, but his aunt would most likely not allow it, and he hadn't disobeyed her in years. But tonight...

With another sigh he turned and urged the small shaggy-haired mountain pony onward to the only home he'd ever known.

The cabin was a single room with a hearth on either end. One side held a table with wooden chairs and a work area which served as the main living area of the house. This hearth was mainly used for cooking. Shelves covered the walls with everything they would need for a season. The other side had two beds, a larger one for his aunt and uncle and a smaller one for him. The hearth at that end was lit mainly in the evenings or when it was cold outside, to keep them warm as they slept. His aunt had put in a curtain between the beds, made of old patchwork blankets, supposedly for privacy, but it did little. Outside the cabin stood another building attached to the back of the house, half of which served as a stable for their single pony and the other half a smokehouse where his uncle cured and dried meat for storage over the winter.

Jais stabled the pony which they'd affectionately named Stout, giving him some grain and brushing him down. He'd left the wagon out in the open beside the house, since there was little concern for thieves out this far from the village, and started to unload the barrels of salt he'd purchased with some of the earnings from the venison, rolling them to the smokehouse for storage before he went inside.

The sun was waning, falling toward the western hills as he finished storing the salt barrels and came indoors to the dim, candle-and-fire-lit cabin. His aunt was there. His uncle was not, probably still out hunting. Jais tossed the remainder of the coins from his excursion into a wooden bowl near the door, and they clanked on the other silvers and copper already there. He sat at the table as his aunt prepared a meal, hoping that perhaps this once, she might let him go to the High Summer Revels, but uncertain if he should ask or simply try to sneak out.

"How was the trip? Were you able to pick up salt?" his aunt asked as she chopped parsnips into chunks. Because of their distance from 'the rest of the world' their local merchant had to make long trips to bring back even the most basic of items. Salt was in high demand and not always available, but because of their need to preserve meat, they needed large amounts of it.

"Yes, three barrels, but it used up nearly all of the two nobles Rolm gave me. The price is going up it seems."

She sighed. "We'll have enough to get through the winter, that's the main thing. If we can't preserve more for the rest of the village, that will limit our winter's income, but we'll survive."

He nodded.

She stopped her chopping and looked at him. He wasn't looking directly at her, staring as he was at the table, lost in his thoughts, but he could sense that her gaze was intent.

"What's troubling you?"

He grimaced. He should have known. She had a way of seeing into his thoughts. Though if he was honest, it wasn't a surprise as he too always seemed to know what others were feeling.

"I'd like to go..." He sighed. "Alnia asked me to go to the revels tonight."

"The miller's girl?"

"Yes."

"She is pretty. She'll make a fine wife for some young

man." And with that Jais' hopes fell. He knew that tone. He could almost speak her next words before she said them, "But not for you. You will stay away from the revels." The tone wasn't harsh or commanding, it was calm and certain, almost sad.

Even as his next thoughts bloomed, she said with a slightly more stern tone, "And I'll know if you try to sneak out. I always do, don't I?"

She did. It was infuriating.

He gritted his teeth, knowing better than to ask why he couldn't go. The response, as it always was, would be a vague reminder that they were somehow different from everyone else down in the village.

The door opened. Jais heard his uncle's gruff voice behind him. "More kroll tracks through the forest. I'm thinking there'll be another attack soon, perhaps tonight."

Jais spun in his chair. "We should warn the village!"

His uncle nodded, shaggy hair and unkempt beard crowding his face. "Run down as quick as you can. Perhaps they'll call off the revels. We don't need that nonsense anyway."

Jais was up in a flash. "I will." He bolted around his uncle and out the door.

Even as he ran he heard his uncle shouting behind him, "Hurry back. I've got two bucks here to clean and skin, and there's still wood to chop."

Jais wasn't the fastest man in the village, but could run for miles before tiring, his strong, sturdy legs made for endurance, if not speed. So he was only a little winded when he burst through the door of the tavern. The drunken crowd was still here, despite the sun being well on its way to the western horizon.

He shouted as loud as he could, trying to make his voice boom over the cacophony of the crowd.

"Krolls near the village!"

It took him three times before the crowd fell silent. When they did a dread hush fell over the entire common room. Jais felt compelled to say more.

"My uncle found tracks in the forest. He thinks there may be an attack soon, maybe tonight."

A large man easily pushed his way forward. Jais grimaced. The man was Damick the smith, Erid's father, and he was the same size as his son with a similar temperament.

"Has he seen the beasts themselves or just tracks?"

"Just tracks, but—"

"Then how can he be so certain there'll be an attack today? Maybe they were heading up to Ostin Vale or down to Eresford." There were grumbles around the room. No one wanted to leave their celebration to risk fighting one of the beasts. It didn't help that Damick was the head of the town's militia and should have been the one marshalling them.

"Are you willing to take that risk? Are you willing to put all of your families, your children, at risk?" Jais' tone was hard. He knew these people toiled for long hours during the year and deserved a celebration, but they were also always afraid of a fight. He should have brought his bow or an axe with him, then he could have seen if they would follow him. But he knew the answer to that clear enough. He was the 'strange-healer-woman's boy,' and there were few in this town who seemed to see past that.

No one moved or spoke. No one stepped forward.

"Fine," he said disgusted. "If you all want to have a great party and die when an attack comes, that's your choice." He threw the door to the tavern closed and stalked off.

He was half-way to the edge of the village down the main road when he heard soft, running footfalls behind him. "Jais, wait." It was Alnia.

For her, probably only for her, he'd stop. He tried to suppress his bitter brooding.

"They're just scared," she said as she reached him, a hand on his back. "I don't know how you can be so fearless. You're out there on your own."

"We wouldn't be if this town—" He bit off the rest of his harsh words. He hadn't turned to her yet. He didn't want her to see his anger.

"They're fools to not see how helpful your aunt is. How... strong... you are." Her breath was warm on the back of his neck. He felt her expectant hesitation.

When he turned to her, she was biting her lip, still flushed with drink, and breathing a little hard from her run, or perhaps for other reasons.

"How certain is your uncle?" The voice from behind Alnia startled him, and he drew his eyes away from her to the speaker. It was Samuar Miller, Alnia's father.

"Of seeing tracks? He'd never mistake such a thing. There's nothing in the forest like a kroll. He didn't say exactly where they were heading, but he seemed fairly certain there would be an attack soon."

The miller grimaced. He too was rosy-cheeked with drink, but he seemed to be keeping a level head. After a moment, he nodded. "I'll make sure we have some men on watch tonight, and—" His gaze flicked from Jais to his daughter with a faint smile. "I'll cancel the revels. There will be many other nights for such things." As the miller he was an influential man in the town and would be able to sway the others.

Good.

"Thank you." He need not have thanked the man, he was doing nothing for Jais directly, but he had listened and that was a lot.

"Now come along 'Nia," Samuar said gruffly.

"I'll be along in a moment, father."

The man grunted, dissatisfied, and threw a stern look at Jais before leaving. The message was clear: 'she's not for you'.

As soon as her father's back was turned, Alnia was next to Jais again, her lips on his, this kiss much longer and deeper than the last. By the time they separated even Jais was feeling flushed and a little drunk.

Alnia whispered, close to his ear, "I hope that will last you until the revels, whenever they'll be." Then she was off after her father, and Jais was left standing in the street a little overwhelmed.

THE SUN HAD SET BY THE TIME HE'D RETURNED TO THE CABIN near the woods, but there would still be light for a while, and he still had chores to do. His uncle was nearly done with the cleaning and skinning of his catch so Jais went to work on the wood. He could split a log with a single blow, and it didn't take him long to finish. Every few days he or his uncle would fell a tree and chop it up in segments, smaller and smaller until it was adequately sized for their hearths. This was the last of a tree felled several days ago.

By the time Jais had stacked the wood near the house, it was near dark. Hot and sweating, he removed his clothes for a quick, cold, dip in the brook, cleaning himself and his sodden clothes before he went in for dinner.

As he entered he heard his uncle saying, "—far too often.

This is the fourth time in three weeks the krolls have come around. I don't think these are isolated events."

"I thought krolls were solitary creatures," Jais said. "I didn't think they hunted in groups."

His uncle shrugged as he chewed a mouthful of stew.

Jais sat at the table, accepted a steaming bowl from his aunt, and began eating.

"No one knows much of the beasts, other than that they're stronger than a bear and only seem out to kill and destroy. As much as they might have the rough form of a man, they are little more than animals, and savage ones at that." His uncle took another bite of stew. "No one knows why they do what they do, and every time someone has tried to communicate with them it's gone... badly."

That was the extent of what Jais knew as well. There had been three previous attacks recently with each escalating in aggression. The first time they had only raided a farmer's barn and taken the livestock. The second time they had hit an outlying farm and the family there had been taken. The third time a farmer had seen them coming and tried to flee. In his haste, he'd lit his barn on fire by accident. The beasts had stayed away from the blaze, allowing the farmer and his family to escape. Everyone in the village thought they were safe, that the attacks wouldn't get closer or wouldn't come to them specifically, but it sure seemed like these beasts were intent on something in this village.

"Should we hunt them?" Jais asked.

His uncle nearly choked on his stew. He shot a glance toward his wife. Something significant passed between them that Jais couldn't decipher.

Aunt Sarelle sighed, and his uncle turned to him. "You've never seen a kroll, so let me enlighten you. The short ones are eight feet tall, and they have more muscles on them than you and that smith boy combined. Their skin is as tough as hardened leather armor, and they carry clubs, which might as well be small trees. They're not smart, but they're cunning, like a wolf. They know how to hunt like any predator. You can track them easily enough, but they'll smell you coming a mile off and be ready when you get there. I doubt our arrows would do much more than annoy them. You'd need to fill one so full of arrows it looked like a porcupine to slow it down. You can fight one, if you have to, if your life is on the line, but no sane man would go looking for that sort of trouble."

"Have you ever fought one?" Jais was hanging on every word, morbidly fascinated.

"Gods no! But I've seen one being fought once. Three knights on horseback had one surrounded. They had lances, swords, and shields and were covered in heavy armor. They killed it, but only one of them survived."

"That's not true," his aunt said softly. Jais looked over at her. "One was as close to death as I've ever seen a man, but I healed him. He lived, even if he was missing an arm."

His uncle grumbled. "I was trying to scare some sense into the boy."

"I think he gets the point," his aunt said. "Don't you Jaistheric?" She'd used his full name. This was obviously serious.

He nodded.

There was little other discussion of such things for the remainder of the meal.

When Jais went to bed that night his thoughts were crowded and too busy for him to fall asleep quickly. Part of him was caught up, lingering in that blissful moment when Alnia had kissed him, and thinking of the... *pleasant* things that might happen if he did make it out to the next revels.

The rest of his mind was a dark mystery of lumbering shapes, with tree trunks for clubs, fighting knights. He wondered if he might be able to hunt one or even fight one. He was the strongest man in the village. How terrible could these things be?

2

CAERWYN WAITED IN THE DARK, HUNTING.

It was a warm night, and there was a humidity in the air which clung to her, making her sweat a little, even though she remained quite still.

The north was not what she had expected. Being from the far south, desert lands, she'd been certain the north would be cold all the time, but this heat rivaled that of some days in her homeland.

She hoped the heat wouldn't keep the animals from coming out this night.

Not many people could hunt with her skill in the depths of night's dark embrace, but then not many people had mystical energies running through their veins, dragon's blood. It had taken her some time to come to grips with the idea that she was the descendant of dragons, but in some ways, she had always known. She'd always been different, stronger than other girls to the point where she was as strong or stronger than most men. Her speed and skill in combat had come partly from years of training, but even her surrogate father had said she'd picked things up surprisingly quick, as if she had an innate talent. There were other abilities as well, her quick healing, understanding any language she heard—then instinctively knowing how to speak it back in return—and of course, her amazing senses, including... night vision.

A wild hen came pecking at seeds and grasses in the clearing she was watching. In silence, she loaded a rounded stone into her sling, clasped the release thong, and began whipping it around. It was an inelegant weapon, but it was the first she'd learned to use. Her real father had taught it to her before he'd been killed.

Several quick rotations, and she released the stone. It hit true. Some people were quite surprised with how accurate you could be with a sling, but she'd been practicing for over thirty years. She ran, silently, from the brush into the clearing, and drew her knife. She plucked up the small bird and removed its head, in case it had survived the blow and was only stunned. Then headed back to camp with the body. She and Barami would have a succulent feast tonight.

It wasn't a long walk back through the forest to where they had stopped for the night. As she emerged from the brush, she saw her tall companion start and reach for his weapon, a great hand-and-a-half sword, which some called a bastard sword, lying next to him. His hand hovered over the hilt for a moment before he pulled it away.

"You're far too quiet, Caer. One of these days you'll surprise me, and I'll lop your head off." His tone was light, playful, which was odd for him. Barami was a stoic man, most would probably call him cold, but only those who didn't know him. Those same people might say he was well past his prime for a warrior. But that was another misconception. He was just past his fortieth year, but he was still strong and able. He knew how to survive, how to win. Every morning he'd work through a calisthenics routine, including sword practice, so he was able to keep muscle on that tall frame of his. She'd known him for a long time. Long enough to see gray filter into the tight-curls of his receding black hair... at least before he'd shaved it all off and switched to a clean, bald head. His skin was darker than hers, a deep, solid brown in contrast to her dark bronze. His face nearly always wore a flat, unimpressed look, eyes stoic, with a tight line between his full dark lips.

She laughed. "You'd have to hit me first, which you haven't yet done when we're sparring."

He shook his head and sighed.

She tossed him the bird. "Clean that up, will you, and put it over the fire. This heat is starting to get to me. I'm going to wash up a little in the river." She rummaged through her pack and pulled out a second set of clothes.

He nodded, and she could feel his eyes on her as she left again.

It was her turn to sigh. The poor fool. She shouldn't have put the image of her bathing into his head.

When would he learn she'd never feel for him as he did for her? Not that he'd ever said anything explicitly to her, but she was keen enough to pick it up. She was certain there was more to his blood oath to stay with her than the fact that she'd saved his life once... and several times since then. There was a way he gazed at her when he thought she wasn't looking, a certain forlorn caring look. She didn't mind, and she didn't care. She admired Barami for his skill and strength, but she didn't want any attachments. She was ever practical, and 'love' was one of the least practical things she could imagine.

Despite the fact that she was on her way to find a mate in this remote northern land.

But that was how she thought of it: mating, nothing more.

She wanted a child, not a husband. She hoped that whoever she found would understand there would be no emotional involvement. In many ways Barami would make an ideal mate, except for his feelings for her. He was certainly seasoned enough as a warrior. A child with him would be strong and capable. But she was looking for something quite specific in her mating companion... dragon's blood.

She didn't know a lot about the dragon-blooded, or drahksani as they were known. She only recently found out she was one. Before that, she'd read a little about them from her foster-father's library. Little was known of how they came to be, but their name suggested they were somehow the descendants of dragons, or otherwise possessed dragon's blood, which gave them their powers. What she had read was mostly stories of their deeds, good and ill. Some had used their powers to help the world and became heroes, but some had done quite the opposite. And it was because of those drahksani with evil intent that her kind was so rare. They'd been hunted down in something called the Great Purge. Her birth parents had died toward the end of that dark period.

And now she felt a drive to help restore her kind.

A little over a year ago she'd been expelled from what had been her home for nearly thirty years. She'd lost everything. She could still recall the look in her foster father's eyes as he'd sent her away. He hadn't wanted to, but there had been no choice. His people would not allow a drahksani in their midst. So, she'd lost a second family, as well as her position as general in her father's armies. And so had gone her purpose and meaning in life. She'd needed a new purpose. Having been a warrior most of her life, she first thought to become a mercenary... but that held little meaning for her, fighting for money. She'd needed something that called to her soul.

She'd decided what she really wanted was to bring new life into this world and help to bring back her kind from the brink of extinction. That was why she sought another drahksan with which to mate. That was also why she was in the northlands now.

She didn't know if it was a trait of all drahksani or just her own ability—she really had no clue what other drahksani could do—but she could sense others with dragon's blood— at least that's what she hoped it was. She'd been following a feeling, a call to something deep within her being, for several weeks now, leading her north. She assumed it was another drahksan, that someone up here had a strong blood line that pulled her to them.

She was close now.

She guessed she was only a day or two away. It wasn't as if the call was getting stronger, but she was able to pin-point the direction much more accurately than she had when she'd started.

As she stood on the banks of the river she and Barami had been following north for some time, she looked out over the dark waters. Her target was almost directly north-east of her, given the positions of the stars. The last village they'd passed through had also told them there was a village probably around the same location called Klasten's Green. She suspected that's where she'd find who she sought.

She removed her weapons, the sword at her hip and the sling in its pouch, and set her spear to lean against a tree. She wasn't concerned about leaving her weapons on shore. The sword and sling were replaceable, and her spear... it was special. She could call it to her hand as she wished. She had a shield she used as well, but it was back at the camp with Barami.

She undressed and washed her clothes, hoping to get out most of the sweat and odor. Then she waded into the river. The rising moon glistened off the soft rolling dark waves. The river was chilly, despite it being high summer. These waters probably came from the distant snow-capped mountains she'd seen to the north, but that was okay. The cold helped to cut the heat of the air around her.

When the water reached her hips, she dove in and came up pushing her hair out of her face. She'd tried to keep her hair short for a long time as a youth, keeping it out of her face during combat, but had found the constant need to cut it tiring. It was easier to keep it a little longer, shoulder-length and tie it back or braid it. That kept it out of the way and was far easier to cut when she wished.

She ducked under again and scrubbed at her hair under the water for a time before surfacing again. She hadn't brought soap with her so she couldn't do much more, but it felt good to be out of the heat.

That thought made her laugh as she made her way back toward shore. She should be used to such warmth. She'd lived for thirty years in the south, where winters were muggy and rainy, and summers far hotter than this. But that was a dry heat, sucking the moisture out of a person. This northern climate, with its wet and heavy warmth, felt like a southern winter. She was still amazed it was like this so far north, but then there was a lot about this world she didn't know.

She dressed in her dry clothes and clasped her sword-belt around her waist along with the pouches that hung from it. She picked up Davlas, her spear, and returned to camp with her still wet set of clothes draped over an arm. Even before she reached the clearing, she could smell the roasting fowl.

Barami may not have been her ideal mate, but he was a rather perfect travelling companion. He could cook, knew how to handle himself in a fight, and mostly kept to himself.

She hung her clothes to dry on branches which arched over the fire, then sat across from him.

He said nothing. She was fine with that.

They ate in silence until she said, "We're getting close. Another day or two at most I think."

He nodded with a grunt. He knew well enough why they had made the long trek up here.

Caerwyn just hoped that it wasn't in vain. If this feeling, this call, did mean there was a drahksan here, she didn't know if it was a man. That was the concern that had plagued her this entire trip. To come all this way only to find a woman would do her no good.

Though, at least she'd be able to find out more about her kind. She knew so little beyond that most humans distained, envied, or despised drahksani. It generally wasn't healthy to let others know what she was.

Barami knew, of course, and it had not changed his dedication to her. That was why, even if she would never consider him as a mate, he was her one and only friend.

The next day Caerwyn and Barami emerged from the forest and began climbing into rolling hills. The river was to their left, running through a canyon it must have carved through these hills long ago, and the sun was rising in the east over more forest which sprawled over much of these hills.

Caerwyn suspected that the village they sought would be on the river. So they hiked down into the canyon and followed that.

They came over the crest of a hill around mid-morning and below, after a few more descending hills, lay a small village. But what called to her wasn't coming from there. She could tell now it was coming from a bit more to her right, east and north. Her eyes were keen, and she scanned the hills in that direction.

"There," she said, pointing.

"I don't have magic sight like you do," Barami said, his rich, deep baritone rolling over the words in his faint Kigasi accent. "All I see is a forest."

"There's a cabin near the woods. The person we seek is there." After a moment she added, "And it might be best not to refer to anything I can do as 'magical'."

He grunted, and they continued on.

Her pace was quick, and being tall for a woman she made good time, her long legs eating up the hillsides. Barami was a head taller than her and easily kept up.

They reached the cabin as the sun was nearing its crest high in the summer's sky. From the far side of the cabin came the noise of someone chopping wood, and they skirted a wide circle around the house to see who it was.

Caerwyn could tell immediately he was a drahksan. The call came directly from the shirtless man working away at a large pile of logs. But there was something she'd never expected... another drahksan was here, in the cabin. Her excitement grew. Perhaps she'd even have a choice. Unless this was a couple, already married, then the woman might not take kindly to Caerwyn trying to mate with her man.

She'd have to approach this carefully.

"Stay quiet," she told Barami, "I need to ferret out some information."

He grunted. Of course he'd stay quiet, it wasn't like he was talkative to begin with.

She approached the man chopping wood.

"Good day!" she called out.

The man was short... or was he? Though not tall, he was perhaps average height, but seemed short because of his great girth. He was exceptionally well built, arms and back thick with muscle. He stuck his axe in the chopping block and turned to her. The expression on his face was one of shock and surprise. He had bright blue eyes set in a friendly, round face framed by a shaggy mop of thick, unkempt brown hair which looked like it had been hacked at with a knife in a vain attempt to keep it out of his eyes and face. He smiled, and it was a pleasant thing on his wide lips. His chest and shoulders were just as heavily muscled as the rest of him. He would certainly make a decent mate, though he seemed a little young, his face looked more a boy's than a man's. The body was definitely that of a man.

She knew from her own experience that drahksani aged slower than humans. She was near to forty but looked like she was in her mid-twenties. So perhaps this 'boy' was a man after all.

"Good day?" he said, definitely confused. "If you're travelers you won't find much here, the village is down there." He pointed out over the hills.

"Tell me, boy, do you have a brother back in that cabin?"

He did look a little young to be married. She hoped perhaps he had an older brother she might talk to.

He tilted his head, his expression growing more confused. "No. Just my aunt and uncle." He took a step back his hand hanging close to the handle of the axe. It only occurred to her then that—with all their weapons—she and Barami must look a bit... dangerous. Perhaps the boy thought them to be bandits.

His answer had shed some light on the situation. If the other drahksan she was sensing was either of the aunt or uncle, then chances are they wouldn't be a viable option. Which left the young man in front of her.

"We mean you no harm," she said, letting her spear drop from her hand to the ground. She put her arms out wide at her sides, palms open and took a few more steps toward him. Barami didn't follow her. Good. "We're travelers, but we're looking for someone specific." She had to laugh, realizing that what she was about to say would sound somewhat crazy to this boy. "We're looking for you. Well, *I'm* looking for you."

"Me?" His eyes darted from her to Barami, and he did grab that axe now. "Why?"

She plucked out her short sword. He tensed, but then she dropped it to the ground. It landed standing on its blade, slicing into the ground. "I'm no danger to you." Another laugh escaped her at the thought of what she wanted. "In fact, you may find me quite the opposite."

His muscles eased as a quizzical look appeared on this face. Yet she noted that his hand hadn't left the haft of the axe.

She needed to just tell him why she was here, but for some reason the right words were hard to find. Well, no, actually the words were simple... 'I want to mate with you', but something about that didn't seem right. She'd always been blunt, straight forward, but this situation seemed different from any attack plan she'd made as a general. She would have to use tact. That wasn't a strong suit for her.

She took a few more steps then stopped.

What could she say?

She didn't know enough about drahksani. Could he sense her as she sensed him? It would make things a lot easier if he did. Did he even know what he was? Presumably the blood-relation within the cabin, the other one with dragon's blood would have told him by this point in this life, but Caerwyn just didn't know.

Perhaps that was a place to start. "Have you ever heard of the drahksani?"

Two voices shouted through the heavy midday air before he could respond. Her keen ears picked out both, despite the overlap. One was a light feminine voice from behind her saying, "Jais. Come quick!" The other was a more mature female voice off to Caerwyn's right. It was stern in its tone, "You there, get away from my nephew!"

She backed off a couple of paces. This put her next to her dropped sword, just in case there was about to be trouble.

She looked to her right, at an approaching woman... who had dragon's blood. She knew it instantly, even if the 'call' within her hadn't told her just that. It was the look of the woman. She looked young still. If she'd been human then perhaps she'd be in her late twenties. It was the eyes that gave her away as drahksan. Caerwyn knew eyes like that. It was the same 'old' eyes in a youthful face she saw whenever she looked in a looking glass or still pond. The eyes of someone who had seen far too much for the age they appeared to be. This had to be the boy's aunt.

There was also a threat in those eyes, like that of a mother bear. Yet when the aunt saw Caerwyn's own eyes she stopped in her tracks.

"Oh," she said softly. "You're... I thought... oh."

Someone raced past Caerwyn. She looked to see a young woman who ran to the boy she'd been talking to and flung herself upon him. A moment later the girl was talking to him in a string of words so fast they were hard to understand.

"Jais, you were right. There was an attack last night. The kroll attacked Ulf's father's farm. Ulf and his family are fine. It only went for their livestock. The village is in a stir, and they're putting together a party to hunt the thing down. You need to come and help. My father and brother are going and so are Ulf and Erid. They don't know a thing about hunting. They're going to get themselves killed!"

Too much was happening at once. Caerwyn's mind was quick and was taking it all in, but she feared her window to make her approach to this boy had closed. She swore softly.

"Jais isn't going anywhere." This from the aunt. She drew closer to her nephew and the girl. "None of you should be going up against a kroll. This is insanity."

"I agree," Caerwyn found herself saying. She approached the group as well. "I've fought them before, and it's nothing for untrained farmers and villagers to attempt."

"I know that," the girl snapped. "But tell that to the stubborn men down there!" She pointed down toward the village as she looked at Caerwyn. Something changed in the girl's eyes then, as if she only now saw Caerwyn for who she was. "Who are you?"

"Yes," the aunt chimed in. "Who are you?"

"My name is Caerwyn Afg—" She cut herself off. That other name didn't mean anything anymore. She stuttered for a moment. "Of... of... well of nowhere at the moment. Just Caerwyn I guess."

"That's a western name. Domaran I believe. You are a long way from home." This from the aunt whose keen eyes looked her over intently, then moved to Barami. "And you have a southern companion who is even farther from home. What do you want here?"

It seemed far too late to make her proposal now.

Everyone was looking at her. A silence hung in the midday air, which seemed oppressive with the beating sun and heavy, wet heat. She drew in a breath and pulled a soft leather glove from her belt, slipping it on.

As she spoke she retrieved a large stone from a pouch at her belt. The stone was the size of her palm, smooth and flat, and roughly triangular in shape, with well-rounded corners. Her words were directed to the aunt, but she kept an eye on the boy, Jais, to see how they might affect him, if he understood.

"You know what I am, what we are, yes?"

The aunt glanced at the girl, then gave a faint nod. The boy looked confused. Interesting. It seemed the boy didn't know what he was.

Caerwyn tossed the stone at him in a non-threatening high arch.

Yet it was the aunt who caught it, grabbing it out of the air, wincing as she did. They all winced... because as soon as the stone touched the flesh of the aunt's palm it blazed forth with a pure white light.

The aunt dropped the stone almost instantly.

"What was that?" This from the village girl.

The boy bent to pick up the stone. His aunt put a restraining hand on his shoulder. "Don't!"

The boy paused mid-bend.

"Pick it up," Caerwyn said. Her tone was soft, easy, but she'd led men into battle many times and knew how to still make it commanding.

The aunt stepped toward her, fire in her eyes. "Why are you doing this? What do you want?" she asked, the pitch of her voice rising with every word.

It seemed petty now, but Caerwyn needed to know. "I need to know if he's full blood or not." The words were vague as she was aware of the presence of that village girl who probably knew nothing of drahksani except what rumors had been spread about them long ago.

"Why?" the aunt said. She seemed rattled. "If you are not a hunter... Now is not the time for this!"

"Aunt Sarelle, what's going on?" Jais asked. Without the aunt there to stop him he crouched next to the stone and touched it. A white light blazed forth for the instant his finger was in contact.

Pure blooded.

The aunt must have seen the flash of light around her and winced. When she spoke next it was with a vehemence, a poorly suppressed rage bubbling up within her words. She stalked forward toward Caerwyn, hand extended. "You. Need. To. Leave!"

Caerwyn felt a pressure on her chest... no *in* her chest, constricting. The pressure turned to a sharp pain on the left side, her heart, and a shortness of breath. The aunt was doing something to her. She backed off, she had to. The pain was too much.

It cut off suddenly as Jais called out. "Aunt Sarelle, what is all this? What's going on?"

The other woman had tears in her eyes as her hand fell to her side.

Caerwyn gasped, as breath returned to her, and fell to one knee.

"There isn't time for this. Jais, you need to come down to the village. They may already be gone!" This from the girl.

Too much was happening all at once, Caerwyn needed to take control of this situation. She stood, despite trembling legs.

"Stop!" This was the next level of her 'command' voice, a crisp shout. It was clear to her now she'd have to put her quest to find a mate on hold. This village needed her help. That and she couldn't risk losing this young man to a kroll attack. She'd need him alive and well for... the other thing.

Everyone looked at her again.

"Why I'm here doesn't matter. What matters is that I am here and I can help you." She turned to the village girl. "You are right. If your family goes to fight a kroll they will most likely all perish. I know how to fight them. I've done so before. I will go with you." Then to Jais and his aunt. "When I'm done with that I'm coming back here." Pointing at the aunt she said, "You need to tell him. He should know the truth." She wanted to say more but with the girl here that was not an option. "After that we all need to talk. That... is why I'm here."

She retrieved her sword then stalked back to Barami and her spear, but turned back to them. "Are you coming, girl?"

The girl seemed surprised and torn. She obviously wanted Jais to come. Caerwyn's intervention had not been what she had expected. But the girl nodded, and with a last look to Jais, followed after Caerwyn.

"I'll be down shortly," Jais called out.

"No, you won't," his aunt said, voice hard.

Caerwyn didn't care anymore. She could hear them arguing as she followed the girl down the hill toward the village.

She cursed her hesitation. It shouldn't have been hard to tell the man she wanted to have a child with him. She'd done many more dangerous things in her life. For whatever reason, this seemed harder than anything she'd ever done before.

But she wasn't going to give up. She knew what she wanted. She just hoped the boy was willing.

3

"YOU KNOW I CAN HELP. I'M THE STRONGEST MAN THEY HAVE!"

"You'll get yourself killed. You can't go. I have to protect you. It's the entire reason your parents gave you to us in the first place!"

"What do you mean? Was I in danger as I child? What did that woman mean when she said we need to talk?" Jais' head was reeling. There were too many unanswered questions, and his aunt was not acting like her usual serene self. Something was wrong, and it seemed to revolve around that stone and the light that came from it when they touched it. It still lay on the ground at his feet. What was it? What had that light meant?

Before his aunt had arrived, that woman had asked Jais what he knew of the drahksani...

"Am I drahksani?" he asked. He didn't even know what that meant. There were vague mentioning's of the term in the village, usually with negative connotations, but he really had no idea what drahksani was.

"Don't say that word!" His aunt glanced around furiously, but there was no one there. "Even when we're alone, you should never say such a thing and definitely not where others can hear. The villagers only tentatively accept me as it is. If they knew... if they suspected anything was amiss, they'd come for me, for us."

"You?" Of course, the stone had lit up when she touched it too. "You're..." He lowered his voice to a whisper. "Drahksani?"

She sighed. When she spoke her voice was also a whisper. "Yes. I am. As are you. As were your parents. It's what got them killed." Another sigh. "And if you're going to say it, say it right. I am drahksan, *we* are drahksani. You add the 'i' for the plural."

"So I am..."

"Yes."

"And my parents... they were killed just for being drahksani? What does that even mean anyway?"

"It's in the ancient tongue. It means dragon-blooded."

"Dragon-blooded? Dragons... aren't real... are they?" That would be a rather stunning revelation. He looked down toward the village. "And whatever you have to say, say it fast. I need to go help them."

"You're not going." She was firm, but he could sense fear in her as well. She was afraid for him.

Well that wasn't going to stop him. He was afraid as well, but that strange woman was going. She didn't seem afraid in the least. He had a sense he could learn a lot from her. "I am going, and there's nothing you can do to stop me."

He saw the shift in his aunt's eyes, the fear turn to anger. "Yes, there is." She stepped toward him, raising her hand.

He stumbled back. That's what his aunt had done to the

woman, and the woman had looked like she'd been in pain. He'd never seen his aunt do anything like that before. Surely she wouldn't do... whatever it was... to him, would she?

He stepped back and felt something poke him in the back. Turning he saw it was the haft of his axe. He moved to the far side of the chopping block and pulled the axe free. He wasn't going to use it on her, he couldn't, but he had to know. "Why are you doing this? Who are you? I've never seen you like this before?" Parts of his world were crumbling around him.

Aunt Sarelle stopped, seeing the axe. She looked at her own outstretched hand, and it fell to her side. "I'm sorry, Jais. I wasn't going to... I was just going to put you to sleep, nothing painful. You can't go down there!" she said, tears coming with the last words.

He lowered the axe.

"You were...?"

Put him to sleep? She could do that? His mind latched onto memories. He'd watched her do many healings, and nearly always she gave the person something to calm them. They often fell asleep during the process. Perhaps it wasn't the draught she gave them that did it. Perhaps it had been her own touch.

His heart raced. It sunk in only then that his aunt had powers, magic, something. Was that what it meant to be a drahksan? But then that meant... he did too?

"I'm..." He couldn't say it.

The axe nearly fell to the ground as his hands went numb.

He couldn't think. Nothing made sense, or perhaps he just didn't want it to. Perhaps it made far too much sense.

He shook his head, latching on to what he knew, what

was urgent in the moment.

"I'm going to help the village." He said it softly, simply.

Sarelle tried to say something but he waved her off.

"We can talk later. I'm doing this. I don't know who you are anymore. Maybe I don't know who I am, but I know I can do this. I'm sorry."

And he left.

She didn't follow.

~

JAIS REACHED THE VILLAGE SQUARE JUST AS A CROWD WAS dispersing.

Alnia saw him and ran over. "Oh, thank all the gods you're here." Her next words were in a hushed, awed tone. "I don't know who that woman is, but she took control here quick enough. There wasn't a man here that tried to argue with her. It was amazing to watch."

Jais was sure it had been. From what little he'd seen of the woman she was certainly... assertive.

It was odd with his axe in one hand, but he pulled Alnia close with his free arm and—not caring who might be looking—kissed her. If he was going to risk death today, he'd do it with the remembrance of her lips on his, and the scent of her hair in his nose. It was a long, lingering, deep kiss, and when their lips finally parted he said, "I don't know what's going to happen out there. Pray to Suur for me."

She smiled. "I'll pray to Lansus, for victory, not just war."

Jais nodded not quite able to bring himself to grin. "Goodbye 'Nia."

"Not Goodbye, just fare well." She levered herself up to give him a quick peck.

Then he was leaving her to seek out that warrior woman. What had she called herself? Carween?

He searched the square for her. She was on the far side, looking directly at him with an odd look on her face. He'd always been good at reading people, but this expression was a bit of a mystery. Could it be envy and disappointment? That made little sense to him. There was no reason for her to be jealous of him nor disappointed, not yet anyway.

He walked over to her. "I'm coming with you."

"Did you speak with your aunt?"

"It was more of an argument... but I think I know... what that stone meant."

"You think?"

He looked away. "I don't know much at the moment. My world seems to be turned on its head, but I know I'm coming with you."

She gave him a stern look. "I see. Do you know how to use that thing?"

When he glanced back at her, he saw she was indicating his axe.

"I can fell a tree quick enough."

"A kroll isn't a tree. For one thing, it'll move out of the way."

He looked her up and down. She had a hard look. He'd never seen a true warrior before, but he imagined this is what one would look like, a weathered padded shirt under a steal breastplate with well-tended weapons. She had dark hair, tied back in a single ponytail. Her face looked young, yet at the same time, careworn. There was a scar on her cheek. It wasn't large, but it tugged at her mouth giving the sense of a roguish grin. It was the eyes, dark pools of brown that made her seem older than her youthful face suggested. Something in his mind clicked at that. His aunt looked a lot younger than she was. Also people tended to call him baby-faced. Was this an attribute of being drahksani?

He shook it off as he resumed his assessment of her. Her lips were full, nose straight. Her body told him more. Square shoulders and an easy, yet ready stance spoke of strength and speed. She carried the spear as if it was a part of her, and the sword at her hip also seemed to fit her look. This woman knew battle.

He shrugged at her questions. "Something tells me you can teach me what I need to know quick enough."

"No." Her tone was firm, final.

He was a little shocked. "What? Why? I'm stronger than any man here, probably stronger than you and—"

"There is more to fighting than strength, much more. You're not going."

He blinked. This wasn't right at all. Why was she being so harsh. He knew he could help. He lowered his voice. "But I'm like you... doesn't that mean something? I'm sure I could take a kroll... if you'd just teach me a little."

She let out a huff. She too spoke softly. "You're strong, sure, and I could train you, but it's because of what you are that I can't let you go. You're... *we're* the last of our kind and I need—" she cut herself off.

What had she been about to say?

"I can't let you get hurt. I... you... your aunt would kill me."

The darker skinned man behind her gave a curt guffaw.

Jais didn't understand any of this. Why did everyone think he was so fragile?

He shook his head backing away. "Fine. You won't train me then I'll go off on my own and find this thing. I'll prove I can fight." He wasn't afraid. He'd show them what he could do.

He turned and stalked away.

"Jais! You can't!"

Oh yes, he could.

Footfalls behind him, running, signaled someone's approach. A hand on his shoulder stopped him.

"Wait."

He turned.

The woman warrior was there. She looked concerned. She needn't have been.

He waited for her to say something, but she just stood there, on the edge of speaking for a long moment. Finally she huffed out a sigh. "Fine. You win, I'll train you.

The older warrior strode up behind her. "He'll never learn what he needs to before we find this beast."

He met the man's gaze, level, unyielding despite the other man's height and obvious battle prowess. Jais' tone was even, stoic when he spoke. "The boys of this town used to pick on me, beat me up. I learned how to fight them quick enough. They only knocked me down a few times before it was them hitting the dirt."

"If a kroll knocks you down... even once... you don't get up again," the man said just as calm.

Jais turned to the woman again. "All I need is a little training. I'll learn quick enough."

She nodded, keeping her gaze locked with his. "I believe you will." She didn't seem happy about it though.

That was it.

They left town as the bell tolled the call of midday. Jais' feelings were a mess of uncertainty and excitement. He only hoped he'd live up to his own expectations... he knew he could fight, but... he didn't want to let this woman down.

And he didn't want to die.

"HERE'S THE DEAL. YOU MANAGE TO KNOCK ME ON MY ASS just once, and I'll train you until Barami gets back, and let you come with us. If you don't... you're going back to your aunt."

They had arrived at the farm where the livestock had been killed. It was abandoned, the family fled. The kroll was nowhere to be seen, so Barami, as the tall dark-skinned man was called, had gone to track the thing and see if it was still close.

It seemed Caerwyn, a name Jais still had trouble pronouncing correctly, had some conditions attached to this training.

He nodded. That seemed fair enough. He was fairly certain he could knock her down once.

They had no weapons. She'd asked to see what he did know of fighting, how good he was with just his fists.

He set himself, stance wide and balanced, fists up and ready.

She stood there. She'd taken off her breastplate to make the fight fairer, but even without her armor she seemed prepared. She shrugged. "Whenever you're ready."

Jais was wary.

He wasn't used to fighting someone who wasn't already

coming at him. He'd been on the defensive most of the times he'd brawled as a boy.

Suddenly he wasn't so sure he could beat her. Sure, he was strong, but he assumed she was well experienced. She had to be used to fighting men stronger than her and probably had some counter ready.

He shook his head. He'd been an idiot to think this might be easy.

He rose from his low stance.

"Giving up?" she asked.

"I don't give up." He moved in toward her slowly, carefully. She began moving as well, to the side, keeping distance between them. He got closer to her and reached out, mostly to see what she'd do. He wasn't punching. He'd hoped to push her shoulder knock her off balance, but she moved quickly, grabbing his wrist and spinning, kneeling as she did. Then he was in the air, out of control, before landing on his back with a grunt of air.

She was up and ready, moving away.

"That's one," she said as he rose.

"One? Do I have a limited number of tries at this?"

"We don't have all day. I'll give you three more."

With how easily she'd put him on his back, he was growing less and less certain of his ability to knock her down.

Last time he'd tried slow and careful. Perhaps this time he'd try all out force.

He charged at her. He'd bowl her over with the force of his attack.

Yet once again she wasn't there as his arms closed around where she had been. He saw what she was doing—despite the lightning speed with which it happened—as she side-stepped, crouched, spun, and kicked out. Her leg caught his, knocking that leg into the other. He tripped, pitching forward and tumbling to the ground.

He rose again, dusting himself off.

"That's two."

There was a hint of a smile on her face now. She knew she'd beat him. But he still had two more shots at this. He wasn't done yet.

The problem was, she was quick. Until now he'd been matching force for force with the boys of the town. He'd never fought someone with grace and agility.

But...

Something clicked in his mind. Just because he was strong didn't mean he wasn't fast as well.

He strode over to her.

He jabbed with a fist, testing, and as he'd expected she blocked his attack—or at least she tried to. He pulled his fist back, chambering his arm quickly.

She cocked her head to one side. "You do learn quick."

That he did.

"Let's see how quickly." She came at him. Two quick punches at his head were easily dodged as he wove around them, stepping back as she moved in.

Some part of him knew that whatever came next would be something new.

He was right.

She kicked, her leg snapping up at his head.

Time seemed to slow. He saw the foot heading for him and raised his hand.

He grabbed her ankle as time recoiled back to its regular pace. His arm didn't give with the force of her kick, and he knew he had her. He smiled.

Now he used his strength, even as she tried to pull her leg

free. He pulled her toward him, dropping to his knees and turning slightly, throwing her leg past him.

She followed her leg and landed in the dirt a few paces away with a huff of air.

He stood slowly.

He'd done it. He'd defeated her!

He couldn't help but grin as she got up. "A deal is a deal," he said pulling himself up to his full height, which still wasn't a match for hers. She was a good half a head taller than he was.

She eyed him. "Where'd you learn to do a throw like that?"

"Just now."

"Truly?"

He nodded.

She tilted her head. "Then perhaps you can learn to fight a kroll in an afternoon." She shrugged. "And a deal is a deal. Go get your axe."

He did, excited to finally be accepted by this strange woman. He didn't know much about her, but he respected her as a warrior. For now, that was all he needed.

He returned with his axe.

"You ready?" she asked.

He gave a nod.

"Then come at me."

He hesitated. She didn't have a weapon. Her spear leaned against the barn not far away and the sword remained sheathed.

"Aren't you going to use a weapon?" he asked.

"I have a weapon. Yours."

"You have... sorry, what?"

She just grinned. "Come at me. If it makes you feel better,

do it slowly. Hack at me as you would with that axe, nice and slow."

He shrugged.

He swung the axe as he would at a log on the chopping block, overhead, coming down at her. Surprisingly she stepped into the attack, also moving slowly. She began talking as she moved. Each movement was sure, smooth.

"Your weapon is end heavy. Not a bad thing, but it means, once you are committed to a swing it becomes hard to change direction." She reached up and grabbed the haft of his axe between where his own hands were placed. Already he could see the head would come nowhere near her, since she'd moved closer. But like she was saying, it was hard to alter his attack, even slowly, especially since she was holding the weapon as well. She was in close to him, her face mere inches from his own. He caught something, some odd look in her eyes as their gazes met.

But he probably shouldn't have been looking in her eyes.

Her free hand hit his shoulder. He wasn't sure how, but it made his arm go numb and his one hand fall off the axe. Her hand then took the place of his and, with the downward momentum of the axe and her two hands already on it, she was able to pluck it from his grip like he was a child. She spun, not quickly, but fast enough to bring the axe down then up at a slight angle such that it came up at his ribs. Even moving slowly he was taken by surprise. She stopped the blade as it brushed his clothes.

"You're dead," she said, letting the weapon fall away.

He could see the blow as it would have happened, up under his ribs deep into his chest. Yes, he would have been dead.

She handed back his axe. "With someone as untrained as

you are, I don't need a weapon. You're more a danger to yourself than your opponent."

"Oh." It was all he could think to say. After the shock wore off he could only grimace. "So how do I get better? Should I be using another weapon, like your short sword?"

"Want to try it?" She raised a brow with a hint of a smile. She seemed... sportive.

Suddenly he didn't want to try it. What made him think he'd be any better with an unfamiliar weapon?

She drew out the weapon and offered it to him hilt first.

He sighed with a shrug. He might as well see how she was going to humiliate him this time. He set his axe against the barn and took the sword. It felt a lot lighter in his hand and he didn't know what to do with his free hand.

"Go ahead, swing at me. Faster this time." Her smile and that suggestion of play was gone: all business. "Don't worry, you won't hit me."

He believed her.

He let out a huff of a breath. He aimed a slice at her shoulder with a slight downward angle. He wasn't moving at full speed, but still quicker than the last time. She, however, moved far faster. She had his wrist, then... everything spun and the breath was knocked out of him as he hit the ground in an all too familiar way.

He was on his back again, the breath blown out of him, only this time she was on top of him. She had one knee on his free arm pinning it. Her other leg was on the other side of him, bracing her. The sword, still in his hand, was at his neck. He had no power over the weapon, something about how she was holding his wrist, all twisted.

She plucked the weapon from his nerveless fingers with

her free hand and stuck it in the ground near his head. Then she leaned over him. "And what did we learn?"

Her eyes were pools of dark brown, intent on him. As much as there may have been a hint of mischief in her tone, those eyes belayed any jesting. She wanted to know what he'd learned.

He grimaced. "Not to fight you."

She cocked her head to one side in a way that was slowly becoming familiar, this time it was accompanied by a dour look. "Jais." Now she sounded like his aunt.

"Maybe if you get off me and give me time to think, I'll figure it out."

She shrugged and released him.

He was up in a moment, massaging his wrist as feeling returned to his hand.

So what had he learned? Well for a start he hadn't learned his lesson from fighting her unarmed. He knew he could be faster, not just in body, but in mind... reaction... seeing what she was doing and changing his tactics. That's the only thing that had won him that fight earlier, and he'd been too preoccupied with actually having a weapon in his hand to remember.

"I can't assume any attack is going to hit, or that any enemy is going to be where I want them to be. I need to react faster."

"Good. What else?"

He shrugged. "I've love to learn that wrist grip thing you did, but I doubt that's going to help me much fighting a kroll."

"Once we've found the beast I'll let you know how it's done. Actually, once we've found the thing and this is all over, I... I wanted to ask you—"

"I found its tracks!" Barami's voice cut her off, ringing through the farm yard as he came around the corner of the barn.

What had she been going to ask him? Whatever it was he saw her swallow the words as Barami approached.

She flashed him an insincere grin. "We'll come back to that later."

She was a strange woman. His innate sense for people... couldn't seem to read her at all. At one moment she seemed standoffish, then she seemed to be softer. She went from teacher to friend to something he couldn't identify too quickly for him to follow. It threw him a little.

He tried to shake the bewilderment off as Barami reported.

"It's odd. The tracks lead away, back east, the way it came. They were deeper, which means it got heavier... I think because it was carrying away the livestock from the farm."

"Why is that odd?" Jais asked.

Barami shook his head at the wrongness of it. "Krolls generally aren't afraid of reprisals. Once they've found a food source they stay there and gorge themselves. If anyone tries to stop it... it just kills them and keeps eating, adding them to the meal. Carrying food away to eat later... that's far from typical kroll behavior." Barami looked at Caerwyn. "I don't like this."

"You don't like anything." But Caerwyn seemed concerned as well. She asked Jais, "What's east of here?"

He shrugged. "Forest." The same large woodlands which sat next to his aunt and uncle's cottage extended down the hills for some ways.

Caerwyn glanced up at the sun. "It's well past midday." She considered something for a long moment before turning back to Barami. "Any chance this thing will come back here any time soon?"

The large man shrugged. "It's already doing things I wouldn't have predicted. I can't say."

She nodded. "It's heading away from the village for now. That's good." She shot Jais a look. "This one's not ready to face a kroll yet, but I promised him I'd bring him along."

Barami raised a brow. "He managed to put you on your back did he?"

So, the man had known what Caerwyn had been planning. She'd probably told him what she'd do. Yet there was something in the way he said it, almost as an innuendo. Jais had no idea why the man would suggest such a thing. Jais wasn't interested in Caerwyn in that way. She was attractive perhaps, in an aggressive-commanding-know-it-all sort of way, but he liked his women a little... softer. Not that he was at all experienced with women. Alnia—if they ever got to a revels—would be his first.

That thought distracted him for a moment, and when he came back to the conversation Barami was already leaving.

"What's happening?" Jais asked.

"Barami is going to track the beast... carefully!" That last was directed at the dark-skinned man's retreating form.

"As if there's any other way," came his gruff call back to them.

"And we're going to stay here and continue to train. You need... a lot more work."

As much as that was the truth it still stung.

"How long did it take you to learn to fight?" he asked.

She turned away walking over to where Jais had left his axe. "Like you, I learned quickly, but knowing how to fight and mastering it are two different things." She picked up the weapon. "I've been fighting for possibly as long as you've been alive. It's all second nature to me." Turning back to him she sized him up. It was an obvious appraisal and made him a little uncomfortable.

Before she spoke again, she looked around the farm yard. He knew why after her first few words. "You're drahk-sani, and from the looks of you, if no other abilities have appeared so far, then you were probably meant for battle like me. It will still take time, but it should come a lot easier for you than any normal man. That's why you learned to protect yourself from the boys in town so quickly."

Oddly the part that stuck in his head from that speech was...

"You've been fighting for twenty years? You can't be that old?" Certainly she didn't look that old... but then he recalled how young his aunt looked. This woman looked perhaps as old as his aunt. "How old are you?"

She raised a brow. "With our kind, age matters little. We age slower than normal people. Other than your incredible build, you look like you're no more than a boy of fifteen to me, if you were human. I won't judge you by that."

Right... never ask a woman her age. He did a little figuring on his own though. She looked to be in her mid-twenties... but then his aunt didn't look much older. Aunt Sarelle was nearly fifty. So, if Caerwyn was a little younger than that—perhaps in her early to mid forties—it would make sense that she'd been fighting for twenty years.

He shrugged. "Well I'm an open book, teach we what you can. I'm all yours for the afternoon."

She blinked at that, and the same look he hadn't been able to identify from before crossed behind her eyes. "Oh, if only." She shook her head. The look vanished. "Let's begin, shall we?" She tossed him his axe.

He caught the haft solidly.

She moved to pick up her sword. Only now, after she'd disarmed him twice did he notice how she moved, so smooth and lithe. He'd seen girls dance as if they were floating, light on their feet, but this was different, more... like a cat, flowing and purposeful. He doubted he looked anything like that when he moved.

She took some time showing him the best way to hold his axe, how to swing it and still keep it under control.

"Remember you're not chopping wood, you're chopping people. Unless they are armored, flesh is a lot... squishier. Aim for soft spots, the neck, the stomach, legs. Mostly with a weapon like this, keep it moving. Learn to flow from one attack into the next. Always remain in control, never overextend yourself."

She showed him how to move to counterbalance the movement of the axe. "You've got a lot of weight to you, all that muscle." She gave him a punch to the shoulder which stung for a moment then faded. "Use that. Keep low, with your legs spaced. Let the axe be just like an arm that can reach a little farther than your own."

The sun had set – the western sky a hazy orange as a diffused twilight settled over them – by the time Barami returned.

Caerwyn was only just finishing her lesson. Oddly, Jais had the dual sensation of feeling like his mind was full, and yet wanting to know more. He felt like he'd learned so much in such a short time, and... he liked the way she taught him, now that she was actually teaching and not throwing him on his ass. What she was showing him made sense to him, although maybe this was his drahksan nature. Maybe it had always made sense to him, and she was just... bringing that out.

He practiced on his own as Caerwyn spoke with Barami for a moment. After the overall instruction, she'd given him three basic attacks to work on. He moved through those, slow and careful, to ensure he was in control at all times, before trying it at speed, to practice what it should feel like.

"Jais!" Caerwyn called over to him.

He stopped. Sweat was soaking through his shirt, and he was starting to smell. He could use a bath.

"What did you find?" Jais asked Barami as he came over to them. He didn't like what he saw in the man's eyes. Jais was fairly certain it was fear.

"I tracked the thing back into the forest." He shook his head. "That's where I found a second set of tracks."

Caerwyn looked at Jais, perhaps to gauge his reaction. But this wasn't news to him.

"My uncle's a hunter. He said he's seen several sets of tracks. Why? Is that odd?"

"Several? That's not good." She raised a single brow again. She took a moment to process that, then said, "Sometimes krolls work together in small groups, but two individuals roaming the same territory isn't in their nature. If they're not working together then one should have killed the other by now. With any luck one will kill the other before we get to them. If not..." She pressed her lips in a grimace and shrugged. "One kroll was bad enough." When she looked at him next it was with the same intensity she'd had leaning over him earlier that day. Those dark eyes firm. "You sure you want to come with us, Jais?"

He wasn't sure. "Yes."

She grinned that same, mischievous grin and slapped him on the shoulder. "You're lying... but you're brave. I like that." But her smile was forced, and it faded quickly. "Just don't get yourself killed."

"Or either of us for that matter," Barami added.

He wouldn't... he hoped.

4

CAERWYN FOLLOWED ALONG BEHIND BARAMI, JAIS BEHIND HER. It was full dark now, and Barami was using a lantern to expose the tracks of the kroll.

She made sure to keep a sharp eye out for trouble, despite her thoughts and emotions trying to distract her. Even with her incredible night vision, she also kept a sharp ear out for any sounds in the dark forest.

Yet thoughts of Jais hovered too near to her awareness. She needed him to be safe. If he got himself killed she'd have to find some other drahksan out there, and she wasn't sure how many more of their kind there might be. She didn't want Jais here at all, but it was better than him running off on his own. The fact that he put her on her back after only three passes had been a surprise. She'd hope that deal would keep him from harm as well. That hadn't worked. She was learning not to underestimate him. He'd learned a lot in their short time training.

She was sure he was like her, a battle-ready drahksan.

Tough and strong and able to learn on the fly in combat, picking up weapons and tactics with ease. But that didn't stop her from worrying about him. Krolls were not an ideal first fight for anyone, drahksan or otherwise.

Barami stopped and knelt, examining the tracks before him.

"What is it?" she asked.

"Look here."

She peered over his shoulder and saw the tracks he was looking at. They seemed a little muddled to her.

"Here are when the tracks cross," Barami said. "They definitely are not travelling together. But... it's odd. The tracks cross enough that it would be almost impossible for each of them not to know the other was around." He looked back over his shoulder at her. "I don't like this. These are strange happenings."

She grimaced and shrugged. "There is a lot in this world we don't understand. Let's just deal with this beast or both of them, then be done with it."

"Yes, we will casually take on two krolls, not a problem." The sarcasm was thick in his voice.

"We've done some amazing things together," she said softly, with a gentle squeeze of his shoulder.

He dropped his head. "We have, yes." When he spoke next he switched to Kigasi, his native tongue, which she understood and spoke as well. "*This is crazy, Caerwyn. Why are we doing this? Just so you can bed that youngling?*"

She didn't know how to answer that. In truth the answer was a simple "yes," but that didn't seem right. What did she care if Barami was upset about her choice of a mate? What did she care if that mate was a tad on the young side? He was still a fine specimen of a man... of a drahksan. He was no boy, despite his youthful looks, and what she had said to Jais had been true. Age for drahksani was not the same as for humans. They came to maturity at roughly the same time, but drahksani remained looking young long after most humans had gray in their hair. By the time drahksani went gray, most humans were dead. It was one reason why relationships between the two races had always been strained. The drahksan member was usually left alone still in their prime, depending on when they'd come together. Not that Caerwyn was thinking of remaining with Jais after she'd been given a child.

She replied in Kigasi, "*This village needs our help. If you're so uncertain about us fighting two krolls imagine how they'd do. And once this is done, I'll get what I came for from Jais and we can move on.*"

Barami only grunted at that.

She sighed. He still had trouble with her doing this. Well, he could have all the trouble he wanted, it wouldn't affect her decision. Barami thought her impulsive. He'd told her so enough times on their way here. But she'd had a year to think about this, and she would hardly call that impulsive. It was true she didn't have to go with the first drahksan man she found, but Jais was a good fit for her. They were both warriors. It would work well.

She looked over her shoulder at the young man. His keen blue eyes gazed off into the forest. He was scanning the area around them alert for danger. That gaze turned to her, and he smiled when it did. She nodded and returned the smile. He moved on looking to other quarters.

He was handsome enough, in a youthful way, but that

didn't much affect her decision except in so far as it suggested a child with him might be handsome as well.

She did feel... something for him though. It took her a moment to identify it. When she did, a sad smile alit upon her lips. She had a student again, someone she could train and mold. Being in command, an instructor and leader of men, was something she'd missed since she'd left the south. She'd had a legion of men to command before... that had all vanished. She'd like those men too, in a joined camaraderie sort of way.

That's all it was. Nothing else.

And just like those men she would take care of him, lead him, teach him the right tactics to keep him safe and kill these beasts. She had decades of experience doing just that. She could keep him safe. Besides, he was probably a lot tougher than he looked... and he looked pretty tough.

Satisfied with herself, she found it much easier to concentrate when they moved on.

After a while Barami stopped again. He turned back to the two of them and said, "I know your kind may not need much sleep, but I do. Shall we make a camp?"

"I don't think I could sleep," Jais said from behind her. Caerwyn glanced at him and found the youth still eager and without sign of fatigue.

"It would be unwise to move on without Barami," she said.

Jais' face turned hard. "And what if those things circle around us and attack the village again tonight?"

Barami responded. "They have enough food to last them. There should be no attacks any time soon."

Jais' firm look left her and slid to Barami. "You're the one who's been saying they aren't acting like usual. So why would they now?"

Barami grunted with a shrug, then nodded.

Caerwyn looked at her old friend. She could tell he wasn't happy. The conflict within him was clear on his face: he could see Jais' point, and yet every fiber of his being told him to rest, that the krolls would be fine for one night. She knew him well enough to read that on his less-than-expressive features, even if he never said a word of it.

Another look back at Jais confirmed he wasn't going to be resting any time soon. She admired the young man's courage, but she wasn't going to let him go on his own. She too wasn't that tired.

"Barami, get some rest, I'll scout around with Jais to make sure the beasts aren't going to attack again. If anything happens we'll come get you."

Barami looked like he was going to object, but after a moment shook his head and shrugged. "Your choice." Then he blew out the lantern, turned, and found a sturdy tree to climb.

"Where's he going?" Jais asked.

"His tribe comes from a jungle, and there, as is probably the case here, most of the threats are on the ground. He'll sling his hammock somewhere up there and sleep in the branches."

"Oh." The boy looked surprised, then laughed. "There is a lot about this world I don't know," he said as she began walking again. He followed up with. "What can you tell me of our kind?"

She'd been expecting something like this. She had no idea what to say.

They were walking in the dark now, but her eyes quickly

became accustomed to the dim light and she could see her way clearly. It wasn't a perfect view, colors were muted toward grays and shadows, but she could see everything around her well enough.

Listening, she heard the songs of several night birds over the rush of wind in the trees. Kroll's weren't known for their stealth so if any were out and about, she'd probably hear them before she saw them. She dropped back to walk beside Jais.

He too was scanning the forest. There seemed no indication that the dark hindered his sight either.

"Can you see well in the dark? Better than others?"

"Yes," he said. "Always have. Is that from being drahksani?"

"I believe so. To be honest, there is a lot I still don't know about what I... what we are. But I'll tell you what I can."

He let out a breath, sounding satisfied, content.

"You've most likely heard rumors of our kind, I'm guessing. That we are some sort of abomination, unnatural, given powers no person should have?"

He made a sound of assent.

She nodded. "None of it is true. It's just a means to turn humanity against us. That's been happening for years." This much she knew from her own schooling as a child. She just hadn't known she was one back then. Luckily, her tutor, her adopted father, had been a historian and scholar and was aware of the facts of the matter in addition to the hearsay. "No one really knows how the drahksani came to be. Many assume from the name—dragon-blooded—that dragons were involved. But since there haven't been dragons in the world for hundreds if not thousands of years, there's no record of what actually happened." She sighed. "Some assume it was a mating between dragons and humans, that dragons could change shape and take beguiling forms, that they seduced young women and left them with child." She shrugged in the darkness. "That may be true for all anyone knows. What is known is that we have powers that human's don't. The range of powers from one drahksan to another can vary, though there are often some base traits. We are stronger than humans of similar build, our senses are sharper. After that powers can vary greatly. Some had great intellects and helped humans advance in science and technology. Some could heal simply by laying their hands on another, perhaps not even needing to get that close. Some—"

"Oh? I think that's what my aunt can do."

"That would make sense," Caerwyn said, thinking back to her interaction with the woman. "I would guess she has other powers as well to affect the body. She didn't touch me but it felt like someone was squeezing my heart while sitting on my chest."

"Is that what she was doing? She said she could put me to sleep by touching me."

"Again, powers over the body. Usually a drahksan's powers fall within a certain realm. Some are combat oriented, like you and I, at least I believe that's what your powers are. Have you found others at all?"

"No. I am stronger and my senses sharper, as you say, but other than that I haven't noticed much else."

"I was always much quicker and more graceful than any around me. My..." She'd been about to launch into a memory of her adopted father giving her a dance tutor and how well she'd done, but that memory only stung now. She didn't want to tell him that. "I could dance easily, and combat training came naturally. I think you might be the same."

He made a pensive sound, nothing more.

"It is said that some drahksani could manipulate the elements themselves, summoning fire or rain. Others were in tune with the earth and animals and could make crops grow or hunt like no other."

"It sounds like everything we did was to help people? Why would humans turn on us?"

She sighed. "Because some of us weren't so benevolent... and because many humans were jealous of our powers. Between those two factors it was only a matter of time before humans turned on us. Some saw what drahksani could do, for good or for ill, and didn't like that we had so much power. They grew to hate us. Over time those ranks grew and they began to spread dark rumors about our kind, that we worshiped dark gods and performed disgusting rituals. Most drahksani didn't think it would amount to much and dismissed it. Our foresight, apparently, was not that good. Eventually, more and more humans turned against us. We were spread far and wide over the world, and when the attacks against us began they were often very successful because there may have been only one or two drahksani families in a city. Easy enough to overpower if a lot of humans banded against us.

"In those locations where there were lots of our kind, wars began, us versus them. Some raged for years, which only served to increase the animosity between us. Some of our kind went into hiding then. But once the bulk of us had been dealt with, the humans trained men they called 'Dragon Hunters' to find the rest of us. Families living in secret were slaughtered."

She swallowed a lump in her throat. "That's what happened to my parents when I was young."

"How did you survive?" Jais asked, she could tell he was well caught up in the tale.

"I ran." she gave a harsh breath of a laugh then. "And I told you I was quick."

"Oh."

After a moment spent calming herself she said. "That's how we got to be where we are today. You..." She trailed off. She'd heard something. She stopped, and Jais did as well.

"What is...?" he asked, voice hushed.

He must be hearing it too.

It was a distant crunching of underbrush. Something very large was moving through the forest, something that didn't care if it was heard, which didn't tend to be most animals.

She glanced at Jais as he looked at her. In the dim light of only stars and under a canopy of trees it was near to complete darkness, but his eyes gleamed, seeming to soak up any and all possible light, like a cat's. She assumed hers looked the same to him.

He pointed and took a step in that direction, but she put a hand on his shoulder to stop him. Thick muscles bunched and tensed under the fabric of his shirt.

"Wait," she whispered. She didn't want to make any noise, but he needed to be warned. "We should get Barami."

"Let him sleep." His quiet words were full of bravado, but she could hear the fear in his voice. He was forcing it. "We don't even know it's a kroll yet."

That was true enough. She couldn't imagine any forest animal, no matter how large, making that much noise, but they should confirm it was a kroll or Barami would be upset for being woken for nothing.

She nodded, and they moved into some thicker growth, picking their way through the underbrush. Their movement was slower now. They had been following a fairly wide game trail through the forest, able to move faster, but now, with twigs and seedling trees, bushes and brush, they had to move carefully.

She was impressed. He could move with near silence through the thick forest. He seemed as at home in the forest as she was. She wasn't sure how he'd learned his skill or if it came naturally. For her, necessity had been her teacher, living on her own as a wildling in the forest and jungles of the west for three years as a child.

She'd been eight when her parents had been killed by the Dragon Hunter. Even now the violent images of the event were locked away in her memory, not to be recalled. Only flashes came to her when she thought of that time, fire, blood, and screaming. What she did recall, vividly, was the time afterward. She'd been living off the land, avoiding any other human soul.

Luckily her father had already taught her to use her sling well enough that she could hunt. She'd learned how to make fire and cook her kills. By a brutal series of trial and elimination she'd learned which plants were good and which would make her sick, but mostly she'd learned to stalk the forest like a panther, silent and deadly.

They were closing in on whatever was crashing through the forest.

The sound ahead of them stopped. Jais paused as well. He tilted his head, listening. She did as well. There was a different sort of crunching sound, the wet snapping of something chomping through bone. She felt an involuntary shiver course down her spine. If this wasn't a kroll it was something that could eat another creature. Nothing to be trifled with.

Jais crept ahead.

A little farther on, Jais stopped and pointed.

She moved closer to him, to see through the brush around them. Pressed to his back, she could feel his hard muscles tense and bunch. He smelled of sweat and earth. It wasn't the most pleasant of scents, but it suited him. She was tall enough to look over his shoulder and down his arm... and there it was.

A kroll certain enough. The gray-green skin wasn't really discernible in the darkness, but the lumpy, uneven quality of the flesh was. Like humans and all other species, no two krolls were alike. They varied greatly in appearance. Whatever tortured mind had created these beasts chose to make them disfigured and misshapen. Some might have a third arm, perhaps fully functional, perhaps only shriveled and vestigial, perhaps only a stump. Others had a second head, usually lifeless, mostly no more than a great lump which tilted their actual head to one side. They were mountains of muscle, but how it was proportioned on the body was wild and odd. Usually there were great mounds on the shoulders and upper body, to the points that they possessed no discernible neck, only a head pushed forward by great, uneven piles of muscle.

This one had great powerful legs, muscles piled on his thighs and upper calves. It sat in a crouch as it ate what looked to be the remains of a deer. Its waist seemed far too thin for something so large, expanding upward to a broad, wide chest. Greater amounts of muscles were piled on its left side, tilting its bulbous, bald head to the right. Its left shoulder was twice as far from its head as the right. The right arm was still as thick around as one of Jais' well muscled legs, the left was a monstrosity of muscle, longer and larger, with an oversized hand, which was holding the entire remaining deer carcass like it was a child's toy. The head was large with great lumps all over and no visible ears, which was deceiving as they often had incredible hearing. It wasn't a pleasant sight.

Pressed against Jais as she was, she felt his shudder of revulsion and heard his heavy swallow. Only now did he fully understand what he was going up against. Even crouching the beast was taller than he was, standing it would tower over them both by several feet.

He turned his head back to her. Where she was, leaning close over his shoulder, this brought their faces to within inches. He whispered, hot breath on her cheek.

"How do we kill it?"

"We don't. Not yet, let's get Barami."

Jais grimaced and rolled his eyes. "It doesn't look *that* bad." More bravado masking his fear.

She shook her head. "Don't be rash. We'll need all the help we can get."

He sighed and nodded.

In the ensuing moment of silence, she heard... nothing, not the crunching of bones from the moment before. The forest was still. That wasn't a good sign.

The kroll roared.

She cursed. Despite their whispers, the kroll had heard them.

"Get ready," she said, and a moment later her shield was out and her spear in her hand. She moved to one side. "Let's not stay in front of it. Move to the side, flank it, keep behind trees if you can!" No need to whisper now.

Jais nodded as he raised his axe. He jogged off to her right.

Gods, that axe seemed like such a small weapon now. But

there was no time to worry about such things. She prayed to Lansus that he'd live through this...

She hoped she'd live through it as well.

The kroll roared again. It was heading for her, not Jais.

Good.

Also, not so good...

5

JAIS CHARGED THE BEAST FROM THE SIDE AS IT BORE DOWN ON Caerwyn.

His heart raced, beating so hard he thought it might burst from his chest. He held his breath, though Caerwyn had told him this afternoon he shouldn't when fighting. His body was covered in sweat, partly from the warm, muggy night, mostly from fear. He kept repeating *you can do this*, to himself in his head.

He wasn't certain what power propelled his legs forward. Only that he couldn't let Caerwyn down. He was terrified of the kroll before him, but the thought of disappointing his newly acquired tutor, for some reason, pricked him even more, helping him overcome his fear and act.

The beast roared and stopped its charge through the forest. Its head reared back, and Jais could see a spear protruding from an eye.

He reached it all the quicker now and yelled a wordless cry as he swung with all his momentum and might. He leveled a great sideways chop at the narrow midsection of the beast, as if it were an ironwood he wished to fell with one pass.

The blade sunk into flesh, cutting deep... but not all the way. It hit bone and stopped, ringing up Jais' arm so hard he let the haft of the axe go as a reflex action.

As it turned out, that was a fortuitous thing.

The kroll screamed again and spun around. His axe would have been ripped from his hands if he hadn't already released it. Luckily he was on its right side, which was its smaller arm. He knew some attack would be heading his way and simply dove away from the thing to escape it. He felt a rush of air at his back, some wild swing of the beast's arm perhaps, then he was rolling to his feet.

He heard a wordless war cry, Caerwyn charging in, and was surprised to see no weapon in her hand. Then at the last moment, she shouted something, he couldn't make out the word. Where there had been nothing before, now her spear was in her hand as she lunged forward, plunging it into the kroll's chest so hard the beast actually lifted from the ground for a moment.

It fell backward, and he heard the crack of wood as his axe-haft was crushed behind the thing.

Jais cursed. That was his uncle's best axe.

Also he was now weaponless.

He watched as Caerwyn relentlessly followed up her attack. Drawing out her spear, she leapt atop the thing as it tried to rise, knocking it back down. She slammed her weapon down into its other eye. Apparently even that wouldn't kill it. With another feral scream it swatted her off its chest with its massive left arm. Caerwyn went flying through the air, crashing into the forest somewhere to Jais' left.

Jais bolted after Caerwyn. He found her lying in a heap, clothes torn and bloody. She was alive, surprisingly. She tried to get up, but winced.

"That's a broken rib," she said as he knelt beside her. Oddly the next thing she said was, "Davlas!" and miraculously her spear appeared in her hand.

He was too stunned to say anything about that but had to ask, "Are you well?" It seemed like a stupid question. She'd already mentioned a broken rib.

A roar from behind them, and the relentless smash and crack of brush and trees gave swift reminder of their foe not so far away.

Jais looked to see the thing trying to rise, but it seemed well injured. It was also probably blind. It flailed about, smashing anything within reach.

"What should I do?" he asked turning back to Caerwyn. For now at least the kroll wasn't getting any closer to them.

She winced as she tried to move and after that kept still. "Krolls heal. If we leave it as it is, it will regenerate given time. Run back to Barami, fetch him, and he'll finish it."

Jais didn't know why she kept assuming he couldn't do such things. "We don't need Barami. I can finish it." He reached for her sword.

Her hand caught his, and despite her injuries her grip was still strong.

"Jais... no."

"Why?"

"I... we can't risk—"

A great single snap from behind him, too close, cut off her words and cause him to look back. The kroll was standing, if hunched. The snap had been a tree it had leaned against and broken. It was sniffing the air and took a tentative step toward them.

He wanted to swear to some god, but the fear of the creature hearing him gripped Jais. He turned back to Caerwyn leaning in close, whispering barely a breath in her ear.

"It's too late. It'll find you if you stay here. I won't leave you. What do I do?"

Her breath was hot on his ear with her response. The words were slow, reluctant. "Take this, finish it. If you call its name, Davlas, it will appear in your hand." She pulled his hand away from her sword and then pressed her spear into his palm.

It wasn't a weapon he was familiar with at all.

"I..." He didn't know what to say. He couldn't do this on his own... could he?

There was no more hesitation in her voice. It was sure, strong. "Trust yourself. You're drahksani. You can do this." She levered herself up to lean against a tree. It seemed to cause great pain to do so, but she was fighting through it. If she could fight, so could he.

He nodded, stood, and stalked back toward the kroll.

His blood was coursing, his breath coming quick. He was terrified and emboldened all at once.

The beast was far too close, four or five more of its long strides would bring it to Caerwyn.

No better time to test his new weapon. He threw the spear as hard as he could, and it pierced deep into the kroll's chest. The thing cried out again.

"Davlas," Jais said, and the spear vanished from the kroll and appeared back in his hand.

He threw again.

This time he charged in behind the spear, and as it sank

into the thing's neck, he threw himself, feet first, at the spot where his axe-head was still embedded in the kroll's waist, trying to push it farther in, complete the cut. He hit it hard, then fell to the ground, scrambling away.

He called for Davlas again. It came to his hand as he reached a small clear spot in which to stand. When he turned back he saw the creature on the ground, flailing around, it was torn in half. The thrashing was slowing now as it lay there, dying.

He crept in carefully, quietly. Then with a leap and a cry he threw himself on the beast and thrust the spear down into where he hoped its heart was.

He followed that strike up with several more, in quick succession, perforating its chest a dozen times.

The kroll stopped moving. He'd finally put the blasted thing out of its misery.

He stood there for a moment, breathing hard, taking in the victory. He'd killed the beast. He... Jais... had defeated a kroll... all on his own. No, not on his own.

"Caerwyn!" he breathed.

PAIN COURSED THROUGH CAERWYN'S BODY. SHE WAS CERTAIN she had a broken rib and arm. There would also be a massive bruise on her right side from where the thing had hit her. She was lucky though. She doubted that had been a full-strength swat.

She admired Jais' courage, going off to finish the kroll alone—as much as she hadn't wanted him to. She wasn't sure if she'd have the guts to go out there again with as little training as he did. He probably had no idea what to do with the spear, but it was all she could think of. It was a great weapon, perhaps that alone would help him. Though... it hadn't helped her.

From her spot, resting against the base of a tree, she'd watched him fight, desperate and brave. Good, he'd kept away from it for the most part until his wild full-body kick at its mid-section. But that had ended it clearly enough.

He was careful after that, and not long later the thing was still, dead.

Jais, pulled Davlas from the chest of the kroll. He hardly looked hurt at all. The boy had a healthy helping of inborn talent.

Thank the gods.

"Well done," she said even though he couldn't hear her. She grimaced at the exertion and pain she could hear in her voice. She wasn't supposed to show pain. She was the near-indestructible Caerwyn Afgenni, General of the Afgen armies and daughter of Prince Ahslam Afgenni, Governor of Rahan Province and seventh in line for the Afgen throne. Even if that life was behind her now, lost to her, those old titles still meant something to her.

Jais was breathing hard and looked over at her. A moment later he was back next to her. "You... You look..." there was an odd... something in how he looked at her then. It vanished in a heartbeat. "You look like you got smacked by a kroll."

She grinned but didn't laugh, that would hurt too much.

"I might need a little help getting back up—"

She was cut off by a ululating roar from not far away. The two of them froze. They knew that sound. The other kroll was near. From the crashing through the forest, which was getting louder, it wasn't just near, it was charging toward them.

6

"Jais—" was all she got out before it broke through the forest not far away. It didn't hesitate, bearing down on them.

Jais turned and threw the spear. It was a good throw, took the thing full in the face, but the kroll didn't slow.

Jais had no time but she saw him spare a glance at her. It was well timed too as she had drawn out her short sword from where it hung on her left hip, and as their eyes met she tossed it to him.

His reflexes were as sharp as hers. He caught the hilt then spun and plunged it into the stomach of the kroll as it rammed into him. The young warrior had come in low, in a crouch, and rose up suddenly with a feral cry, using the momentum of the kroll against it. The beast was tossed up and over him. In that single instant, she saw Jais' immense strength, those compact muscles on his stocky frame bunched and bulged as he lifted the beast off the ground. But the kroll had gotten in an attack as well, bashing Jais with a mangled club-fist. The end result of the encounter was the kroll rolling off in one direction and Jais another. Luckily Jais was knocked toward her.

"Davlas!" she called, and the spear appeared in her hand even as the kroll landed on its back. She looked down at Jais who was grimacing with pain.

"That hurt," he said, but he was already getting up. Apparently it hadn't hurt that much. Yet he was moving awkwardly, hobbling a little and favoring his right leg.

She had to get up, get back in the fight. She'd fought through worse injuries than this... hadn't she? She would certainly like to think she had. Yet every movement set new parts of her body on fire. Despite her wounds, and carefully working around the worst of it, she managed to roll to her good side, then lever herself up to a kneeling position. She was sweating hard from the agony and the humid night air by the time she'd done that much. She hissed through gritted teeth and rose. Her legs were okay, only battered and scraped from the fly through the branches. Yet as she tried to walk, pain shot up her right side, sparking through her shoulder and down her arm. She winced and ground her teeth.

"What are you doing?" Jais hissed. "You're in no condition to fight!"

"Maybe not," she said handing him the spear. The kroll was already on its feet again and would be at them in a moment. "But I'm not going to lay there doing nothing either." Mostly she couldn't let him die and was willing to risk a great amount of anguish or injury—anything short of death —to ensure that.

He nodded, taking the spear. Then he turned to the kroll.

This one was as different from the one they had just defeated as two could get. Where the other had had a narrow waist, this one had a great bulging belly which overhung his hips in front. The legs seemed too thin and narrow to support it, but were still thicker than Jais' and the young man had legs like none Caerwyn had ever seen before. The upper portion of the kroll was odd with a shriveled chest, but great balls of shoulders, then narrow upper arms and huge forearms. One of its hands was clubbed and deformed the other seemed to work just fine as it plucked the short sword from its stomach. The head seemed shrunken as well as it needed to be to fit between those two mountainous shoulders.

It roared at them and came on again.

Jais returned the roar and charged as well. She wouldn't have recommended a head on attack with a kroll, but then... he had survived a head on clash with the thing just a moment before. Jais leapt, surprisingly high, and came down jamming Davlas between one of those great shoulders and the kroll's head, the spear sunk in deep. The thing cried out, and it bashed Jais out of the air. This wasn't an off-balance hit as the last one had been, and Jais too cried out as he was sent flying into a rather unforgiving tree. There was a nasty crack that came as the young man hit, then another when he hit the ground.

He didn't move.

"Jais! No!" She couldn't run to him, she could barely walk.

And her cry had alerted the kroll to her presence. The thing was stunned. It paused, perhaps regaining some strength, but it was clear she'd be its next target.

"Blast," she cursed. "Davlas!" She called the spear back to her. Sure... she could take this thing.

She was actually fairly certain she was about to die, but well, she did always imagine her end would come in battle. What did it matter if she died now anyway if Jais—the man she needed to fulfill her dream of having a child—was dead as well. She hoped he wasn't, but wouldn't have time to check. If she didn't kill this kroll, it would finish them both off quick enough.

"Come and get it you ugly bastard." She pushed off from the tree she'd been leaning against and took a step toward the thing.

A ragged war-cry caused both her and the kroll to turn.

Barami raced into the clearing and with a great, two-handed swing of his hand-and-a-half sword lopped off one of the kroll's shriveled upper arms.

It roared and reared back, which gave Barami—an experienced warrior—the time and opening he needed to cut one of the beast's relatively skinny legs from under it. To be fair the long blade didn't quite sever the limb, but it did enough damage to make the kroll fall back. From there the fight was fairly determined. Barami was fresh and too quick for the injured beast. Two more hacks to keep flailing limbs away from him, and he sank his blade deep into the kroll's chest. He repeated the motion a couple more times even though the beast had stopped moving. It paid to be certain these things were dead.

Not caring if more might arrive, Caerwyn collapsed to her knees, using her spear to keep from falling over completely.

"Caer!" She heard Barami's voice. There was concern there.

"Check on Jais first," she said nodding her head in the boy's direction. She heard Barami moving around, then grunting. From across the clearing he called over. "He'll live. Tough hide on this one."

Caerwyn nodded to herself. She couldn't bear the thought that she'd brought this barely trained young man to a fight which had ended him... and her hope of a child.

Secure in the knowledge Jais would survive, she slumped to the ground and let the darkness, which had been hovering at the edge of her senses, take her. Her last thought was a practical one. Barami was a competent healer, he'd take care of them.

Jais was aware of things before he was fully conscious. It was an odd state of semi-consciousness where he floated in a soothing darkness, but could hear things around him. A crackling fire, the sweep of wind in the trees, and morning birds calling out to each other.

"...didn't know better I'd think the second one of those things was coming to help the first from everything you're telling me." The voice was thick and deep with an accent he couldn't place at first. It wasn't a voice he knew well, but he seemed to think he'd come to know it recently.

A woman's voice answered. At first he thought it might be his aunt, but no, this was sharper, with an edge like a knife to it, crisp and cut. "Krolls shouldn't act this way. They don't care about each other like that. They'll band together to take down a city or large food source, but after that it's every kroll for itself. They don't fight to protect each other. At least I've never known one to." There was something behind this female voice, a bit of anger or perhaps pain, as if it hurt to talk.

"It seems your new young father-to-be has a strange problem. Are we going to be staying long enough to help?" This – from the male again – didn't make much sense.

"Perhaps we might," said the woman.

A grunt answered the woman.

Then pain lanced through Jais, and his eyes fluttered open as full consciousness and awareness came to him. It was light out, but not the blazing brightness of full day. Just after dawn perhaps. Above him leaves attached to a hatch work of branches, twitched and swayed in a light breeze with the sky above a deep azure blue.

He groaned.

That caused the man, Barami as Jais knew him to be now, to laugh. "Stay still, brakka."

"Brakka? Is that me?" Jais said, though it hurt to talk. His entire left side was throbbing and incredibly sore.

There was a painful sounding grunt of exertion then Caerwyn drifted into view. Her hair was tied back as usual but her face was battered. A bruise was forming over most of the left cheek, and that eye was mostly swollen over.

"It's a term of endearment... sort of," she said settling next to him with another groan. "A brakka is a beast of burden in the south. Think of the tallest, largest horse you've ever seen, but with the girth and breadth of the largest ox, then give it hide like rough leather armor and spiky horns over its face and body. They are known for their toughness, durability, stamina... and stubbornness."

"Ah." After a moment he asked, "Do I look worse than you?"

She gave a bit of a laugh, then grimaced as if regretting the action. She nodded. "Just a little."

Jais tried to think back, to recall the fight, but details eluded him. He remembered the first kroll, but of the second there was only flashes, glimpses. "Remind me what happened?"

"Well aside from being tough and stubborn, you have a significant streak of bravery. You went in against a charging

kroll with only a short sword. You're also stronger than you
look, and you don't look weak. You lifted that monstrosity
clear off the ground and threw it several feet. It hit you,
sending you flying as well, but you got right back up and
went in after it again. The second time it hit a little harder,
and you went flying into a tree. I thought for certain you were
dead, but no, just knocked around a little. Speaking of which,
what hurts? Barami patched you up as best he could, but
without your input he couldn't be sure if there were any
internal injuries."

There was an odd look in her eyes. She was concerned for
him, which made sense, but there was something beyond
that. He faintly recalled some strange comments she'd made
yesterday about "not wanting him to get hurt" or "keeping
him safe". He couldn't recall exactly. That didn't make any
sense to him, and for the moment he put it from his mind.

Instead he took stock of his ills. He hurt all over, head
to toe. He tried to identify how he hurt and where specifically. His entire left side was one giant sore spot. He was
guessing he would be quite black and blue. He knew the
feel of bruises from his brawling days and that's what this
felt like. It was the scope of it that was amazing, from not
far under his shoulder all the way down to his thigh and
spreading around to his stomach and back. But there
weren't any sharp pains in that area so he assumed nothing
was broken. His arms were generally sore, but that felt
more like exertion than pain. They were also covered in
small sharper pains, cuts and scrapes, but nothing that felt
serious. His head similarly felt like it had a plethora of
scrapes, but not much more. He did have a raging
headache, though, and a sore spot on his left temple. It was
the below the waist where the real pain was. Aside from the

myriad cuts and scrapes all over his legs, his right thigh had an intense stinging, throbbing area, more than just a cut. He'd never had a broken bone, but he imagined it might feel something like this. That and his left ankle, which was afire with pain. It was a general area, but still strong and sharp.

"Left side is not bad, bruised, but I don't think it's much worse than that. Lots of cuts all over"

"That would be from the branches you crashed through the second time you were hit."

"Ah. Also my right thigh hurts like Holn, and my left ankle is quite painful." He couldn't see her at the moment so he rolled his head to the side to gage her reaction.

She nodded. "Good."

"Really?"

"Yes. Your ankle is swollen, you probably won't be able to walk on it for a day or so, but Barami thinks it's only twisted, sprained, nothing more. Your right leg... well we had to take a sizable branch out of it. That's probably what you're feeling. He's put a poultice on it to stop the bleeding and help the healing, and bandaged it tight." She shrugged. "You're alive and not losing too much blood, so you'll be fine. Most minor cuts won't be bothering you in a few more hours. The bruising, well I'm sure you know it doesn't slow us much, the pain will dull quickly, and the color will fade just as fast. Larger wounds like that one in your leg, they'll take more time, but it and your ankle should be well enough for you to walk in a couple of days."

He nodded. It now made sense why his pain and bruises as a kid had never lasted long. He'd often been able to get away with his aunt and uncle never knowing he'd been in a fight at all, unless he'd been hit in the face.

Though even a couple of days off his feet felt like an eternity.

A thought came to him. "If you can get me to my aunt Sarelle, she's a healer."

Caerwyn nodded slowly. "That's right, you mentioned that yesterday. We'll see what we can do. Moving you will be tricky for at least a little while. If I was at full capacity I might be able to carry you, even with your rather... dense musculature, but I've got a broken rib, and Barami had enough trouble just getting you to a semi-flat place to lie down, and he's no weakling."

After a moment she added, "But perhaps Barami or I could go and get your aunt and bring her back here. I don't know how happy she'd be with us for pulling you into this mess—"

"I came of my own will. It's not your fault."

She grimaced. "No, but training you was."

He shrugged at that. It only hurt a little to do so. "I survived, didn't I?"

She smiled. "I think that was less because of my training and more from your natural toughness." Caerwyn seemed lost in thought for a moment, an odd look on her face, pursed lips and distant eyes that gazed at him but didn't see him. "That girl who came to your house to ask for help... are you...? Is she...?" Uncertainty didn't suit Caerwyn. Seeing her stumble over her words was like watching a sure-footed stallion trip over its own feet.

Jais wasn't quite sure what Caerwyn was asking. He responded with, "I like her... and I think she likes me." Though as he recalled back to her invitation to the revels he might amend that a little. It seemed fairly clear that Alnia was rather intent on him. Perhaps she felt more than just a 'liking' toward him. Did he himself feel more? His heart twisted a little. Yes he did, but there was fear and doubt. He knew he was different now, and the question remained... what would Alnia think when she found out? There had been a time, so very recently when he'd thought he was normal, thought he might want to marry Alnia and have children, a family, a normal life.

But he wasn't normal. He knew that now.

Perhaps that was why his aunt had always tried to keep him away from the revels or getting to close to anyone in the town. She knew what they were, and she too had been scared.

Jais sighed. "I honestly don't know what's happening with Alnia or anything else right now. Everything seems so... confusing and uncertain."

Caerwyn looked away from him then. "I did that."

Jais thought about it. "Well, in part, maybe, but actually I think things had been heading that way for me for a while. My aunt... she'd never said anything about what I was, but I think she was getting to the point where she was going to have to tell me. I can't say for certain, but given the things I was doing, it seems likely I'd have been told one way or the other soon enough. I just don't know what this all means; drahksani and powers, being... different."

Caerwyn sighed then, and her tone was a little thick with emotion, a little haunted when she spoke next. "It means your life will change forever. It means people will despise you. They may not want to, not really, but they've been taught that our kind are evil for so long that eventually they'll all turn against you." She still wasn't looking at him, but her gaze seemed even more lost than usual. When she finished speaking, her jaw set tightly and she swallowed hard. She looked like she was trying not to cry. He couldn't imagine her ever crying, but something about what she was saying was affecting her deeply. It seemed obvious that people had turned against her at some point, presumably when it had come out that she was a drahksan. "I'm sorry Jais."

Now didn't seem like the time to ask her more about whatever was bothering her. So he simply said, "Barami is still with you."

She nodded and after a moment of deep breaths the emotion within her seemed to have passed. "Yes," she said finally. "You're right. There are a few good souls out there who will always see you for who you are and not... *what* you are." She looked at him then. "I truly hope your girl is one of those." She tried to smile, but it was forced. Jais could see that she didn't really think it would happen.

He looked away then, rolling his head back to gaze at the forest canopy. He hoped Alnia wouldn't turn on him when he told her what he was. He knew he would tell her, he'd have to at some point. He couldn't keep something like that from her if they were going to be together. He wanted to believe she wouldn't despise him... but honestly he didn't know.

Caerwyn groaned. She was getting up, he could see it from the corner of his eye. Even with a broken rib she was acting as normal.

"I'll be back by... well I don't know when. I'll fetch your aunt."

Then she was gone, at least from his immediate area. He caught her voice a moment later a little distance off saying, "keep an eye on him while I go get some help."

Barami replied with, "You shouldn't be going anywhere."

She replied with a flat tone, "You're the healer. I'm no good to him if he gets any worse. You stay, I'm... well enough."

There was a deep grunt a moment later. It seemed Barami wasn't happy with the choice but he wasn't going to fight it.

Not long after that Barami came to him with some broth and helped him drink it, lifting his head. The old warrior wasn't one for words. They didn't talk.

After that Jais just closed his eyes and rested.

CAERWYN WASN'T LOOKING FORWARD TO THIS ENCOUNTER. NOT only did she have to ask the woman who'd tried to kill her for help, but she had to tell her that her nephew was wounded. Depending on the woman's temperament and abilities, this might not go so well for Caerwyn.

Frankly she wasn't sure she deserved the woman's sympathy. Gods, but she'd truly messed up Jais' life. Well in truth, it had only partly been her and partly this strange series of events with the krolls. Jais would have gone after these beast whether she'd been here or not, and no matter what had happened it would not have turned out well for him. Either he'd be dead or he'd have shown the village just how different he was.

She knew what it was like to be exposed as different, and pushed away because of it. She wished that on no man.

And here she was, complicating that whole situation with her own desires. She felt a surge of guilt at stringing the young man along, and frustration at not being able to tell him what she wanted. She was usually so clear-headed and practical, but this whole situation had her turned on end. She knew what she wanted, but didn't know how to ask for it or explain it to him.

It didn't help that he seemed to already be in a relation-ship. Could she ask this of him? Should she?

Her thoughts couldn't settle, and she fought with herself as she made her way to Jais' aunt.

It didn't take her long to find her way out of the forest, a few hours only. Thanks to her gift of sensing other drahksani she had an unerring sense of direction to where Jais' aunt would be. It would also help her get back to Jais later. Moving through the forest wasn't much trouble either. She'd learned early on in life how to survive in the wild, mostly forests, and that included how to move like the animals did, quickly and without disturbing things around her. Even with only one good eye she made excellent time. So midday found her approaching the small cottage where Jais and his family lived.

She was feeling a little better than she had the night before. Her rib still bothered her, but she managed to keep from jostling it while moving, most of the rest of her injuries were healing well. She blessed her drahksani nature for that. She couldn't imagine how normal people must feel, having to wait for days or weeks to recover.

Caerwyn paused before the door of the small house. She drew herself up, drawing in a long breath. That made her rib sting, and she winced at it, but it was the price she paid for preparing herself for what was to come.

She knocked.

The door was answered quickly. It was Jais' aunt. There was a play of emotions over the other woman's still youthful face, hope quickly replaced by anger, then fear and anxiety, finally settling on concern.

"You're hurt. Come in." The woman moved aside to let Caerwyn into the dark confines of the single room home.

This was not the response Caerwyn had been expecting.

Her mind worked for a moment. She'd expected yelling, a tirade, or at the very least some sharp comment in the vein of 'where's my nephew!' This kindness caught her off guard. Though after a moment she supposed as a healer the woman would have a strong desire to help those who were hurt. Still it didn't help Caerwyn adjust from the harsh reaction she'd been expecting. "Jais is safe," was all she could think to say as she ducked through the short doorway.

The woman nodded. "Thank you," came the clipped reply. There was a heavy sound of relief with that as well. "Now, this way."

Three small windows and several thick candles were all that lit the interior. It was enough with the strong summer's sun that Caerwyn's eyes did not need to adjust much to the dimmer light. She was ushered to a bed, but before Sarelle laid her down she went about stripping off Caerwyn's clothes. This too was a bit of a shock, but only for a moment. Caerwyn was not shy or modest. She'd lived and fought among men for most of her life, and it made sense that the other woman wanted to discard her soiled clothes before putting her in a clean bed.

"By Thadros! What have you done to yourself woman?"

Caerwyn couldn't help but grin at the fact that Sarelle swore by the god of healing, art, and inspiration. He wasn't the usual god people chose for their expletives. "I didn't get out of the way fast enough. This particular kroll packed quite the..." She laughed a little at her own pun. "Punch."

"Kroll? You found it then?" Sarelle was laying her down now, eyes scanning Caerwyn's body, noting the bruises, cuts and abrasions making soft 'tsk' noises. "Is it dead?"

"It and the other one with it."

Sarelle's eyes met Caerwyn's, growing wide. "There were

two?" After a moment that sank in, and she continued with, "and you defeated them both?" Before Caerwyn could answer Sarelle was back observing her wounds and finished with, "And this is all you came away with? You must be a great warrior." The other woman turned away heading into the kitchen area of the house. While doing so she gathered up Caerwyn's clothes and boots and dumped them by the door.

"Actually, it was your nephew, Jais, who did the bulk of the work." Caerwyn watched Sarelle carefully. The other woman paused in her brisk trek around the foot of the bed. When Sarelle responded there was a slight quaver in her voice.

"And you said he is well?"

She moved on after this to retrieve a metal box from under the other bed in the hut. She set it on that bed and opened it, pulling something out then closing it and placing it back under the bed.

Caerwyn worded this precisely. "He is well enough. He is alive and awake, but he will need your healing. He fought bravely, but took far more punishment than I did. Yet his gifts from our shared heritage seem to be along the lines of great strength and endurance."

As Sarelle returned, carrying a small pot. The other woman's face displayed a false serenity, poorly concealing her worry. She scooped out a dark goo from the pot and began applying it to the worst of Caerwyn's injuries. "This is your fault, you know that," she said tight-lipped.

"I know." After a moment Caerwyn added, "But with gifts like his he would have some day tried to test them. Better he do that with others who can help to protect him, don't you think?"

Sarelle once again flicked her gaze up to meet Caerwyn's,

unimpressed. She continued on with her work. Sarelle began muttering to herself. A rather intense tingling filtered into Caerwyn's body. There was a nasty pain around her broken rib, and she gasped. Was the other woman trying to hurt her more?

"What are you doing?" Caerwyn breathed out between clenched teeth.

"I'm healing you... hastily. I figure that will get us both to my nephew quicker. But healing is painful work at times." The other woman met Caerwyn's eyes again, and this time there was a hint of gleeful spite in that look. "I figured you were tough enough to handle it without my usual pain killers. That would have taken longer anyway."

The tingling intensified but oddly the pain around her rib didn't, it was slowly fading. It felt awkward, like feeling returning to a once numb limb, but it wasn't truly painful. In truth this wasn't that bad.

The door to the hut opened.

"The forest is quiet today, I wonder if Jais and those two strangers had any luck with..." Jais' uncle's voice trailed off as his gaze came around to see where his wife was. "Oh!" He looked away after a moment. Not that Caerwyn cared much if men saw her naked. The man had some decency, though, and she could respect that.

"There are clothes by the door, take them out and wash them." Sarelle's tone was stern, and the man nodded, following the order. He was gone shortly.

"My apologies, I didn't expect him back this early."

Caerwyn was surprised at the tone in the other woman's voice. Was it actual remorse?

"I care little about such things. But I thank you for tending to me and my clothes."

"It's what I do," was the stoic response. After another moment, as the tingling began to fade, Sarelle spoke again. "Usually I put my patients to sleep when I heal them. It takes a lot out of the body to recover, and sleep is needed. You are going to be tired when I'm done, but I'll give you a little energy so you can take me to my son." It wasn't until a long moment later that Sarelle corrected herself. "My nephew."

"You think of him as your own don't you?"

Sarelle nodded.

"I am truly sorry he got hurt." Chances are he would have gotten hurt whether Caerwyn had been here or not, but she could have done more to protect him.

The tingling faded to nothing, and Sarelle stopped massaging the dark goo over Caerwyn's wounds. She sat back heavily, not making eye contact, and sighed. "You're right. He would have gone out on his own at some point. I wouldn't have been able to stop him." She laughed a disheartened, mirthless chuckle then. "Well, I am perfectly capable of stopping him. It is within my powers to keep a body from moving..." Another sigh. Now she looked up, and in her eyes Caerwyn saw a deep concern. "But I couldn't do that to him. He's been testing his limits more and more, and one of these days he was going to do something foolish. You're right. At least you and your companion were there to help him."

Caerwyn tried to raise herself to a sitting position but failed, falling back. She was truly exhausted. "Oh," she said softly.

Sarelle laughed truly now. "I told you."

Caerwyn blinked. "I thought you said you'd give me some energy?"

"Oh, I will," Sarelle said rising. "In a minute. I like you this way." She walked around to the other bed in the room and rummaged around in a chest at its foot. "I don't think anything of Jais' or Perrick's will fit you, and I don't wear shirts and pants like you, so I hope a dress will do." She rose, holding a utilitarian dress, long and shapeless with a belt at the waist and no sleeves. "We are of a size, though you have more muscle on you. This should fit."

Caerwyn grimaced. She hadn't worn a dress in... actually she hadn't worn a dress since she was a child. Since she had lived with her birth parents... before they had been...

Perhaps it was her state of fatigue or something else, but tears came to her eyes. She did not cry... ever, especially about this. She'd long ago accepted her parent's fate, but for some reason with this woman helping her, so... motherly— even if Sarelle's ministrations weren't particularly gentle— Caerwyn found some pain in her soul leaking through to the surface and suddenly could not contain her sobs.

She had only briefly known her mother and even now had trouble remembering the woman's face. That seemed so wrong. Some voice in the back of her mind poked at that sting in her soul saying: *and what sort of mother would you be? You know nothing of being a mother and you want a child so much? You're being selfish. Had you ever thought of the child and what it would need and want?*

Sarelle was there a moment later, laying the dress down at Caerwyn's feet before sitting at the head of the bed. "I'm sorry, I..." She stroked Caerwyn's hair. A soft soothing warmth emanated from wherever the other woman touched her. It eased the pain despite that this was not a physical wound.

"Hush now," Sarelle said softly. "I'm sorry. I did not know you had such deep pain." After a moment she added. "I suppose we all do."

Caerwyn wasn't sure what that meant, but she felt better soon enough and was sniffing away the last of her tears. "It's I who am sorry. I don't know where that came from."

Sarelle knelt next to the bed so their heads were closer. "Oh I think you know exactly where that came from. I wager you are old enough to remember the Great Purge. I do not doubt you've lost much and lived a hard enough life. It is our fate as drahksani, I fear." Sarelle reached out again and laid her hand on Caerwyn's forehead. "Take this." Suddenly a great feeling of peace and living energy flowed into her. Caerwyn watched and could see the toll it took on the other woman. She was giving of her own resources to restore Caerwyn to herself.

"Thank you," she said, and the words could not express her actual gratitude. She sat up slowly now, much more able to move and reached for the dress. It was not what she would ever choose to wear, but it was a gift from a woman who had already given her so much so she accepted it without comment.

Sarelle rose and began gathering a few things, packing them into a satchel.

Caerwyn found the dress did not fit well, but again she said nothing. She could live with it. She was a slightly taller and larger woman than Sarelle. The cloth was quite snug at her shoulders, bust, and hips. The hem of the dress fell to her knees where she suspected it was mid-calf for the other woman. Moving, especially through the forest, would not be easy in this, but she would make do.

"Thank you," she said again, not knowing what else to say.

A business-like manner had returned to Sarelle. "You can thank me by taking me to my s— nephew."

Caerwyn nodded and they left.

Sarelle called out to her husband as they passed by him cleaning up Caerwyn's things. "We'll be gone for a bit. May not be back before dark."

He waved his acknowledgement then Caerwyn was leading Sarelle into the forest and to her kin.

7

BARAMI DIDN'T LIKE ANY OF THIS.

Not this new young pup with his wild strength and endurance, not Caer's desperate need to find a drahksan to mate with, not being this far north. But mostly he didn't like what was going on with these krolls. He couldn't figure it out, and it bothered him.

He knew his own limitations well. He wasn't a scholar or a great thinker. His mind had been honed on fighting, how to survive, and tactics. So he was aware that he knew precious little about krolls. But what he did know was fairly common knowledge, and generally 'common knowledge' came from a long series of observable, similar instances. People just know that some birds flock together while others fly alone. Some very few might know why, but most don't care, they are just aware of these facts. It was the same with the krolls. They were solitary, only generally banding together to hit a larger target, but then quickly doing their own thing once that target was destroyed. 'Helping' a fellow in need... that wasn't anywhere in the general knowledge of the beasts.

Something was wrong. The annoying thing was, he was certain he should know what it was. There was something... some scrap of knowledge tugging at the edges of his thoughts. He was certain that if he could recall that, this would all make much more sense. But it wasn't coming. There was too much else on his mind.

Jais groaned... again. The boy was still only semi-conscious after his one awakening earlier that day. Barami sat next to him, restraining him when he tried to move too much. It wasn't easy, the boy was ungodly strong, even when he wasn't really trying.

Jais' leg twitched, the tip of his boot wavering. It wasn't anything serious, just some dream most likely. Barami looked Jais over.

This was the man Caerwyn wanted?

All he could think was: the boys' boots needed new soles.

He rose with a sigh, then paused.

A noise in the woods alerted him of someone approaching. For a second he was torn, stay here and guard the boy or find a better vantage point to see who was coming. He stayed. Caer would kill him if he left the boy. He drew out Oken-adi, his long-bladed sword. The name, translated from his mother tongue, meant 'stalwart friend'. It had been given to him by Caerwyn. A prized possession.

Whoever was coming knew something of forest lore. They weren't crashing through the brush, but they were far from silent. He did not think it would be Caer, she was much more careful, like a panther moving through the jungle. Nor did he think it was another kroll, it was moving too slowly and carefully and soon he could hear human voices, speaking the common tongue of the north that Caer had taught him.

"Well, where to now?" This one seemed commanding, but the voice was young and brash with a hint of arrogance.

"Give me a moment. The tracks are not that fresh, and the ground here is dry." No expert tracker, but someone who knew enough to follow the three of them here. This voice was also young, but more uncertain, if deeper and richer sounding.

Both voices were male, and the third which spoke up a moment later was as well. "Alnia will be a wreck if anything's happened to Jais."

Barami grimaced. So, these were townsfolk coming to look for their friend. He lowered his sword and waited for them. They pushed through the brush a short while later.

"What did you...?" One of them, a boy who was reed thin and tall, going through a growth spurt no doubt, began speaking but his words trailed off as the full scene unfolded before him. Barami hadn't moved Jais far, to the nearest spot of clear and level ground, which meant the bodies of the two krolls were still nearby. The eyes of all three boys went wide as they took in the two dead beasts and the rest of the scene around them.

Next to the reed thin one was a boy who was nearly all man now, taller than his companion by a half a head and well filled out, built like an ox. "What happened?" that one asked.

Barami wasn't one for extensive conversations. "Your friend killed one kroll. I killed the other." It was an adequate summary even if it lacked a lot of the more important details.

All three sets of eyes turned to him now. He knew how he looked, old and weathered, no hair, but nearly more gray than black in his eyebrows and stubble. He wasn't the image of a young hero, except for the large sword he wielded. He slung it back over his shoulder into the sheath on his back.

The three boys waited for a moment, perhaps thinking he'd say more. He didn't.

The skinny one asked, "how is Jais? He doesn't look so good."

"He's tough. He'll be well soon."

The big one stepped forward, inching toward the dead krolls. "How did you do it?"

Barami didn't have much patience for frivolous people. These boys were more interested in the fight than the people themselves. He could spin a yarn about a fight for those who appreciated it, those who understood what it meant to put your life in the balance and come out the other side, each battle changing you, never quite the same. These boys were not such men. They wanted something interesting to tell their friends or impress the girls. They wanted to claim fame by association. Well perhaps that was unfair. The other two seemed appropriately shocked. It was the big one who really seemed too eager to learn about things no one needed to know.

"Quickly."

The large boy turned to him, a confused look on his face. "That's it?"

Barami didn't deign to respond to that one.

More noises in the woods came to his ears. The boys flinched, but a wafting voice came to Barami, a familiar one. Caer was returning.

A moment later, she and Jais' aunt emerged from the woods, and the other three boys relaxed.

Caer looked around, concerned. "What are you three doing here?"

"We were looking for Jais," the shortest one said. He was

the tracker, Barami associated that deeper voice with what he'd heard earlier.

It was the aunt who responded. "Well you've found him now. Run back to Klasten's Green and let the rest of the town know everyone is safe and the krolls have been killed." When the boys didn't move right away she added a clipped, "Now!"

The three started and nodded, moving off through the woods as a group.

The aunt and Caer exchanged a look. There was something there, some shared knowledge, some secret. Barami frowned. Caer had never had many secrets, especially from him.

He wouldn't ask. He never did. If she wanted to tell him she would. Caer caught his gaze and made her way to him. She was moving easier, well healed by the look of things. This healer-woman really did have some special powers to fix a broken rib that quickly. Except Caer wasn't in her usual leathers, but a simple dress. The cut wasn't flattering, but seeing how it clung to her tall frame, too tight and too small, made his blood quicken. A part of him wanted to tell her she looked good, beautiful, but that wasn't their relationship, and it wasn't his place. Plus, she was a warrior first and a woman second. He knew that much about her. She wouldn't care for such silliness.

"Can you follow those boys and be discreet?" Caer asked, voice hushed. "What's about to happen here, we don't want others to see."

Barami nodded, and would have left without another word, but turned back to her after a half-step away. He'd had a thought. "Those boys have seen Jais now. If he starts walking around like nothing happened…"

Caer nodded with a frown. "I know."

Barami gave a curt nod and left.

He wasn't a tracker, not like some he'd known back among the Kigasi, his tribe, but he knew the basics. In this case that meant moving quietly through the forest looking at the signs the three boys had left behind. As he had expected, not long after the three had left the clearing one of them, the large one, had broken off from the other two. The other two had headed back to the village, the big one had doubled-back. Barami found him creeping through the forest toward one of the dead krolls; doing a decent job of staying quiet for one of his size.

Barami got within ten feet of the boy before saying, "You shouldn't be here."

The large boy jumped and spun, terror in his eyes, which quelled rapidly as he saw who had been following him. "I just wanted to get a better look at the krolls; never seen one up close before."

"Pray to Suur you never do, dead or alive. Things like that never leave you."

The boy let out a nasally breath of a laugh, acting tough. Perhaps he thought that Barami was weak for being haunted by such demons. If so, he was wrong. Living with such memories was not for one who was weak of spirit.

"I think I can handle a dead one just fine," the boy said, flush with bravado.

Barami thought of what Caer was doing in the clearing. This kroll wasn't that close, but there was a risk that the boy might see too much.

"Leave. Now." Barami didn't need to puff himself up. He leveled his gaze on the boy, years of battle and hard living behind that look. The boy flinched but didn't otherwise exit the area.

"You're not my keeper. I can do as I wish."

Barami didn't want to harm the boy... well, he may have wanted to teach him a lesson or two, but he knew it wouldn't end up well for any of them.

The boy's retort had been loud, defiant. Barami couldn't see the clearing from where he was. He wondered if the others had heard it. If so, perhaps they wouldn't proceed. But if they had already started and couldn't stop... he didn't know enough of how their powers worked. He couldn't risk this boy seeing too much.

Perhaps the threat of violence would work. He drew his great blade off his back. It, much more so than the short sword at his hip, would intimidate. If the boy had known anything of combat he would have known such a weapon was near useless with all these trees around.

The boy didn't and stumbled back until he hit a tree. Barami came onward, and the boy bolted, crashing through the forest back toward the village, away from the clearing.

Barami sighed and returned his weapon to its sheath. There would be a price for that action later, but for now Caer was safe. He returned to the clearing.

Jais had been stripped down, and the boy's aunt was rubbing a dark grayish goo on his wounds and mumbling. Jais twitched and moaned, but didn't otherwise seem to notice.

"It's miraculous what she can do," Caer said moving over to him. "I was healed in a matter of minutes, broken rib and all."

"I am glad you are well."

She looked at him with 'the look' in her eyes. He knew that look well. It was the one she gave him instead of saying how she felt about him. He knew she couldn't, that it was complicated, and she didn't want to lead him on by saying the wrong thing. It made his heart constrict anyway.

"What's next?" he asked, hoping to change the topic and her mood.

She looked away and shrugged. "I'll talk to the boy and see if he's..." She pursed her lips. She was not good with her emotions or words which related to them. "If he's available for... mating." She'd lowered her voice. Perhaps she didn't want the aunt to hear.

"What do you think of him?" Barami was curious. He hadn't asked what he'd really wanted to ask: 'did she have feelings for the boy?'

Caer had only known Jais for a couple of days, but he'd seen looks between them. There was something there that broke through their lack of familiarity. He guessed it was their shared heritage. They had found someone who was like them. That was nothing to dismiss.

"He's... everything he seems to be: tough, strong, brash, and young." After a moment she went on, but her voice had changed, there was something strange in the timbre now. "Fearless and brave. A warrior."

And that was the moment he knew he would never be with her. He'd known in theory for some time, but those few words, which described him as much as the boy, had been said with a faint longing, a distant hope. She didn't just want a fearless warrior, if so she'd have chosen him long ago. No, she wanted a specific fearless warrior... and it wasn't him.

He grunted, not trusting his words.

"He'll make a strong child," she said softly. There was pain in her voice though. Was she questioning her choice? Or perhaps she was regretting having turned this young man's life upside down? He didn't know.

"You need to say something to him." Barami said evenly.

"I will." But her tone wasn't firm, there was still a question there.

He shook his head. This wasn't the Caerwyn he knew. This whole quest for a child had changed her. The changes were small, and he wasn't even sure if she knew it yet, but he could see it. The lack of certainty, the self-questioning. This wasn't the woman he knew.

Yet... he knew she'd still never choose him. That was a certainty. He'd never be who she wanted. He wasn't drahk-sani. That thought soured his mood. That boy was going to give her something Barami himself never could.

Barami nodded and turned away. He made a pretense of tending to the fire, but he just needed to not be facing her. Not while that tear was on his cheek.

8

Jais ducked under Caerwyn's blade, raising his own to block her quick back-handed strike. He came up on her right side and with his free hand grasped her shoulder and pushed her off balance. If they hadn't been practicing at half speed, and if he had actually put his full strength behind the push, she probably would have fallen, but she stumbled to one side, catching her balance.

"Yes!" She was grinning. "Now you're getting the idea of using everything at your disposal. That free hand of yours can be doing so much more than just hanging at your side. With your strength, you can punch or push people around the battlefield to gain an advantage."

"What about using a shield like Barami does?" Jais asked. He'd been fighting both of them for hours at a time for the last day or so.

His aunt had healed him then left, returning to her usual duties. She'd wanted to bring him back home, but knew he couldn't be seen anywhere near the village for at least a week. She wasn't supposed to be a miracle healer, just an exceptional one, and given his injuries, he wouldn't have been up and about and looking completely healed for at least several days. So he'd stayed in the forest and trained more with Caerwyn and Barami. It was edging toward evening on the day after he'd been healed. In that short period of time, with such intense training, he felt like he had learned so much, and was on his way to becoming a more-than-decent warrior, like the two who taught him.

"You could," Caerwyn said with a noncommittal sideways nod of her head. "It would help protect you. But you'd probably be better off learning to fight with two weapons, long sword and short sword perhaps."

"Oh?" Jais was curious about this. He'd never seen anyone fight with two weapons at once.

"It takes a lot of effort to learn to use your off hand as good as your primary hand, but if you can..." She took the step over to him and put her short sword in his left hand, moving it around as she spoke. "You can use that weapon, or either weapon really, to block attacks like you would with a shield, but at the same time you can also attack twice as much as well." She was close to him, using both her hands to help his left hand get a feel for moving with the sword. Her left side was pressed into him. With her taller stature that put her shoulder at his chin and he could smell her leathers and sweat. It was an odd scent for a woman. Alnia smelled of crushed flowers or berries or some other perfume she'd picked up from the merchant's shop. She was one of only a few girls in town whose father had enough wealth to buy such things. Alnia smelled as beautiful as she looked. Caerwyn smelled as rough as she looked.

Unbidden Jais recalled when he'd woken yesterday and seen Caerwyn in one of his aunt's dresses. He'd had to look away. The simple frock was practically scandalous on the warrior-woman. The way it pressed tight to her bosom and hips, accentuated by the belt around her waist, and ended at her knees revealing strong well rounded calves. She'd not looked like herself.

Caerwyn was saying something but Jais' mind had wandered.

"What was that last bit, sorry?"

She turned toward him, still close, her body brushing his. "Did I wear you out already? Need a rest?"

"No, I'm good to keep going. You were talking about how to use two weapons?"

Her face, so close and slightly above his, broke into her usual lopsided grin, that scar on her cheek tugging at the one side of her mouth. "Probably easier to show you anyway. Something tells me with your natural gifts for this, it will come easily enough." Stepping away, she left her sword in his off hand. She retrieved her spear from nearby. "Barami, let's test this boy out!"

The bald warrior was sitting by the fire. He'd seemed sullen ever since Jais had awoken, and he rose slowly. "What do you need?"

"Your sword. We're going to walk through a scenario with Jais. Two people, each with weapons of greater reach attacking him, while he defends with two weapons."

Barami grunted and made his way over.

"First a few quick lessons." This was to Jais. Caerwyn stood before him spear at the ready. "You remember all the blocks you learned with your right hand? Think you can do that with your left?"

Jais shrugged. "We'll find out."

She jabbed in at him slowly, calling out her attacks.

"High." She poked at his shoulder and he swung the blade in his left hand around to block it. "Low." She poked at his thigh, and he swiveled his hand around to bring the sword sweeping across his body to block that. "Head." She swung her spear first in an arc horizontally at his head, he ducked a little and raised the sword high to block. "Head." This time she swung downward at his head, and he stepped back bringing his blade up horizontally to block the blow.

"You've got the basics. Now let's see if you can keep track of two people attacking you." Her grin was no longer quite so friendly, more mischievous.

Barami stepped up. There was a fair space between him and Caerwyn, as would be needed for him to swing that large sword. At this point they were both still in front of him, but he could see how easy it would be for them to split farther apart, so he'd be fighting at his sides or with his back to one of them.

"Nice and slow, we don't want to kill the boy... yet," Caerwyn said and set the pace with a slow jab in at his chest. Barami began moving at the same time, starting a grand swing over his head which would eventually come down on Jais' shoulder or neck.

Jais swept Caerwyn's spear aside and did the thing which made the most sense to him. He was fighting two people with longer reach weapons, so he got in close to one of them. Stepping in closer to Caerwyn, keeping his one blade on her spear, he swept a blow in at her neck as he drew nearer.

"Well done!" she said as she moved, ducking, and at the same time switching her grip on the spear to bring the blunt end of the haft up into his gut. He bent back spinning away while moving the blade still touching the spear down the haft toward her hands.

She dropped the spear, calling it back to her hands a moment later as she too stepped back. Jais continued his spin and moved away from her, trying to keep her between him and Barami who was moving in still.

"Good. See if you can keep me between you and Barami!"

She stepped in once again, this time jabbing higher at his shoulder. He blocked with his opposite hand as he spun turning his back to her for a moment, and bringing his other sword around at her midsection. But as he spun his head around, she wasn't there.

"Never turn your back on an enemy unless you know you're faster than they are." He felt the spear haft push into his back. It would have been a jarring-pushing blow at full speed. It also seemed to wrap around him as he turned and ended up pushing him toward Barami. He ducked an upward blow from that massive sword, crouching low to launch himself at the warrior, both blades committed to a slicing action across Barami's mid-section.

The pommel of Barami's sword came down, thankfully slowly, on the back of his head. Again at full speed, that might have completely felled him. As it was, it knocked him off balance, and he fell to the ground at Barami's feet. Two separate points touched his back.

"You're dead," Barami said with a faint note of glee.

Jais stayed down for a moment. The mosses of the forest floor filled his nostrils with their earthen scent.

He rolled over.

"It seems so obvious that I need to get in close when you both have longer weapons, but with people moving around so much it seems impossible to stay in close."

Caerwyn had withdrawn Davlas and leaned against it, offering a hand to help him up. "It doesn't help that you're fighting two experienced warriors who are also well coordinated in fighting together. Some people wouldn't be as quick as we are. We call them 'dead'."

He accepted her hand and got to his feet, crouching to retrieve his two swords.

"On the positive side, you seem to naturally understand the concept of two weapon fighting. When you have two weapons and your opponent doesn't, keep them threatened and moving. You did that well enough."

Something occurred to Jais then. "But you have two weapons too."

She nodded. "A spear can be wielded more like a staff, making its haft a weapon too. It was the best tactic, once you were in close, to use the spear that way; countering your two weapons with my two. Shall we go again?"

He sighed. There was a lot he'd just learned. "I think I need a moment to take this all in,"

Caerwyn shrugged. "Have a seat, and I'll go over some of the finer points of two weapon work." She waved in the direction of a tree while moving away to retrieve a waterskin.

He sat back against the tree, and she joined him a moment later, handing him the waterskin after she'd had a long pull.

She didn't say anything right away. After a long moment of silence he looked over at her. The expression on her face was hard to read. She almost seemed nervous, a look which didn't suit her and was not one he'd expected.

"Before that..." Her mouth hung open for a moment before she closed it, lips pressed. "I wanted... There was a reason that we... that I came to find you. I..."

"Jais!"

He turned to find Alnia running across the small clearing

at him. At the forest edge behind her stood Danz, her brother, with a quizzical look on his face.

Caerwyn swore softly beside him as he was engulfed in the other woman's embrace. Alnia fell next to him, planting a rather sudden and passionate kiss on his lips.

When she pulled back she said, "See I knew you were just fine. To hear Danz talk about it, you were on the brink of death!"

Jais didn't know what to say exactly. He hadn't been on the brink of death, but he was fairly certain he hadn't looked very well yesterday before he was healed. Judging by the stunned and confused look Danz was throwing his way he shouldn't be up and walking, not yet anyway.

It was Caerwyn who spoke first while Jais' mind reeled, searching for words.

"It looked a lot worse than it was, and with a little of his aunt's care and some poultices, he was on his feet in quite little time."

Alnia spun around to Danz. "You scared me half to death! I told you it couldn't be as bad as you thought."

"But..." Danz was still stupefied.

Barami stepped up beside the lanky young man. "Take it from a warrior who's seen many wounds, your friend looked bad, but most of that was dirt and scrapes, easily cleaned and healed. Nothing was that serious." The old warrior lied easily, it seemed.

"Oh." Danz blinked himself back to reality. "Good to know." Though he still didn't seem completely convinced.

Jais' attention was torn from that as Alnia filled his vision again, pressing her lips to his once more in another urgent and potent kiss. This one lasted far longer than Jais was comfortable with, while others were around. Yet he didn't want to break it off either.

When finally Alnia did pull away it wasn't far. Her long auburn hair created a curtain around them, since she was slightly above him leaning over. Their eyes met in the dimming light of day, and there was an intoxicating intensity to her look. They'd been deprived of the revels, but it was clear she meant to mend that wrong. She leaned in closer, cheek to cheek, hot breath on his ear sending pleasant sensations through him as she whispered, "I'm glad you're well. Perhaps tonight we can have our own revels." There was an urgency in her voice, a semi-choked desire which drilled a similar need into him.

"I'd like that," he whispered.

She wore a broad smile as she pulled back.

She rose and before anyone else could say anything, said, "It's getting late, I don't think we'll have enough light to get back to Klasten's Green. Do you mind if we share your fire?"

It was a moment before anyone spoke. Each person's expression made their thoughts clear. Danz did not want to stay, Barami did not want the two to stay, and Caerwyn was conflicted, though about what, Jais wasn't sure. It was she who answered.

"Of course you can stay with us."

And it was settled.

Jais spent some time telling Alnia—and Danz, who listened while pretending he wasn't interested—about the fight with the krolls, glossing over the more gruesome and damaging bits. Caerwyn disappeared for a while and returned with a small wild boar, on which they supped.

After dinner, as the light in the sky above faded to darker shades of blue, and the first stars appeared, Alnia stood and, having had Jais' hand in hers, gave it a tug for him to rise.

"Excuse us," she said. "I'd like to take a walk with Jais in the woods. We may be a while." Danz half stood, but she waved him away. "We'll be fine. Jais will protect me."

Jais' heart was pounding hard. He knew what Alnia planned and was at once terrified and excited. He was certain the others would see his blush, or his chest thumping with the beat of his heart, but no one made any comments. His gaze caught Caerwyn's as he rose, and there was something there. Was it regret? That seemed odd.

Then he was being led off into the woods by Alnia, intently pulling him along behind her. They wandered for a bit, and Jais made note of markers so he'd be able to find his way back. After a short while he was leading—his night-vision much better than hers—and helping her over any difficult parts. They made certain they were far enough away from the camp that they could not see the fire, after that... it was merely a matter of finding a comfortable spot.

There was a bower, a small area of soft mosses in a curving little dell between two larger trees.

"Yes, here," Alnia said softly, her voice had even more of that choked, breathy nature. It was quite dim, but their eyes had had time to acclimatize to the darkness. It still wasn't full night yet, the bits of sky Jais could see through the dense foliage above were still a dark azure.

Alnia unclasped her cloak and laid it on the ground. She wore a pleasant summer's dress beneath. The color was hard to discern in the dim light. The cut was made to emphasize her bust, belted beneath her bosom with a long skirt which fell to her ankles. She reached behind her and pulled on the bow of the belt, and that strip of cloth fell away.

The night wasn't hot, like some summer nights could be. It was a middling warm, but Jais was growing quite heated as she turned around and said, "Help me with this?"

The dress laced up the back, and his fingers were trembling as he reached for the strings. He fumbled with them for a moment, his hands feeling thick and clumsy, before he'd untied the laces.

His heart was pounding.

Oddly it was she who said, "My heart is racing!" Her voice was only a breath, a whisper.

Her dress began to slip down, and he laid his hands gently on her shoulders, running them down her arms, feeling the soft skin, pushing the dress lower. It fell in a pool at her feet. His breath caught. She was naked, her back smooth and lean, her hips round, buttocks high, legs strong and well-shaped. For a moment, he didn't want her to turn around. He didn't think he could handle seeing her. His heart was already bashing against his ribs like some wild animal in a cage.

His hands fell from her arms, and she did turn slowly. His breath caught again, or perhaps he'd never resumed breathing, he certainly felt light headed. He swallowed hard at the sight of her, the beauty of her face, the way her hair fell splashing around her shoulders. His gaze dipped to her full breasts then her slender waist and hips again. He felt his own arousal keenly.

She took a step toward him hands placed on his chest. She was smiling tightly, lips pressed together.

"Your heart... it's beating as hard as mine." After a moment one of her hands slipped down to clasp his and raise it to her chest, pressing it there against the soft and yielding skin. He too felt her manic heartbeat.

She left his hand there, and he didn't want to move it. She returned her hands to his chest and the laces of his shirt.

After that things blurred a little. His clothes fell away, and they spent some time exploring each other's bodies by touch, or standing close, pressed together, kissing passionately. Then he laid down, bringing her atop him. He didn't want her back pressing into any rocks or roots. He didn't notice any himself, but he was rather preoccupied with what Alnia was doing. That went on until it was quite dark, and they were both well spent.

9

CAERWYN HOPED SHE HADN'T LOST HER OPENING WITH JAIS.

They were on their way back to Klasten's Green. It was a beautiful, warm summer's morning, and they had just left the forest behind, revealing the vast clear blue sky above. Ahead of her Jais and Alnia were holding hands and quietly tittering and laughing. Caerwyn had missed her chance to speak to Jais last night. She'd hesitated, and that had been all the gods had needed to intervene and tell her she'd taken too long to ask him for what she wanted.

She couldn't help but feel bitter and disappointed at this. Indecision had never been an issue for her before now, but this one thing had her all befuddled.

She was a... no... she *had been* a general! She should have enough courage to ask a man to mate with her. It didn't even mean anything! Well it might not to her, but perhaps to him. He seemed to be quite close with that girl, Alnia. They weren't married yet... though perhaps consummation was kin to marriage in these parts, and she was fairly certain there had been some consummating last night. So maybe he was married?

By Suur! This was confusing and infuriating. To make matters worse, she was fairly certain Barami was smugly grinning because of all of this. She was quite certain he didn't like the thought of her with anyone else.

Her teeth were grinding, jaw clenched. The hand holding Davlas was trembling, white knuckled. She was furious with Jais and that bouncy, beautiful girl, and angry at Barami. Mostly she was livid with herself. In truth she had no one else to blame.

Stupid, tongue-tied, coward of a woman!

She didn't even know why she was upset! There were other drahksani out there. There had to be. They couldn't all be dead. Why was she so set on this one in particular? Yet it had taken her a year to reach this one, and she had no clue if she'd find another suitable match any time soon.

Perhaps that was it. Jais was... suitable. He was a good match for her and as such would produce a child that was a good match for her as well. At this very moment he was her best chance of having a family and one that suited her lifestyle. She wasn't sure what she'd do with a kid that wished to pursue books or tend to nature or any of the other possible drahksani abilities.

It wasn't as if she had any feelings for Jais. Well... perhaps she did. She respected his strength and warrior spirit, but there wasn't anything more.

Was there?

For a moment an image flashed in her mind. She and Jais sitting in a small cottage with a couple children, living a simple life, happy and... bored stiff. Yet even as she thought that another image came to mind of her and Jais together. This one was far different though, with them fighting side by side against some faceless horde. The enemy being no match for their combined battle prowess. And there was a child there too, strapped to Jais' back as he fought, squealing with joy as the enemy fell. That... seemed quite plausible and enjoyable.

Then, within that same daydream, an enemy sword slipped through Jais' defense and lopped off his head.

She snapped out of her reverie with a clipped, "No!"

Everyone looked at her. It took her a moment to realize she'd said that out loud. She waved them off with an abashed: "Sorry." But she could feel herself blushing.

Gods! She never blushed! What was wrong with her?

She knew she didn't want Jais with her. That would just be someone else she might lose. All she needed was the child. She could look after a single child. She would keep it close and make sure nothing happened to it.

She wasn't going to lose anyone else she loved.

So no, she didn't need Jais to like her. And she was certain she had no affections for him beyond respect as a warrior. All she needed was the child.

She could ask him for it still, even if he was with Alnia. She could ask them both and see if the other woman understood.

She was decided.

She wouldn't waste any more time. She would talk to him... them.

Now.

She hurried to catch up to the others. They were just cresting a hill, and as Caerwyn rejoined them, she could see the village below them. It wasn't large, clustered along the slow meandering Eresvan River, with a few rough roads, little more than wagon tracks, leading away from it, mostly to nearby farms.

She was about to call out to Jais when Danz pointed at something. "What's that?"

Gods, why was there always something just when she wanted to speak!

Alnia responded with a glib, "That's our mill, silly." Indeed the direction the man was pointing was toward the mill, the large water-turned wheel making the building easily identifiable.

"No, out beyond it. Those shapes, they're moving."

Caerwyn's sight was exceptional, as was the case for most drahksani. She and Jais saw what the boy was pointing toward at the same time. She knew this because they swore in unison.

"Krolls!" Jais breathed in disbelief.

It was indeed hard to believe, mostly because there were three of them. She could see their large misshapen forms heading straight in toward the village. Straight for the mill actually.

"They're... headed for the mill?" It sounded like Danz was questioning his own words, as if he didn't want them to be true.

Alnia spun on Jais. "Do something!"

The problem was that even with their greater than human speed, if Caerwyn and Jais ran as hard as they could to the mill, they still wouldn't get there in time.

Jais sprinted off anyway.

"Jais!" Caerwyn called. She wanted to say more but instead just swore and bolted after him. If the others followed she didn't know and didn't care. Jais was strong, fast, and tough, but she highly doubted he could take three krolls on his own. He just didn't have the combat experience. By the Shadows of Holn, he didn't even have a weapon! And against three krolls? She didn't even think she could take three krolls herself.

She caught up to Jais. Her longer legs gave her the advantage in running despite his raw power. But at these speeds, running all out, talking was a near impossibility. She grabbed him by the shoulder, squeezing, hoping he'd stop.

He slowed.

It was enough for her to find the breath to speak as they jogged along, side by side.

"Jais, don't do this. You can't take three krolls. You'll never reach the mill in time anyway, it's already lost. And you're only killing yourself arriving to a fight already winded. Stop and let's make a plan!"

"I can't stop. I have to do something. And I'm not stupid. I know fighting would be silly, but Alnia's family is in there. I was hoping to help them get away. Then we can plan!"

That made sense, even if she was fairly certain that mill was going to be in pieces long before the two of them got there.

She didn't try to convince Jais of this, instead she picked up her speed as he raced forward once more. At this point her goal was simply to save Jais from himself.

She quickly found out that although she was faster, Jais' stamina exceeded hers. Her lungs were burning, breath hard to find, her legs ached and began to slow. He kept on running. They had crossed more than half the distance to the mill. She had to stop and take a moment to catch her breath.

She glanced behind her. The other three were all making their way as fast as they could, but they were still a ways behind. She and Jais were at the outskirts of the village, having found a path that ran along between two farmers' fields.

She rested for as long as she dared, then began another sprint. It was harder this time, but she forced her legs to churn. She could see Jais ahead, pulling farther and farther away. She had to get to him, had to help him. She found strength in that thought and pushed herself onward.

Her prediction had been wrong. She pulled within sight of the mill as Jais reached it. It wasn't in pieces. The krolls had only just arrived. She could see small forms fleeing.

Jais threw himself between the krolls and those forms. The lead kroll, wielding a small tree as a club, slammed it down on Jais.

Her heart lurched.

She ran faster.

10

JAIS THREW HIMSELF OUT OF THE WAY OF THE MASS OF branches descending on him, but was too slow. Smaller limbs tore through his shirt into his back. He landed hard, rolling to his feet quickly, but the kroll wasn't wasting any time either. It slammed the tree down toward him again. This time he ran in toward the thing, dodging the branches. The kroll missed. Jais lunged, throwing himself bodily at one of the large beast's skinny legs. Those looked like its weakest parts.

He'd gotten a look at the three krolls as he'd sprinted nearer. This one was taller than the other two, all rangy limbs and mostly narrow body, though the torso flared out through the chest and shoulders, making its body look almost like an even-sided triangle with limbs.

His tackle worked, and he knocked the legs out from under the thing. It collapsed in a heap as he too hit the ground. Again he rolled away, this time quicker. The kroll had dropped its tree, and thankfully, the other two were more intent on crushing the mill instead of the people within. So it seemed that Alnia's family: mother, father, and two younger siblings, would have a little time to flee. He'd done what he came to do.

The kroll roared, and the other two turned their attention toward it... and Jais.

Now he needed to get out of here.

He was breathing hard, his lungs raw, legs aching, burning.

A feral scream came from his left, and before he could look to see what it was, a spear took the lead kroll clean through the head. It was Davlas, and Caerwyn must have thrown it with immense force to pierce the thing's hard skull twice, front and back.

Against all Jais thought possible, the lead kroll still rose to its feet, reaching for the tree that was its weapon.

His stomach sank.

Jais didn't have any weapon on him. All the ones he'd been practicing with were either Caerwyn's or Barami's, and they had them back now. He was defenseless... except for.

"Davlas!"

The spear appeared in his hand. Still he needed to get away from these three monstrosities. So he ran.

They ran faster.

He needed shelter.

Luckily he was running directly for The Grand Bazaar, the merchant's shop. Just before he reached the door he spun and threw the spear with all his might. It took the lead kroll in the shoulder but the creature hardly seemed to notice.

Jais bowled through the door to the merchant's shop, yelling for Ambrast, the merchant, to get his family and get out. The shop was empty, and Jais didn't know if the owner and his family were still here, but he yelled it again anyway. He leapt onto the back counter with its shelves displaying wares worth fortunes then jumped again, this time grabbing an ornate long sword off the back wall. He'd seen that sword many times while ogling the merchant's goods, and it had been all he'd thought to go after now.

A tree slammed down into the merchant's shop sending bits of wood, either from the tree or the roof, in all directions. As the roof caved in at the front of the shop, Jais ducked behind the counter which protected him from most of the flying debris.

Somewhere outside he heard Caerwyn's distant voice shout for "Davlas" and hoped she was faring well. He rose, spinning to face the lead kroll as it withdrew the tree from the shop. There were barely any complete branches on the weapon anymore, only jagged, spiky stumps.

Jais charged the beast, hoping he'd be able to get to it before it could swing again. The front door of the shop was already broken open, from when he'd barged into the place, so he ran through that opening and, with both hands on the hilt of that fancy sword, leapt up and swung a great overhead chop at the arm holding the tree. He didn't know if it was the sword or his strength or his momentum, but he cut cleanly through the thing's spindly arm, landing on the far side of it. Even before it had a chance to turn he was in action. He sliced high across its back, the blade biting deep and drawing a lot of goo, which Jais assumed was akin to its blood.

As the kroll turned, he swung again at its leg. The sword cut cleanly once again, and he severed the beast's leg. The kroll screamed a feral cry.

There was a stupefied moment as he looked at the sword. This blade was certainly something!

Then the kroll fell on him.

He raised his sword—the only thing he could think to do,

in the fraction of a moment he had—before a great weight slammed him into the ground. The impact blew the breath from him, which was a problem, because the weight of the beast pressed on him so hard he couldn't draw breath.

Thick goo from the wounds on the thing's back oozed over Jais' legs and chest. The sword, still stuck in the thing's back, had just barely missed Jais, ending up between his arm and his body, the cross guard biting into his side. The kroll wasn't moving, and Jais was fairly certain it wouldn't. It was dead, or wounded enough as to be unconscious.

He had landed on his back and, when the sword had been torn from his hands, he'd tried in vain to 'catch' the falling beast. So his hands were both facing outward, on it, but pressed back into his shoulders at the moment. His only hope was to try to push the thing off him.

His lungs had already been worn ragged from the run, and they ached for air even more now. He pressed upward. He'd lifted a kroll off its feet before but that had been using its momentum and himself as a pivot point. This was far different and required raw strength. His wrists protested first, then forearms, then his upper arms and shoulders, even his chest strained to push the beast off him. He would have been grunting and yelling if he'd had any breath to do so.

Harder and harder he pressed, putting everything he had into the effort, growing more and more desperate as his heartbeats ticked away the moments without air.

It was only an inch, but he managed to lift the kroll.

He gasped in a desperate breath, then gulped in several more, while still holding the thing only barely above him, his arms straining, shaking. But he could breathe now, and air made all the difference.

Now he did shout, a savage cry as he pushed at the

thing. His trembling arms moved farther, pushing harder. He felt every muscle in his body grow taut, and with a final bellow and a single forceful shove, he threw the thing off him.

He had a moment to recover. Yet even in that moment he sensed more danger close by. From his prone position he tried to see what was going on.

He rolled his head around and scanned what he could while still catching his breath and giving his body a break. He caught glimpses of Caerwyn, still upright and dancing around in a deadly display of her incredible prowess. She was facing both of the other two krolls and somehow keeping them both at bay.

He rolled his head to the other side and saw Barami sprinting toward them to help. He also saw Alnia staring at him, eyes wide and mouth agape. She'd seen him push the kroll off, it was clear from her expression. Danz, it seemed, had missed it... perhaps... as the other boy was nowhere in sight. Jais groaned, knowing this was going to require some explaining later.

He rose slowly. There wasn't a part of him that didn't ache, but he seemed to have escaped any major damage, which was lucky. As he drew to a sitting position he saw that with both Barami and Caerwyn in the fray the two krolls were being pushed back, farther and farther away.

He should help.

He pulled his newly acquired blade from the kroll's back as he rose, then plunged it in again a few times to ensure the beast was dead and not just unconscious.

As he drew the sword out the final time, he heard a tentative voice nearby. "Jais?" It was Alnia of course. She'd drawn closer.

He turned to her. Her face was a mask of confusion, fear, and joy. Her hands were trembling at her sides.

"How...?"

"I need to go help the others, I'll explain later."

She nodded, the motion seemed more habitual than in response to his words. He took the two steps over to her—nearly stumbling on his aching legs—and gave her a light kiss on the cheek. Her hand came up and touched his face almost as if to check to see if he was real.

"I saw..." Her eyes were distant.

This was going to be a long conversation.

"I know. I need to go. You shouldn't be near here. Run off to the Ox and Axe. I'll see you there when we're done."

She nodded. Again it seemed more out of habit than a response to him.

"Good." He kissed her again, then made sure she was on her way before returning to the fight.

He took in the scene before him. The mill was half crushed and burning, the merchant's shop was partially caved in and would need a new roof. Several other buildings nearby had taken minor damage as well.

The two remaining krolls were both injured, but the wounds seemed minor. It was clear from several pinprick holes, that Caerwyn had been peppering both of them with Davlas, but he got the feeling she'd been doing more avoiding than attacking, until Barami had arrived at least. Now the two warriors were facing off against their respective beasts, but even so they were still mostly on the defensive. The two of them seemed tired, both breathing heavily and swaying on their feet.

The krolls they'd fought in the forest had been more aggressive, charging in and taking damage. These two beasts seemed to be a little more cautious, avoiding damage where they could. Jais didn't know much about the creatures, but somehow that seemed odd.

Hopefully with him joining the other two, this would end quicker.

The excitement of battle made his aches dissipate, his pain a distant thing. He came around the side of one of the beasts, the one Barami was fighting, and with a shout, leapt in suddenly as it swung down at the aged warrior. Barami was blocking the blow with this shield, which looked a little dented at the moment, but Jais' attack caught the kroll's arm and—with his new sword, which he was quickly learning to like—severed the creature's limb. The arm fell to the ground and Jais landed next to it. Barami looked up surprised, but said nothing, moving in to attack.

Jais followed.

Between the two of them they cut that kroll up fairly quickly. It bellowed as it went down, before Jais removed its head.

He was panting like a spent horse, shoulders and chest heaving.

Not far away Barami was doing the same, kneeling and leaning heavily on his shield. "By the gods I didn't think I could do that!" The dark-skinned man then looked at Jais with a new respect in his eyes. "And you..." He shook his head, perhaps at a loss for words. Jais nodded back, admiring how a man of Barami's age had run here then gone straight into battle. That couldn't have been easy.

"It's getting away!" came a distant shout from Caerwyn.

Jais looked. She was throwing Davlas in a last ditch effort to stop the thing, but it was sprinting. Long, strong legs carried it quickly away. Jais was certain none of them would be able to catch it. Davlas did little to hinder it, and Caerwyn called the spear back as she stopped her pursuit.

"What in all the Shadowed Places?" This was from Barami close behind Jais. "None of this makes any sense! Where are all these Shadow Spawned things coming from?"

Jais had an uneasy feeling about this whole thing himself. Whether it was the number of them or how they had fought so carefully, he wasn't certain, but he just felt like something was terribly wrong. Some voice in his head screamed at him that there was more going on here.

He jogged over to see how Caerwyn was doing. She looked exhausted. A few strands of hair had escaped the tied back pony tail and were plastered to her face. She was leaning over, hands on knees, breathing hard.

She looked uninjured.

"What happened?" he asked. She turned her head toward him, and her face lit up.

"By Lansus! You're alive!" She was up in an instant and rushed to him. He was quite surprised to find her arms tight around him in a fierce embrace. "I saw that thing land on you and..." Her words were a little muffled, her face in his shoulder.

He didn't know what to make of this. She'd never shown him this degree of affection before. Perhaps this was just her way of congratulating him?

She was nothing like Alnia: smelly, sweaty and hard, and certainly much more aggressive in her affections. Alnia's embrace would be a soft and yielding thing.

"I'm glad you are well too," he said slowly. He gave her a perfunctory hug with a pat on the back.

She drew back suddenly. She was breathing hard still, and she gave him an odd looking smile. "Yes, of course. I am well. We are... well." An odd expression passed over her face, almost as if she were arguing with herself about how she felt: intimate and friendly or assertive and commanding. "I'm just so glad you're alive." She settled on an all-business look and nodded to him. Then she flashed a smile that didn't seem completely genuine.

Jais didn't know what to make of any of that.

Then she spoke, and words seemed to burst forth from her almost as if she had little control of it. "Jais, there is something I need to ask you before anything else happens. I've tried so many times, but something keeps getting in the way, and I won't allow that to happen anymore. I don't know the right way to say this, so I'm just going to say it. I want to have a child, a drahksan child. And I need another drahksani to help me create that child. I don't want a husband. I'm not looking for anything emotional. I plan on taking care of the child on my own. But I need you to help me with this. Will you help to give me a child?"

Her eyes were wide, seemingly surprised at herself and her own words.

Jais was more than a little taken aback by this as well. He didn't know what to say. He stood there dumbfounded for a long moment, blinking. His only utterance was a drawn out, "Ahhhhhhhh."

The worry and shock on her face turned to a pained expression of need.

She stepped closer and took his hand. "Please, Jais. I need this, and you're the only one who can help me."

"I... I don't know," he managed to stammer.

Her lips tightened, and she nodded. She gave a weak smile, which looked so very out of place on her face. Letting his hand drop she turned away. He was certain she was on the brink of tears—something else which seemed foreign on her.

"I understand," she said with a quaver to her voice.

"I don't!" Barami said stepping up to Jais. "You're going to listen to me boy!"

11

SHE'D DONE IT.

She finally told Jais her desire, asked him for his help. She'd found words, even if they'd been awkward, and—well it didn't matter that now wasn't a good time, she'd needed to say them.

And Jais had stood there struck dumb.

She'd had to turn away to hide her tears. She felt as wrecked as the town looked. The village around them was in shambles. The mill was still burning, the merchant's shop a mess, and several other buildings had suffered from the wrath of the krolls. But they could be repaired. Could she fix this strange tear she felt in her heart?

She'd bared her soul to this man. She knew it was a lot to take in, but she'd thought at least he might be... flattered? She hadn't known what he'd say, how he'd react, but that look of shear panic on his face hadn't been it. It wasn't like she was asking for him to give his life for her or anything so demanding. She didn't think it would be a big thing. He'd probably enjoy it... but then...

Perhaps that was it.

Never once before in her life had Caerwyn questioned her looks. She'd never cared to, never needed to. It didn't matter how she looked in a fight. Looks only seemed to matter if one was looking for a life-partner. She wasn't even doing that, but perhaps she was just so hideous that the thought of mating with her wasn't even a pleasant concept?

She tried to put a quick lid on that line of thought. It was petty and childish and not like her at all, but still her thoughts whirled and pounded inside her head. She was still exhausted from the sprint, then straight into a fight. She didn't feel strong in any way at the moment, and it was a terrifying feeling for her.

How had this gone so wrong?

Then she heard Barami talking.

"You're going to listen to me boy!"

Jais didn't respond, and Barami barreled on. "I know you've been through a lot these last few days, and this was probably the last thing you were expecting, but Caer just did something very difficult for her. She deserves something more than an 'I don't know'."

"But..." Jais still seemed as stunned as he had before.

"But nothing!" Barami was getting angry. "I can't believe you'd..." Barami huffed and there seemed a long moment when she could hear him drawing long deep breaths.

"Do you understand what Caer asked of you?" Barami asked.

"Yes," Jais stammered.

"All she wants is the child. Once she has that we'll be on our way. You won't have to see either of us again. You won't need to leave your girl, though I suspect there will be an awkward conversation as you try to explain this all to her.

That's all it will cost you. That and a little time and energy which I can't imagine would be so horrible. I know she caught you off guard, boy, but what's the problem?"

"I... I don't know. It was a bit of a shock. People generally don't... ask for something like that."

"But you understand why—?"

"Yes," Jais said. "I know why it has to be me. I get that. I just... well people don't ask that sort of thing!"

"Well she is, so get over yourself. Either tell her yes or tell her no, and we'll be gone from this place. Which will it be, boy?"

"Barami," Caerwyn said, the man was being too hard on Jais. Yet even as she said it Jais spoke in unison with her.

"I'll do it!"

She blinked the tears from her eyes and risked a glance at him. He had his arms up in the air in a sign of defeat. So it would be a hardship for him?

She didn't know why that stung, but it did.

Jais' gaze caught hers, and his arms fell.

"Caerwyn..." The young man's words failed him. "I'm sorry."

Sorry? What was he sorry for? He wasn't the one putting her on the spot by asking such a thing from her. She should be apologizing. She looked away again.

"I'm sorry I reacted like that."

Oh.

A strong hand fell on her shoulder. Jais' voice was closer this time. "I know that must have been hard for you, and I didn't react well. I'm sorry. I don't know how I'm going to let Alnia know of any of this, but you've done so much for me that... that I can repay you with this." Though when he said *this* it was with a hesitation. He still wasn't so certain of *this*.

"Thank you," she said softly.

"Holn's Dark Depths, boy!"

Caerwyn turned at Barami's curse. Jais turned as well. Barami was looking at the young man's back. "You've got a lot of deep cuts and with dirt packed into all of them. Let me take a look at you." The big man strode over and began inspecting Jais' wounds, clucking like an old farmwoman over weeds in her garden.

Jais stood there for a long moment, and when he turned his gaze back to her, it was laden with mystification. "I'd forgotten about that."

For some reason that perplexed look on Jais' face and Barami doing his best impression of an old healer woman seemed like the most hilarious thing Caerwyn had ever seen.

She let out a breath of a laugh, followed reflexively by a few more. Once she started, she couldn't stop.

Jais' confusion turned to a smile, then he too was laughing with her.

All the pent-up emotions within her suddenly released through her hooting and chuckling, and it only got worse... or better. Her stomach knotted with the effort, but she didn't mind. This felt good, and Jais was joining her, laughing for no reason and every reason.

Some little while later, after Barami had told them to stay put so he could get some water and bandages, Caerwyn finally settled and—completely exhausted—just sat in the road.

Jais sat with her.

"So that's why you came to me that day," he said softly, gazing out, perhaps into his own memories. "You said you were looking for me... now I understand. Now... well a lot of things make sense." He swung his head to look at her. He wasn't entirely smiling but he was sincere when he said. "I'll give you a child, if I can, Caerwyn."

She smiled back, and some part of her soul healed just a little. "I know it's not something that normal people ask for." It was her turn to look away. "But we're not normal." She couldn't help a little melancholy slipping into her voice at that. "I didn't want to disrupt your life. I'm not looking for a family or a father for the child, just a man to help me have it."

He gave a soft laugh. "No, you don't need a man to help you with anything do you?"

She didn't.

But...

Then why had those words stung. He was stating what he saw in her, a confident independent woman. His words had had no malice in them, but they hurt all the same. As much as it was true she didn't need anyone, she already knew that it was nice to have... friends around. That's what Barami was.

She didn't need a man, no.

But Jais wasn't a bad man to have around, either.

That image of the two of them fighting side by side returned to her. She swept it out of her mind.

No, that wasn't what she wanted. Her soul constricted at the thought.

No.

She wouldn't let anyone get too close, not anymore.

She softly but sternly said words which cut her to say, "No, Jais. You are right. I don't need anyone. We'll be moving on soon enough, and all I want from you is a child. Thank you for agreeing. It means a lot to me."

He sighed heavily. "And when you go, what will there be for me?"

"What do you mean?"

"This has been—well not fun, but this fighting..." He drew in a long breath. "I feel like I'm finally being myself for the first time in my life. This all feels... natural. Defending people and fighting monsters. That's strange I know, but..."

No, it wasn't strange, it was exactly how she felt; more at home in a fight than at most other places.

But, Jais was no adventurer. He may have longed for a fight, longed to venture away from his home, but he didn't really know what that meant. There are few who truly do. What it means to leave behind those you love for long periods; risk never seeing family and friends again. She'd never wanted to have this life. It had been forced on her, and she wouldn't wish it on anyone.

"It's who you are," she said softly. *It's who we are.* "But you will have to go back to your life after this. Trust me there is no 'adventure' out in the world. Only the pain of being away from those you love."

"Oh," he said. "Oh."

Then Barami was returning with supplies and tending to them both. First to Jais and his myriad wounds, then to her and the few light injuries she'd sustained. Though Caerwyn wasn't sure she needed the bandage on her arm. The cut was not deep and would heal quick enough. What did it matter if she had another scar? But she had no strength to fight Barami.

Jais rose.

"I should go and find some way to tell Alnia about this." He sighed. "There is a lot I need to tell her." He turned back to them with a nod, then was off.

Caerwyn watched him go.

"Well that was awkward," Barami said quietly.

Caerwyn had to laugh. "Oh? I hadn't noticed."

Barami grunted. "He's a good enough lad."

"You've come around?"

He looked at her then, those dark eyes intense. "You deserve only the best." But then perhaps having said too much he looked away. "I'm glad he'll give you what you need."

"Me too," she said with a sigh. "Gods, but I need a rest."

Another grunt from Barami was the only response.

12

Jais' mind spun, as he made his way toward the Ox and Axe and the center of Klasten's Green. The sun was high, just past midday, and he was dressed like a nobleman. The merchant, as upset as he'd been about this shop, had been thankful that Jais had fought off the kroll, keeping the damage to what it was. So thankful, he'd gifted to Jais the sword he'd used in the fight. Jais had tried to return it, but Master Ambrast had insisted he keep it and even given him the scabbard and a new finely tailored shirt as well.

Jais was still exhausted. So much had happened in the last short while it was still all just settling in for him. The fight, Caerwyn's request, everything seemed so immediate and... big.

He grimaced.

How in the Deepest Shadows of Holn would he ever ask Alnia if he could...? He couldn't even say the words to himself.

He sighed. Gods he was worn out. But there was still so much to do, and while he knew he looked impressive in his new clothes, his insides were all a jumble with confusion and uncertainty.

When he'd been with Alnia the other night, it had been an expression of their feelings, something shared and intimate. He wasn't certain he could just... do that... with Caerwyn like a business transaction. That seemed somehow wrong. She'd made it quite clear that she had no feelings for him. He could see she didn't need him... or anyone else in her life.

So how could he go through with this? How could he even talk to Alnia about this? His tongue was dry, no words in his mind.

He was about to turn around to go back and tell Caerwyn he couldn't do it, when a voice called out his name.

He couldn't place the voice until he turned around and saw Alnia's father, Samuar Miller.

"Jais." The man hurried over. He was wearing his heavy apron, his work clothes, not the finery he often wore to village events. "I know the mill is gone, but it can be rebuilt. Thank you for your bravery. I think that's all that allowed us to get away."

Jais was touched and a bit uplifted by the comment. He'd always dreamed of being a hero, of saving others and fighting monsters. It only really sunk in, at that moment, that that's exactly what he'd done today.

"You're most welcome, Master Miller. I am glad I could help."

The man laughed with a bit of surprise. "You did more than that. And look at you now! You are the proper vision of a hero, and one from our little town." Samuar beamed. Jais was uncertain what to say to that. Before he could say anything the other man went on. "I think I was wrong about you, my boy. I had thought... well... seeing you with Alnia I didn't think you a good match for her, but perhaps I was wrong. If you're willing to risk your life to save myself and my family..." The man shrugged. "I'm sorry I misjudged you. If you are interested in formally courting Alnia, I think perhaps that could be arranged. If that goes well perhaps you two could be betrothed at the harvest festival."

Jais' lack of words changed to stunned silence. The thought of being betrothed to Alnia before the end of the year...

This certainly was a turn about from the dour looks the man had thrown Jais' way before today.

Jais found some words, though he could only stammer them out. "I... think that... would be great! Thank you. It would be an honor... my honor."

The other man clasped his shoulders with a nod before embracing him. Jais winced as the man's arms pressed on the cuts on his back. Samuar let him go, still beaming. "I'll set it all up, don't you worry."

Jais nodded.

"Would you like to tell 'Nia, or should I?" Samuar asked.

Jais' request to her about Caerwyn now seemed even more awkward. "I will. I need to speak with her anyway."

"Great! I'll see you later then."

Samuar was off, heading back toward the mill.

Jais didn't know which direction to go. He was suddenly even more conflicted than he had been before that talk.

Was he a hero? Sure he certainly looked like some valiant knight—without the armor—at the moment. He had defeated monsters in defense of his village, saving lives. He'd done heroic things, but... he didn't feel like a hero. He still felt scared and uncertain and... himself. And... if he was going to be betrothed and eventually marry Alnia, could he still be a hero? Did heroes have wives? Perhaps, but usually, in the tales he'd heard, it was some princess they found and settled down with when their 'heroing' days were over.

Was he done being a hero now? Did he want that? He honestly couldn't answer the question. On the one side, it would certainly make things less scary and more peaceful. He didn't want to have to charge at monsters. He knew he'd escaped death and serious injury only barely today—a couple of times. There would always be the risk of such things if he was off being a hero, the risk one day he might not come back to his wife. He'd only survived today because there had been other heroes around to help.

What if Caerwyn and Barami weren't here? Someday soon they wouldn't be. What then? Who'd help him then? But... on the other side, the rush of battle, and the cama-raderie of fighting alongside great men and women to defend the weak and innocent was what he'd always wanted. He wouldn't be able to do that if he stayed, if he was bonded. He'd probably end up taking over his uncle's job as a hunter and woodsman. That wouldn't be a bad profession, but it wouldn't be the same as adventuring and being a true hero.

He didn't know what he wanted. He needed to talk to someone.

He set off purposefully toward the Ox and Axe... and made it only three steps before stopping sharply.

Who could he talk to? He didn't have a close friend to confide in. His aunt and uncle had their own desires for him; they would not be impartial if he asked them such things. None of the boys in the village were true friends, just men of a similar age who respected his strength enough not to test it. Most of them had beaten him up as a kid. They only respected him now because he could fight back. They weren't real friends. Who did that leave? The village girls? The girls might give him a willing ear, but he thought them more likely to run and tell someone of his deepest worries than help him with them. That left Alnia. He trusted her. But part of his concerns were about her? Could she be that objective? Did he have another choice?

Caerwyn and Barami?

Maybe just Barami.

He spun around and headed back to where he'd left the two.

The aging warrior was sitting next to the semi-demolished merchant's shop tending to some nicks in his sword. Caerwyn wasn't around.

"Can we talk?" Jais said crouching next to the man.

"We are both able to do so, yes. I am often not inclined to do so at length, however."

Jais wasn't really sure what that meant and took it as an affirmative. "I talked to Alnia's father. We're going to be betrothed."

"Congratulations."

"Thank you, but..." What exactly was his question? "I don't know if I want to?"

"That's not a proper question."

"No." This wasn't going as he'd hoped. He just spoke his thoughts. "I've enjoyed learning to fight and helping fend off these krolls. It's exciting, and working with you and Caerwyn makes me feel more... at home, than anything else I've ever done. And yet, it's dangerous work, and I've already taken more injuries these last few days that I think I have my entire life, certainly more serious injuries. I know this is dangerous, and I don't think I could honestly do it if I were bonded. I'd be putting myself too much at risk. So what do I do? Do I not get married and go off and be a hero? Or do I give this all up for a loving wife and family and all that?"

Barami grunted.

That wasn't a helpful response, but Jais waited in case there was more.

After a moment Barami elaborated. "What we do, Caer and I, is not 'being heroes'."

Jais waited for more, but it didn't seem to be coming. "What do you do? What would you call it?"

"We walk. We hunt. We search for more of... your kind. That's it."

"But you're fighting here?"

Barami only now looked up from the work of smoothing out his blade, stopping his slow repetitive hand motion. "To save you. To save them." He nodded out toward the town. "Not because we want to. Not because it's fun. Because we are the best able."

"Some would call you heroes."

"They can call us what they wish."

"Your life certainly seems more interesting than mine... than living some normal life with a family and wife."

"More interesting... perhaps. Better? I am not so sure."

"Would you have a wife if you could?"

Now Barami looked away, beginning the slow motion of his work once again. It took him a long time to answer. "Yes."

Jais sat back on his haunches and sighed. So even this warrior would choose a safe life if he had the choice. Perhaps he'd seen too much battle? But Jais had hardly seen any. Would it be enough for him? He'd have a few tales to tell his kids. Not many, but they'd be good ones.

"So I should get bonded and forget this life?"

Barami shrugged. "Your choice, not mine."

That didn't help.

"But you would if you had the chance?"

"Yes."

Jais nodded. "Thank you." He rose and turned to go when Barami spoke again. "You still going to help Caerwyn with her... request?"

Yes, that.

What an interesting conversation that would make: *hello Alnia, we're to be bonded and I'm going to give up being a hero for you. Do you mind if I lay with another woman first? She'd really appreciate it.*

Yet he still responded with, "I will." He'd consider it at least. The two of them had done far too much for him not to, as awkward as it would make his life.

Jais found Alnia with her family at the Ox and Axe. She caught sight of him and left her mother and siblings to come to him.

"Can we talk, outside?" he asked.

She nodded.

Once they were out in the glorious noonday sun he felt a little enlivened. "Your father came to me. He said we can court each other, formally."

"Jais, that's wonderful!" Her good humor quickly died away. She looked into his eyes, her clear green eyes cautious, concerned. "Jais. I saw you fighting and it was..."

He enfolded both of her hands in his. "Yes, about that."

"I thought you were dead," she whispered. He could feel her hands trembling. She was so fragile, like a leaf. "That... that thing landed on you, and I thought... but then you..."

He'd lifted the dead weight of a twelve foot tall creature off himself and thrown it to the side. He still couldn't quite believe that himself. He had no idea how he could explain it to Alnia.

He sighed. He had a lot of explaining to do. This would have to come before he spoke to her about Caerwyn.

"I'm different," he said softly. He glanced around, but they were out in the open not far from the front of the inn. He didn't want to talk here. "Come, let's go somewhere a little more private."

She nodded, and he led her around to the alley between the tavern and the baker's shop.

His words from a moment ago must only have sunk in now for she said, "Different?"

Once again he took her hands in his.

He didn't speak for a long moment as he debated what he would say.

All his life... well his adult life, since he and Alnia had come of age at roughly the same time, the two of them had had a bond. Somehow he had always known he would be with her. But how could that happen now that he was... something else? He considered telling a falsehood. Perhaps he could claim that the gods had helped him in that moment and that's how he'd lifted that thing. Yet lying to her didn't seem right. If he was going to share his life with her it couldn't be based on a lie. Last night she's shown him the true depths of her feelings for him. She'd been truly open, giving herself to him. Now he needed to be just as open. He was what he was, and if he was going to be with her, she needed to know.

His pulse pounded in his ears drowning out all sound but his voice and hers. This was it. He had to tell her the truth. "I don't get hurt as easily as most people." That was an easy way to start.

She only blinked at him, uncomprehending.

"I heal faster than anyone here and can run faster as you

saw. I am far stronger than even I thought I was, and seem to have a natural affinity for battle and hunting. My senses are sharper than most peoples. I can see in the dark better than most." He lowered his voice for the next part. This was the true test of how she felt about him. Would she react well? "Alnia, I'm drahksani."

Her eyes went wide, and he saw a flash of fear in them. But she didn't pull away or try to run. Instead that fear turn quickly to confusion. "Drahksani?" She lowered her voice. "The demon spawn?"

"No, Alnia. It means that I have the blood of dragons in me. It's not evil at all. It's... it's like a sword. A sword isn't evil, but instead can be used by men of good intentions or bad. You don't think me evil do you?"

"No of course not. But..."

"I'm not, Alnia. You know me. I just have abilities. What I do with them... well you've seen what I do with them. Was fighting those things evil?"

She shook her head, but still seemed confused. She looked down, her thoughts heavy perhaps.

"I know there are lots of terrible things said about drahk-sani, and before now I believed them too, but then I found out I was one and what I could do. I'm still the same as I was before. I have the same good heart. A heart that... loves you, Alnia."

Looking up at him she blinked. Slowly through the fog of fear and uncertainty, he saw the light return to her eyes.

She smiled. "Yes, of course. I know you're not evil Jais. And... I... love you to."

He smiled with her. With a quick look around he lowered his voice again. "But you have to be careful how much you speak of this or how openly. This is a secret of mine you cannot tell anyone, ever, not even your father or family."

"No one?"

"No. It would put me in danger. Others may not be so easily swayed. They may judge me harshly, no matter what I've done to help the village." He was whispering but lowered his voice even further, drawing her closer. "People feared the drahksani so much they hunted us down. That is why you can never tell anyone, otherwise my life—the life I want with you—would be in danger."

"Oh! Jais that's horrible. I'm so sorry."

"I am trusting you with this because I know we were meant to be together, Alnia."

"Together, yes. Your secret is safe with me."

He gathered her in a soft embrace then, thanking the gods he hadn't lost her. But that was only one part of what he needed to say to her.

And some part of him told him he needed to tell her now. He had a sudden feeling, some strange premonition like something was horribly wrong. There was this hard, cold feeling in his gut telling him that somewhere out there, things were falling apart. It was like nothing he'd ever felt before. He needed to get home.

But before he could do that, he had to tell Alnia about Caerwyn's request.

"There is something else I wanted to ask you."

"Oh? What?"

How could he possibly say this? Yet that sensation of distant panic insisted he find a way. Perhaps if he worked his way to it. "The two southerners, they've been really helpful, fighting off several krolls, wouldn't you say?"

"Of course."

"They didn't have to, they owe us nothing. They were just passing through, but they did help us. That deserves a reward, doesn't it?"

"Yes, I would say so. Have they asked for something?"

He grimaced. "Yes." He pursed his lips trying to find the right words.

"Jais? What is it?"

"They have asked for something, but they have asked it of me only. I'm the only one who can give them what they want, but I don't know if I can do it. I... don't know if you would want me to do it."

Alnia was concern, confused. "What is it, Jais?"

The sensation of something horrible happening intensified. It was like a scream inside his head. He needed to be home... Now!

He shook that off for the moment. "Remember what I told you about... what I am?"

"A drahksan?"

Jais winced and made a hushing sound. She hadn't been that loud, but he'd hoped to avoid mention of the word all together.

"Sorry."

"It's okay, but, well... that woman, Caerwyn, she is one as well."

This seemed to sink in slowly for Alnia, but after a moment she nodded. "That makes sense."

"And... she wants me to—"

"You're drahksan? That explains why you're so strong!" The voice came from behind him.

Jais spun, terrified.

Erid stood just inside the alley, eyes wide.

Jais looked back to see if Alnia had known the other man

was there, but she seemed just as surprised as he did.

"Erid, you—"

"You're the spawn of a demon. No wonder I can't beat you at grip-wrestling." Erid wore a nasty grin on his face. His gaze flicked to something behind Jais... Alnia. "And you knew did you? You're a sympathizer with a demon?"

"Erid, no." Alnia tried to help. "You know he's not—"

"—Human? Yeah, I can see that now. We'll have to burn him to ensure all the shadows are purified from his soul."

Jais was stuck between fear and uncertainty. Was Erid really threatening him or just playing with them.

"Erid, you can't believe that. I've only ever helped this village."

"All a ruse, apparently." The man sneered.

Jais had had enough, he stalked forward, getting in the other man's face. "What do you want? I can't believe you're callous enough to want me dead. So what is it?"

Erid straightened emphasizing that he stood head and shoulders above Jais, and glared down at him. He wasn't stronger, but he was intimidating with his sheer mass. Jais had learned long, long ago that he had nothing to fear from Erid, but he was a little worried for Alnia.

Erid's voice, when he spoke was a lethal whisper, venom dripping from every word. "I want you to go. Leave this village and never return. Stay up in that hut of yours and never show your face around here. Tell everyone you've contracted some nasty disease that even your aunt can't heal and..." He trailed off, the look on his face changing from loathing to a dawning comprehension. He nodded to himself after a moment. "Your aunt is one too isn't she? That makes sense. So for your sake and hers, leave us all alone."

Jais was growing more and more furious. Erid knew too

much and Jais couldn't risk him telling anyone else. But he also wasn't going to let the man dictate the terms on which he lived. He was still formulating a response when he felt Alnia behind him, having drawn closer, pressing herself to his back, hiding from Erid. Her voice came from over his right shoulder.

"It's well, Jais. I'll go with you. We can live in peace away from these nasty people."

Jais wasn't sure what to think of that either.

Erid said, "No. You stay, Alnia. It sickens me to think of a beautiful woman like you living with a demon-spawn." Erid's gaze fell back upon Jais. "That's another of my terms. You stay away from Alnia... forever." The man grinned.

"You can't—" Alnia cried.

"I can, and if you don't both agree I'll tell everyone what you are."

Jais had had enough. "Alnia step back." There was death in his voice.

"Jais?"

"Just step back."

He felt her go, never taking his eyes off Erid. Erid too backed up a few steps, shaking out his arms. He knew a fight was coming. He had to know he couldn't win.

Apparently he did know.

He'd backed up far enough that he'd cleared the end of the alley... then ran.

Jais swore.

He knew where Erid was going and knew he'd not catch him in time. But he had to try. He sprinted after Erid. His legs were still sore from his run this morning, but he pushed them as hard and fast as they would go. He caught Erid just inside the door to the Ox and Axe, tackling him to the ground, crashing through a table. Ale and food went flying, covering them.

He rolled Erid over, it was far too easy. After dealing with the inhuman strength of the krolls even the strongest of humans was little challenge for him. He drew his right arm back.

Erid flinched away, closing his eyes.

But Jais didn't let his fist fall.

He couldn't kill Erid, as much as the man was being annoying and childish. He couldn't kill a man. He could kill a kroll, they weren't human. But the thought of bashing in Erid's skull, as much as that would satisfy his rage, wasn't in Jais. And if he couldn't kill him he was stuck. Even if he broke the other man's jaw Erid would still be able to communicate what Jais was to someone at some point. The secret was out, and there was nothing he could do.

He leaned in close as Erid tentatively opened his eyes, probably wondering why Jais hadn't hit him. "Do not tell a soul. You understand?"

Erid met his gaze, terrified. But after a moment his gaze moved to Jais' poised fist. The look in his eyes changed to something else... superiority, defiance. He laughed in Jais' face. "You can't do it, can you? You won't hurt me." The man sniffed, grinning. He knew he'd won. "So what's to stop me? My offer still stands. I won't say a word if you leave this village —and Alnia—behind."

Jais slammed his fist down... into the floorboards next to Erid's head, breaking them, his fist plunging through easily.

"Last chance," he said to Erid, hoping his bluff would work.

Erid had flinched away, but now was even more defiant. "No, Jais, it's yours. What will it be?"

Jais growled, grinding his teeth.

His decision was made for him as Erid, taking advantage of his hesitation, shouted, "Jais and his aunt are drahksani!"

The words rang in Jais' ears.

The next words hurt even more. "So is that woman warrior passing through. She and her southern pet probably summoned these krolls so they could act like heroes!"

Jais did hit him now. He couldn't' help himself. Erid's words cut too deep. Caerwyn and Barami had only ever tried to help this village. The blow wasn't to the young smith's face, but to his shoulder, his off hand, and Jais pulled it enough that it would hurt like blazes for a while, but he wouldn't break any bones.

Erid cried out as other men hauled Jais off him.

There were several men on him and though he knew he could probably throw them all off, he didn't struggle. He was pulled to his feet and brought to face Erid's father, Damick.

"When you were boys I could stand you rough-housing," Damick bit out, obviously upset, more red-faced than usual. The man was well respected in the village, one of the 'elders' along with Alnia's father and a few others.

Jais couldn't help himself. "That's because when we were kids Erid always won."

Damick slapped him; a meaty hand hitting him hard with the full force of the smith's not-insignificant strength.

Jais hardly felt it.

Damick looked at him closer then. He didn't say a word for a moment. "Is there any truth to this?" Damick searched Jais' eyes. "You a drahksan, boy?"

Jais said nothing, thinking silence would be best.

"Ask her!"

Everyone turned to Erid, who was sitting, massaging his

shoulder. He pointed to the doorway, and everyone's gaze shifted again... to Alnia. Her eyes were wide, her face flushed.

It was Danz who hurried over to her. "Alnia, is any of this true? What do you know of it? Is Jais a drahksan?"

It seemed she didn't know what to say either. She flushed even more, her cheeks a deep crimson. She swallowed hard, her eyes finding Jais', searching them.

Danz grabbed her arm, more forcefully than he should have, his knuckles white. She gave a sharp cry, but Danz shouted over it. "Tell us, Alnia! Is Jais a drahksan? Did those foreigners summon the krolls to plague us, so they could extort us after they ran them off?"

"You're hurting me, Danz."

"I'll hurt you more if you don't answer me!"

"Why would those two summon the krolls? They wouldn't. Jais, tell them!"

Danz shook her, hard.

Jais had had enough. He couldn't see Alnia hurt like this, not for him.

It was far too easy to throw off the men around him tearing himself from their grip. They toppled around him, losing their footing. He rushed to Alnia and pried Danz hand from her arm, the skin underneath was bone white.

"He's a drahksan, surely!" someone shouted from behind him.

He cursed himself. He'd just given them the proof they'd wanted.

"Run," Alnia breathed with urgency.

He did.

14

CAERWYN SWAM TO SHORE AND CLIMBED OUT ONTO THE MUDDY banks of the Eresvan River. She removed a drying cloth from her pack and patted herself dry before dressing.

The splash of water on her face when she'd first come to the river side had felt good, but not enough. She'd been sweaty and dirty and just wanted a bath. So she'd found a spot a little farther upstream behind a clump of bushes and stripped down for a swim.

As she emerged, dressed and ready, from behind those same bushes, she found Barami rushing toward her.

"Everything's gone black as Holn. We need to leave this village now!" The immediacy in his voice startled her.

"What? Why? What happened?"

"They know!" It was his look, the intensity of those dark eyes boring into her that told her everything she needed to know. The village had found out she was drahksani.

"Jais?" she asked.

"On the run."

"Seven Shades of Holn!"

"I know. We need to go. Now."

She sighed. She was tired of running. She'd run from her parents as a child, run from her adopted family a year ago. She wouldn't run anymore. She was fairly certain the wrath of this little village would not be as bad as the entire Afgenni Empire after her.

"No."

"No?"

"Jais and his aunt will need our help." She found herself quite calm in saying so. Perhaps it was her calm that halted Barami from responding right away.

He took a moment, perhaps to see if she was joking.

"You're serious."

"I am." She drew forth Davlas and her short sword.

"What are you going to do, slay this village? These are innocent people."

"Not if they're trying to kill me they aren't."

"Oh, by all the gods, you're serious. This is crazy!"

"Let's go."

A certainty filled her entire being, but deep down she surged with rage. All her life she'd been cast out of whatever existence she'd had because of what she was. As a child she'd had no power to change it. When exiled from the Afgenni Empire she'd had little choice. To fight would be to die. There were thousands of warriors, even some she herself had trained, who would hunt her down. To have this little village in the north up in arms over what she was—what Jais was— was the last straw for her. She wasn't going to run, and that certainty of direction made it that much easier to act.

Barami caught up to her and readied his shield and bastard sword as they headed through the city.

Oddly the first man they encountered seemed happy to

see them. Caerwyn didn't know him, but he was poking through what remained of the mill, so she guessed he was the miller. He waved to them as they passed and thanked them for helping his family.

Her emotions were too confused by this to respond kindly so she simply nodded to the man. It seem so peculiar that perfectly normal and polite men like that could turn into hate filled monstrous shadows of humanity when they thought someone was different.

The real challenge came as they approached the middle of the town.

Caerwyn didn't want trouble. She wasn't aiming to encounter people. She needed to reach Jais and was taking the most direct route to do so. This took her near the center of town, but not directly into it. Still, she drew close enough to garner attention.

Someone shouted about 'the foreigners' which seemed to be repeated several times. It didn't take long before there was a crowd gathering, following them.

Then a group came around some buildings to block their way out of town. Caerwyn didn't even stop walking. She kept her pace even and moved toward them, cold and calm.

She called out to them, "I seek only to help Jais. Let me pass. This is your only warning."

That caused some to back up, especially those she was heading directly for.

There were mutterings among the group before them, growing more concerned the closer she got. They backed up farther, but then apparently the braver, or stupider, ones among them stepped in.

"What are you going to do? Kill us like the demons you are?" one shouted.

She spun Davlas around and threw it. The man was close enough that even throwing the spear the wrong way around was no issue. It bonked off his head, and he fell in a heap.

"Davlas," she said softly, and the spear returned to her hand before it hit the ground.

There were other mutterings now of "demon" and "demon weapon." Four larger men stepped out in front of her. Two had swords, though only one of the weapons was in decent shape, the other hadn't seen use or care in years. The other two men had staves.

"Barami, don't kill them if you don't have to."

She heard his grunt from behind her. He was very skilled with using his shield as a weapon, bashing and bludgeoning. It would prove less fatal than his sword.

She adjusted her short sword in her hand so she'd be using the flat of the blade if needed.

The four men didn't advance, holding their ground.

She threw Davlas at the man with the nicer sword, calling it back with precise timing just as it hit the shoulder of his sword-arm. The wound would be nasty, but not fatal. It would hinder his ability to use a sword greatly. After that, she was in melee and let her battle senses take over.

The man with the other sword swung clumsily at her. She blocked the blow, moving with far greater speed, and thrust the blunt end of Davlas into the man's belly. He doubled over, and she brought the pommel of her sword down on him, dropping him. The man with the wounded sword arm tried to punch at her with his off hand. It was a solid swing. This man was an experienced brawler. She batted the fist away with the flat of her sword and slapped him in the side of the head with Davlas. He staggered to the side. She had a quick moment to sheath her own sword and pluck his from this grasp. She then spun around behind him and slapped him hard on the arse with the flat of his own blade before kicking him back for Barami to deal with.

Now the other two with staves were backing off, but still kept themselves before her. She tossed her newly purloined sword to the ground in front of them as she drew nearer. As expected, one of them thought it would be a better weapon than his staff, a silly move since they were probably much more adept at using their staves. She lunged forward and bashed him on the top of his head with Davlas as he bent over for the sword. He went down yowling. She moved past him for the last man.

He fled.

There was no real resistance after that, people still followed along behind them or a ways to the side, but no one got in their way.

Caerwyn sensed a problem though. She was on her way to try to help Jais, but all she was doing was leading a mob, angrier by the minute, straight to him.

"Barami?"

"Still here."

"How do we get rid of our friends?"

"You could run."

"You'd be stuck here with them. I don't know if they know you're human. They might try to lynch you once you're alone." She'd lowered her voice for this, not wanting to give any ideas to the crowd.

"I can handle myself."

"Like you did in Numedia?"

"That was against a group of Blood Warriors, not peasants."

"True." She was conflicted. She wanted to run off and

help Jais, but Barami was a solid friend and companion, she didn't want to abandon him. "You could run ahead, and I could keep these folks from following?"

"I've had enough running for one day. Holn, I've had enough for a week. I'm no longer the warrior in his prime you met all those years ago. You go."

She had a bad feeling a cold gnawing fear in her gut that if she left him she'd never see him again.

When he spoke next, it was from closer behind her, he'd drawn near to her back, his voice was low. "We both know you're the better of us. You have a long life ahead of you. I'm just an old warrior. I always knew I'd die in battle anyway. I'd prefer that to wasting away in bed."

The words stung, partially because of their harsh truth, partially because she knew how he really felt for her. She'd saved his life long ago, that's why he'd dedicated himself to following her. But now it was even more than that. He loved her and was so very willing to repay that life debt.

She found tears in her eyes.

"Try not to die," she said, hoping her emotion didn't come through. She wanted to be strong for him.

He gave a breath of a laugh. "I always do. Just because I expect to die in battle doesn't mean I plan on doing it today."

She stepped to the side and paused for a moment, letting him catch up to her so she could give him a friendly kiss on the cheek, "Thank you."

He beamed a white-toothed grin, setting off the dark contrast of his skin. "Today is a good day to beat the stuffing out of some ignorant villagers."

She nodded then turned away from him and ran for Jais' cottage.

Her legs were still sore from her run earlier that day, but

being a drahksan, probably a lot less so than any human's would be. She was able to sprint up the hills around the village toward Jais' home.

Even before she got there, she knew there was trouble.

Smoke, too much to be just a cooking fire, was billowing in dark plumes before her. She picked up her pace.

15

BARAMI DIDN'T KNOW WHAT WOULD HAPPEN, BATTLE WAS always like that... unpredictable. You could be in a one on one fight with an untrained inexperienced fool, and he could still get lucky and stick you. The fact that he wasn't trying to kill any of these men made it harder for him. He could bash and smash and hinder them, but unless they were knocked out completely they'd still be in the fight, still be trying to get him. He didn't know if they thought he too was a drahksan, and if so whether that meant he needed to be killed on sight or saved for some formal public sham of a trial and execution. There were too many unknowns. So he stopped worrying about them and focused on keeping himself alive.

In his prime, fifteen or even ten years ago he would have relished a chance to prove himself against a mob like this. Now he was older and more experienced, but he also knew he was slower and would tire quicker. That run earlier today had nearly broken him. He did a range of exercises daily, but he needed to run more apparently.

The crowd closed in around him. He put away Oken-adi and drew his short sword. He didn't want to use lethal force, but he might, if he was threatened. Otherwise he could use the flat of his blade to bash them, in addition to his shield.

There were some who had left, following after Caer, but they wouldn't catch her, not until she stopped. At least he'd kept a good many of them here.

"I'm not drahksani," he called out. He wasn't sure anyone would believe him, but perhaps if they did, they might go easy on him.

"Even if that's so, you were still the pet of a drahksan," someone responded.

He was no one's pet.

"What do you think you will prove with this?"

"You brought the krolls!" This from another man.

That was just crazy. What exactly did these people think drahksani were? They had spoken of demons earlier, were they silly enough to believe demons walked so openly with men? In his culture demons were great and powerful beings that towered over humans, dragging them away to darkness and torture.

"Were there not krolls attacking before we arrived?"

"So you could swoop in and act as heroes."

Barami couldn't quite understand how these people had come up with these ideas. All he and Caerwyn had done was help, and this was their reward.

"We don't want your kind here!"

That seemed to unleash the torrent of emotions within the crowd who began shouting all manner of vitriol.

Barami just shook his head. Oddly he wondered, before the fight began in earnest, what was prompting all these krolls to attack the village. These villagers would find out soon enough once he and Caerwyn were gone that it had not been them inciting the creatures to attack.

Someone threw a stone, and he raised his shield to deflect it. Two or three others charged in at him with clubs and rough weapons. He blocked one, sidestepped the second, and batted the weapon out of the third man's hands with his sword.

Then others charged in. He was quickly inundated by a wave of angry humanity attacking him en masse.

ALNIA SQUIRMED AGAINST THE ROPES THAT RESTRAINED HER.

After having tried to help Jais, and with Erid's condemnation that she'd been working with him, she'd been tied to a chair to keep her at the Ox and Axe while the others went to find Jais and... Gods she hoped it didn't get that far.

To think that her brother had been a part of this, had helped to restrain her, a certain intent glee in his eyes... it was more than she could bear, given everything else that had happened.

She had shed her tears. Now she was intent on freeing herself, though all she seemed to be accomplishing was chafing herself against the ropes and wood.

She honestly couldn't believe the town had turned on Jais so quickly. She didn't have that much of an idea what a drahksan really was, but it couldn't be that bad, could it? Jais and his family had only ever helped the town or kept to themselves. Even once Jais had become strong enough to fend off the beatings by Erid and the other boys he hadn't ever tracked them down to start a fight. He was kind, a good man. Why couldn't anyone else see that?

"This is just silly. Why are boys so stupid?" The voice, a woman, had come from Alnia's left. She looked to see Esrine, the tavern keeper's daughter approaching with a short knife. Esrine quickly sawed through the ropes restraining Alnia.

The other woman was younger than Alnia by a couple of year, but old enough to brave the rough seas of humanity as a serving girl. She was a waif of a woman, slender like a stick, though her legs and arms were filled out, not bony as some girls are. She had blond hair, kept long, but tied back in a braid at the moment. Her eyes were blue and fierce. It was probably that same gaze that got men worked up... and kept them at bay.

"Now you don't be stupid either," Esrine said, scolding while still holding the knife. "Don't go after Jais, there is nothing you can do. He'll either get away or he won't. You'll only hinder him or get in the way and cause more trouble."

It was sage advice, and Alnia wondered how one still younger than she had come by such wits. Certainly she'd been thinking of going after Jais, but it was true... what could she do?

She knew what she couldn't do... nothing.

"Give me that knife, Essy," Alnia said holding out her hand.

Esrine's shoulders slumped a little. She frowned, but she handed over the knife. "You're going to do something stupid, aren't you?"

Alnia felt the rough wood of the handle and looked down at the short blade. It was a knife for cutting vegetables, but it was still sharp enough. "Yes. I am."

Esrine heaved a sigh and shook her head. "Why am I the only sane one here?"

Alnia's answer was under her breath. "Because you haven't found someone to be crazy for."

Jais was shaking, his mind whirling, trying to make sense of the chaos that had been his day. That feeling of dread he'd felt while trying to tell Alnia what he was, had lingered with him. It spoke of disaster, and now he knew it hadn't been lying.

Before him, the house he'd known all his life was nearly destroyed. The roof was smashed in on one side and the other, where the cooking fires had been, was smoking heavily, smoldering with the beginnings of a fire. He blinked but little comprehension came to him. All he could think was that somehow the villagers had gotten here before him and taken his aunt then destroyed his home, but... that wasn't possible. He was faster than any of them, and he'd seen the smoke soon after leaving the village. They couldn't have done this, but then... who... and why?

Nothing made sense. He'd lost everything he knew in a matter of moments, and that still hadn't fully sunk in. He'd needed to find his aunt and uncle, tell them, talk to them, get them to flee with him, but... they weren't anywhere in sight.

He hadn't ventured into the wreckage. He was, somehow, quite certain they hadn't been in there when it collapsed.

But then... what had happened?

It came to him slowly as his mind began to work through what he saw around him. Footprints: very large footprints... which meant...

Krolls.

More than one? Yes, at least two. But given the timing... it would have to have been happening right around the time the others had been attacking the village.

He wasn't able to fathom the depths of what this portended. He couldn't make sense of it. Why were there so many of these Holn-spawned krolls? What did they want?

Nothing made any sense to him anymore. Too much had happened in too short a period. His life as he'd known it was gone, and he couldn't accept that, not yet. So he stood there for several long moments just staring at his home, trying to wrap his mind around any of this.

Why?

Why did the villagers turn on him? Why did they hate drahksani so much? What had he done to deserve their wrath? Why were there so many krolls intent on destroying everything in this area?

As he asked that last one a new 'knowing' sprouted dark wings in his gut, cold and heavy. He wasn't able to decipher it yet except to feel that there was far more going on here than he yet knew. Something bigger was at play, and he was caught up in that as well as everything else going on around him.

He needed to do something.

He forced his feet to move. He made his way around the house to the shed at the back, it too was damaged, but not as bad. He'd thought to retrieve Stout, their pony, but the animal was gone. He stood staring at the empty stable for a long time. Did this mean something?

"There he is! Get him!" The voice snapped him out of his dark thoughts. He turned to see a group led by Erid and Damick. They were armed, marching up the hill toward him. At a quick count there were eight of them.

Something snapped in him then. All of the confusion and frustration and destruction around him, all if it seeped into his soul and turned him hard.

Let them come.

He drew his sword.

Yes, let them come. They wanted him dead. That was obvious by their manner and the open weapons they carried.

He said nothing as they drew closer, did not taunt or goad. He didn't even hear their exhortations. He was cold inside waiting for them to get close enough to strike.

They sensed this perhaps, for they halted a short ways from him, fanning out to surround him. He closed his eyes to slits and slowed his breathing. He was calm, yet with a core of fury. He smiled, only the barest hint, thinking that perhaps this was how Caerwyn felt going into battle.

He could sense the men behind him: hear their footfalls on the grasses and their heavy breaths, smell their heady, sweaty stink.

They had quieted, perhaps thinking he'd just give himself over to them, or uncertain what to do now that they had him.

"I'll take him if none of you will!" It was Erid, of course. He had a sword in hand, a sturdy enough weapon, probably from his father's forge. The large man fell into a battle stance, but even Jais with his limited training knew it was all wrong. He was standing like he expected a brawl, too exposed, too wide.

Erid stalked in toward Jais, and his action must have stirred others as Jais also heard movement behind him. He took a half-step back, turning so the two men coming at him were at his sides. Then he waited to see who would act first. He knew the men of his village... no, not *his* anymore... they were not fighters. Only a few had ever seen any real combat, guards from the capital who had retired up here, and none of those were in this group.

From the corner of his eye Jais caught Erid nodding to the man on the other side of him. A signal. That man would attack first, and when Jais turned to fight him, Erid would stick him in the back. A good enough plan.

The man to Jais' right lunged in, a wild attack, swinging in a wide downward arc with his weapon, a heavy bladed broadsword. Jais raised his own blade to block, easily catching and stopping the attack, probably jarring the other man's arms quite hard.

Erid was moving in. Jais stepped slightly back and toward the first man, with a quick flick of his blade he knocked the broad sword down. Still moving he lowered his sword as the man beside him lost his balance, over-extended. Jais drew his blade along the man's side as he stepped behind him, it was a solid cut. That man would be out of the battle. The man clutched his side as Jais kicked him toward Erid, who was still charging in. The first man fell, his blade nicking Erid's leg as Erid flailed wildly to avoid the man.

Another man was moving behind Jais, and he spun to face the man as a voice stopped them all.

"Stop and surrender, you have no chance!"

Jais couldn't help but grin at Caerwyn's confidence.

He hazarded a quick look in her direction, she looked winded, having just run here from the village it seemed. Her sword was drawn and ready. Davlas as always was in her other hand.

The men around Jais were startled and turned to see who the newcomer was. There was a sudden and cold realization which swept over the other men in a wave. They were facing two drahksani, one of which was a battle-hardened warrior... that and they had already lost one of their number. Jais was guessing that eight against one had seemed safe to them, but with seven on two... they were reconsidering.

Caerwyn drew closer, and Jais took advantage of the distraction to rush one of the men around him, knocking aside a hastily raised weapon and bowling the man over, running past him. Now outside of their circle he edged toward Caerwyn. The others regrouped. For a moment they were uncertain, which was good, because Jais wanted a few words with Caerwyn.

He made sure to keep his eyes on the others as he talked, not letting himself get distracted.

"Where's Barami?"

There was something odd in Caerwyn's voice when she responded. He wasn't looking at her so he only had her tone and timbre to go by. She seemed upset. "He's back at the village stalling the rest of the villagers so I could get here to help you before they did." After a moment she added. "Before most of them, anyway."

"I can handle this troop, but we have other issues."

"Oh?"

"Krolls attacked my house. My aunt and uncle are missing. Something strange is happening. They must have attacked here the same time as the village. I can't make sense of it."

"The krolls are these folks' problem now. We need to get your aunt and uncle and get far away from here."

The cold dark sense in his gut churned. "I think... I think my aunt and uncle may have been taken by the krolls."

"Oh."

"I need to go after them." Of that he was now certain. It seemed the only thing he was certain about.

"Well we can't have these goons hunting you while you hunt for your family. I can take care of them."

Jais didn't want to leave Caerwyn behind, despite a strong certainty she'd be just fine against these brutes.

"I..."

"Go." It was a command.

He sighed, his heart torn. But the choice had already been made. He had to go... now.

"I'll see you soon," he said softly.

"And I you."

He hurried away keeping an eye on the group of men. Three broke off to come after him, Erid leading them.

"I'll take care of them. Go!" Caerwyn was following along behind him.

Smart.

"Jais!"

He nearly toppled over his own feet, missing his stride, stumbling but not falling. He knew that voice.

He turned to see Alnia riding up on the back of a long-striding filly, small and lean. The woman was riding bare-back, clutching the neck and mane of the horse with her arms, her legs tight on the mount's flanks. She was riding astride the beast, the skirts of her dress pushed up high revealing slender pale legs. Both horse and rider looked a little frantic.

What in the name of all the gods was she doing here?

Alnia drew up close and threw herself from the filly landing close to Jais. From a pocket of the apron of her dress she drew forth a small knife.

Her hair was a wind-swept tangle, her face blanched, eyes red from tears. "I'm sorry," she said softly. "I came to try to make things right."

"Get gone from here, woman," Caerwyn commanded. "There is nothing you can do. You're going to get yourself killed!" Caerwyn was adamant, and Jais had to agree.

But there was something in Alnia's eyes, a wild devotion. Jais knew she wasn't going anywhere. "Take my horse. Flee," she said, taking Jais' free hand and planting a quick kiss on his lips.

It wasn't a bad idea, but leaving her here was.

"Go! They won't hurt me."

Jais wasn't so sure of that. He glanced back at Erid. The man had halted his advance as stunned by this new arrival as everyone else. But there was hate in the man's eyes, and it wasn't solely directed at Jais.

"Come with me," Jais said urgently.

She shook her head. "That horse will have a hard enough time carrying you, let alone both of us." Jais could see the truth of that quick enough. The young mare was a fine mount indeed, but he was a big and heavy man, and it was still young and lean.

"I'll only go if you get yourself gone from here now. Run back to your father."

"No, I—"

"Go, or I won't."

She pressed her mouth shut and nodded, turning away from the fight and stalking back down the hill.

Jais glanced at Caerwyn who nodded. He mounted and felt the horse tremble at his weight. He kicked it forward, and it ran, though it must have been exhausted.

He was away.

He needed to find his aunt and uncle, but a part of him stayed back with Caerwyn. He wished he'd have been able to fight beside her once more.

He put that thought aside as the horse drew near to the forest, then plunged into the leafy shadows.

16

ALNIA WATCHED JAIS GO, THEN TURNED BACK TO HELP THE drahksani woman. Jais had been right in saying that the woman and her companion had only helped the village and deserved something in return. Well Alnia's help may not be much, but she'd lend it now. She was tired of being a woman fought over by men. She was going to do something to help.

Caerwyn was handling herself well despite being nearly surrounded by large, angry men. She had already dropped two of them, Alnia was uncertain whether they were dead or unconscious. They weren't moving.

The remaining five men seemed to be pressing hard, all attacking at once. No one seemed to be that concerned that Alnia was around. That would be their mistake. She snuck around the fight to one of the prone men, sticking her little knife in the ground next to him and taking his blade. It was heavy, and she had to hold it with two hands to swing it, but now at least she wouldn't have to get right up next to someone to hit them.

And she knew exactly who she wanted to hit. Both Danz

and Erid had come with this group. She hated her brother at the moment. He'd changed, turned into someone she didn't know, over the course of one day. She still couldn't believe that he'd grabbed her like he had, shaken her, yelled at her, his own sister!

He'd even been the one to suggest she be restrained. There was something vastly different in his eyes, a hatred she'd never seen before. Yet with all that, she couldn't bring herself to hurt him. He was still her brother, and as nasty as he'd become she wouldn't turn into a person like him, hurting his own kin. She had no such qualms however about hurting Erid. The man was a brute, and she had not liked one bit the way he'd looked at her when telling Jais she had to stay behind. It made her skin crawl. He'd been a friend, sure enough, but he'd always looked at her just a little too greedily, as if he owned her. Well he'd stop looking at her like that after today.

She snuck up behind the big man and with a yell, partially to release her pent up anger and frustration, partly just to help her lift the sword, she swung at him.

He half turned at the last moment. Her blade bounced off his left shoulder in an awkward blow. She lost control of the weapon as the shock of the strike paralyzed her arms. It fell to the ground.

Erid screamed and turned on her.

Terror froze her. She wanted to run, wanted her feet to be moving, but was stuck, wide-eyed as he faced her.

He raised his own weapon high, but paused for the barest of moment as he seemed to actually see who it was who had hit him.

"Alnia?"

His eyes went wide then, and he grunted, falling forward, a spear in his back. He landed on his hands and knees

Caerwyn ducked through a hole in the battle created by Erid's absence, and slid out to Alnia. "What are you still doing here? Get away, before you get hurt."

Alnia nodded, but her feet still didn't want to move, at least not quickly.

"Die, demon!" Erid it seemed wasn't out of the fight. Despite being on all fours, he swung up and back with his blade. It took Caerwyn in the stomach, in a long slash across her abdomen.

The warrior woman brought the handle of her sword down hard on Erid's neck, and he pitched forward with a rather sickening crack of bones. But after that Caerwyn dropped her sword and clutched at her stomach, lurching forward toward Alnia.

"Davlas," Caerwyn said through clenched teeth, and her spear appeared in her hand. She used it as a crutch for a moment to stagger a little farther from the other men.

"Go!" she hissed at Alnia, but the most Alnia could manage was a stiff legged step or two backward. She must be blanched pale. All this blood and death and the noises of battle were getting to her and she felt sick.

Why had she thought she could help?

She fell back on her rump, also holding her stomach, but for a different reason.

The three remaining men came after Caerwyn. One of them was Damick, Erid's father. He looked furious.

Caerwyn seemed to know they were coming, despite that they were all behind her. She got an intense, determined look on her face and forced herself to stand from her bent position. With a quick turn she threw her spear and one of the men went down.

She said something, and the spear returned to her again just in time to block a great overhand swing from Damick. She tilted the haft of the weapon, so his sword fell off beside her, then flicked out with the tip of her spear and a red line appeared across Damick's throat. He gurgled and fell to his knees, eyes wide with the realization of his own death.

The last man swung at Caerwyn's unprotected side, or what he thought was unprotected. Caerwyn moved her hand from her stomach, catching the flat of the blade with the side of her hand as it descended, knocking it away enough to miss her. Then her spear was in the man's chest, and he too went down.

Alnia had been too shocked and stunned at what Caerwyn was able to do while mortally wounded to remember her own discomfort for a moment. Then Caerwyn fell next to her, bleeding and exhausted, her stomach wound belching blood.

Alnia turned away and was sick.

It took a torturous few moments for her stomach to empty, her throat raw, a vile taste on her tongue. She spat a few times to try to clean her mouth out as best she could before daring to look back at Caerwyn.

The woman was still conscious, but there was a sheen of sweat on her face, and her breathing was shallow. "Get me something to put on this, as clean as possible," Caerwyn hissed through clenched teeth.

Alnia nodded and, trembling, rose to her feet, looking for anything to help. She looked around for a long moment not finding anything clean. Everything the men had been wearing was either soaked with sweat or blood or covered in dirt. Oddly, it was her own dress which was mostly clean. She ripped off a sleeve and knelt next to Caerwyn. But she couldn't bring herself to touch the wound.

Caerwyn nodded and took the cloth, pressing it to the long gash. The white material immediately blossomed with red, soaking through quickly.

"Now go. See if you can get into that house. Under the bed furthest from the door there's a metal box, I hope. Get it." That seemed to take up a lot of the woman's strength as the tension seemed to drain from her after this, her eyes closing.

Alnia didn't know how much longer Caerwyn would survive, but if she needed that box, Alnia would find it. She sprang up again, glad for the distraction, and ran around to the front of the house. The door was half-caved in and blocked, but there was a small window which seemed intact. Alnia glanced inside to see the two beds with the roof collapsed at the foot of them. There was still a fire burning at the other end of the house, but it wasn't burning quickly, just smoldering with licks of flame. She'd be fine if she got in and out quickly. This side of the house seemed to be mostly intact, other than the caved in roof, thankfully. She climbed in through the window, tearing her dress, but caring little. She needed to help Caerwyn. The woman wouldn't have been wounded if she hadn't have been trying to help Alnia. She owed her.

The roof was close, slanted down with several beams broken and blocking the way. She clambered around them and over the first bed. Then ducked down looking under the second bed, but could see little in the dimness. She reached her arms under, moving them around until she crashed her fingers into something hard and cold. She found the box and pulled it out.

In her haste to leave this place and get back to Caerwyn, she tried to rise from her knees... forgetting the roof had fallen in. She bumped her head on a roof beam. Stunned, she staggered to one side, falling on one of the beds, tears in her eyes.

Whether from her hitting the beam or pure coincidence, part of the roof behind her collapsed even more, in a shower of wood chips and thatch. She let out a scream even though none of the debris landed near her.

For a moment she lay very still, in near darkness, as the dust settled.

She tried to calm herself, but her heart was racing. She didn't know if she'd be able to get out.

After a moment of silence, glad to still be alive at least, she tried to look around. To her surprise she could still see, if only barely. The way she had come in was blocked, but there was light coming from somewhere, if not much.

She looked the other way and found thin beams of light, filled with dancing dust, coming from between the slats of a shuttered window on the far side of the cottage. She hefted the box, though it was quite heavy. She slid it over the top of the bed and climbed over herself. She left the box there and opened the window, throwing the shutters wide.

It was a much smaller window than the first. She wasn't sure if she'd be able to fit through. She returned to the box, grunting as she lifted it, then took it to the window and, hoping there wasn't anything too breakable in it, dropped it out the other side. It didn't fall far. She looked to see a small pile of wood below the window. That would make it easy getting out the other side at least.

She had to half-turn to get her shoulders through, then had one arm stuck for a moment as she was half-in and half-out, but finally managed to squeeze through onto the wood pile. This time more than just her dress was torn, she had cuts and scrapes all over her arms and legs. But she knew it wasn't anything like what Caerwyn was going through, so she gritted her teeth, hefted the metal box, and staggered her way back over to where the other woman was.

The thud of the metal box on the ground startled Caerwyn awake, if she had been unconscious. Her eyes opened, and she moaned.

"Is there a curved needle and thread in there?" Caerwyn asked, breathing still shallow.

There was no lock on the box, thankfully, Alnia opened it to find several small clay jars as well as some other odds and ends, among which was the implements Caerwyn had asked for. The thread was waxed silk, not what Alnia was used to.

"You need to sew up my wound," Caerwyn said.

Alnia trembled at the thought. "I can't. I can't even look at it. I'm sorry."

"Then give it to me, I will. Is there any alcohol in there?"

Alnia searched again and found a sturdy glass flask. The fluid inside was clear, but there was no label. She unstoppered it, and smelled the heady waft of strong alcohol. She handed that to Caerwyn too.

"Is there anything labeled healing goo in there?"

"Nothing is labeled, there are these little jars though."

"It's worth trying. Do all of the pots look the same?"

"No, the tops are different colors, blue, black, and white."

"If you open them, what's inside?"

Alnia lifted off a lid from each colored jar. She grimaced; apparently the lids were descriptive of the contents. "blue stuff, black stuff, and white stuff."

"Let me smell the blue and the black."

Alnia shrugged, uncertain what the other woman was looking for. She wafted the blue under Caerwyn's nose first. The other woman shook her head. "Too pleasant. Try the black."

Alnia did, and Caerwyn's nose wrinkled. "That's it. Leave that out. Is there another jar of that?"

"One more, yes."

"Take it, find your brother. He shouldn't be too hurt. Put it on any wounds you can see."

"What will it do?"

"Help him, heal him, I hope."

Alnia nodded and left Caerwyn to her work. She nearly dropped the small, but heavy, clay jar a moment later when an ear-piercing cry shattered the hillside around her. She glanced back then away again quickly. Caerwyn had poured the alcohol on her wound; that explained it.

She found her brother, his wounds seemed mostly superficial except for a nasty lump on his head. She applied the dark goo anywhere she could, not certain how thick to apply it or whether to rub it in or not. She was probably using too much, half the jar seemed to be gone when she was finished. Danz didn't wake.

She returned to Caerwyn who was thankfully done stitching herself and was applying dark goo to her wound.

She seemed a bit better, still sweating and breathing hard, but clearer of eye, more coherent of speech. "Is there bandage in that tin?" she asked.

Alnia nodded and retrieved it for her.

Caerwyn sat up gingerly, slowly, wincing often. Then wound the bandage around her midriff, using it up almost entirely. Then she lay back, gingerly, breathing hard and quick.

"Gods this hurts."

"Better than being dead." It was something her father used to say.

Caerwyn gave a short, clipped laugh. "That's true." After a moment she added. "I need to find Jais."

"You shouldn't be going anywhere, not now."

Caerwyn sighed. "I know." And with that she closed her eyes and her breathing evened.

Alnia sat beside her, unsure what to do.

17

BARAMI WOKE IN A RUSH FROM SOME DEEP UNCONSCIOUSNESS... and immediately groaned. He hurt... badly... all over. Breathing involved a stinging sharp pain in his chest, probably a broken rib. Agony radiated out through all parts of him, some dull and aching, bruises most likely, most were sharper pains, cuts or worse.

The problem was, despite his eyes being open, he could see nothing. He was in the dark... somewhere, and was fairly certain he was losing blood. He couldn't move his sword arm, but his other he could managed to feel around a bit and most places his fingers came away sticky. He was certain if he was left like this, he'd die here, wherever 'here' was.

One thing was quite clear, he'd not managed to win against the horde of men who'd swarmed him. They were most likely waiting for him to die on his own so their consciences were mostly clear. Either that, or they were keeping him here until they decided to hang him or burn him, or whatever it was they did with 'demon sympathizers'. Perhaps they were still figuring that out. If they were decent men, those deliberations would take some time. It was never easy to condemn a man to death. Better to let him die on his own... from wounds you may or may not have inflicted in a general melee.

Which meant he probably had time.

If he could move, that might be useful. But at the moment any advanced movement like sitting or walking was out of the question. He already knew, from the numbness he felt, that one of his legs wouldn't work like it should.

So what were his options?

Stay here and die or... what?

So he did something he didn't usually do. He prayed.

First he prayed to the god of his people, Noa Oki, god of the southern reaches, of heat and storm. He prayed for forgiveness that he had left his people, had left the south, left the heat. Then, after a while, when nothing had happened, he prayed to Hakan, god of the wilds and the hunt. Barami had always been a hunter, though mostly he'd hunted men in battle. But he thought it perhaps fitting to speak to the god of the hunt to give him one more chase, one more chance. When little came of that he tried speaking to Doa Nosi, god of victory and mercy. But he gave that up quickly. He had lost his fight, so he doubted he'd get far with this plea.

Then he tried the god of healing, Juuta. Perhaps if he was healed, he could change his ways, focus more on healing than war. He had some skills, they could be nurtured. After that he turned to the god of war when no one else had answered his call. Kan Akan was a god he knew well. He'd been in many wars, many battles. If he was closest to any god, it would be Kan Akan. But in the end, he knew that such a god also knew that the outcome of war was only pain and suffering, which Barami was currently experiencing. He would get no pity, no help from that god, which is why he hadn't prayed to him first.

His last prayer was to Ini Moa, goddess of peace. If he couldn't win and wasn't going to be healed, at least he could die in peace. He lay there for some time, feeling the life and energy drain out of him. Slowly his mind clouded and grew less aware, he started to care less and less about his body, it felt distant, even the pain seemed far away.

As darkness closed in, and his mind wandered even farther from this world, a light shone around him. He smiled. He was moving on to Lokana, the silent jungle.

But then the light coalesced into a form, a woman, kneeling next to him in the darkness.

She looked familiar.

Was this Ini Moa come to take him to the peaceful lands?

Yet the glowing form had a strange, almost confused look on her face.

"You?" She seemed confused. "I was seeking for my nephew."

The words swam in his mind and took a long time to make sense. It was only when he finally understood them that he saw her more clearly. This wasn't Ini Moa, this was Jais' aunt. Barami had only seen her a couple of times, but he was certain of it now.

"You're not doing so well, though, are you?" She grimaced, shaking her head. "I don't have much strength as it is, especially in this form." Then a sigh. "But I'll do what I can."

She laid her hands on him.

He felt... it was hard to describe. With his mind still hazy it could only really comprehend what he felt as pure life and energy flowing back into him. His mind cleared, his body—

the pains returning to him—was slowly soothed, his wounds healed. Yet as this happened the woman's light grew dimmer and dimmer. The room was returning to darkness.

"That is all I can do." Her voice sounded distant. "I hope it is enough." Then she was gone, and he was returned to full darkness.

But he felt much better.

There was still pain, far too much for his liking, but feeling had returned to his numb leg, and there was no more stinging when he breathed. He was fairly certain he could sit, could walk. That gave him options.

Now he just had to find a way out.

JAIS WALKED BESIDE THE WORN OUT FILLY. HE SHOULD LET HER return to wherever Alnia had taken her from, but something prompted him to keep the mount around. Perhaps it was that deep feeling of dread still lurking in his gut.

That dark feeling now had a companion: guilt. He felt horrid about having left Caerwyn to fight his battles for him. He should have stayed and seen it through. Yet he had to know what had happened to his aunt and uncle. He was torn. There was no good choice to make. He hoped Caerwyn had fared well.

He'd been following the trail the krolls had left through the woods. It was quite clear to anyone who was observant enough. They'd stomped through shrubs and broken a lot of branches. They weren't trying to be stealthy, if they even knew how. It was also fairly clear they were heading some-where specific or at the very least directly away from Jais' house, as they were moving in a fairly straight line.

He came to the Blackbush Run, a shallow but wide creek which carved a clearing through the forest. Depending on the year and the rains, this watercourse was sometimes just a rough path of stones, dried up. But this year it was still gurgling along well enough.

Still pondering his situation and uncertain what to do, Jais stopped for a sip from the cool waters. He sat back on his haunches afterward and sighed. He had nothing with him, but that which he'd had when he left the village, the clothes on his back and the sword at his hip. He hadn't had time or the inclination to gather anything from his home. He'd thought it destroyed, but there were probably still some things he could have recovered from the wreckage. A bow would have been nice, something with which to attack krolls at range instead of going toe to toe with one.

Gods, what a fool he was.

He rolled his shoulders and stretched his back. The wounds from earlier that day felt tight and itchy, already healing. When Barami had cleaned and bandaged them, the old warrior must have done a superior job—or Jais' natural healing was kicking in—as he hadn't noticed the wounds for some time. But he could feel the pull of the cuts now that he moved his back. He had never seen them so he had no clue how bad they were, but he was fairly certain none would hinder him much, even if reopened.

He sipped at another handful of water from the stream, and stood.

Only then did something catch his eye.

Movement.

Something in the shadows beneath the trees. It wasn't a kroll, it was too small, human sized. He left the filly still drinking from the brook and crept into the brush toward where he'd seen the shape.

It had been odd, like it had a lantern or something, as if there was light, but an odd color.

Once on the other side of a large bush, he caught another glimpse between two trees farther on. He moved carefully to that point, making no noise on the loamy forest floor.

When he reached those trees the flash came again, to his left. He looked then blinked. There was a body there. The face was turned away, but suddenly Jais' dread solidified into an anguished squeezing of his heart. Those were his uncle's clothes.

He rushed over and threw himself down next to the man. Turning the head confirmed two things: this was his uncle and... he was dead. There was no pulse at his neck, and his face was ashen white, eyes staring into oblivion. There were also the three great gashes across his chest and abdomen, widely spaced... claw marks. No animal had anything like that. This was the work of krolls.

"Uncle Perrick!"

He slumped over the body, tears coming to his eyes as he was flooded with a wave of emotions, not the least of which were anger and grief.

He allowed himself to weep for a long moment before thinking of his aunt. Where was she? Also who had led him here? The last question didn't really matter. He was here, and that was good enough.

He rose and rushed back through the brush, bringing the filly back to the place where his uncle lay. It was surprisingly easy to pluck up the body from the ground. His uncle was a tall and well-built man, not huge like Erid, but big enough. Jais draped him over the back of the filly.

A thought struck him, and he took a moment to search the area. He found his uncle's hunting bow and his pack not far from where his body had been. The nearly full quiver at his uncle's hip gave him twelve arrows. He now had a ranged weapon. He wasn't sure what arrows would do to a kroll. They seemed to shrug off Caerwyn's spear, and these projectiles were much smaller. But it was something, and he'd take it.

He returned to tracking the krolls with a mounting sense of urgency. His aunt was still out there, and whether she was still alive or dead... Jais didn't know.

Barami was in a cellar, he knew that much now after exploring the walls. He'd found, by banging his shin into it—as if he didn't have enough pains already—a stairway up to a horizontal door in the wood panels above him. It was barred or locked down, and he could find no other way out. The cellar was large and contained several barrels and hempen sacks. He'd searched it thoroughly by touch.

Once he was coherent enough and stopped to listen, he could also hear voices above him, though they seemed distant, like they were not directly above him but in some adjacent room.

He took his time, planning. It was hard to tell time down here in the dark, but after a while he knew he was hearing three separate voices. Unless there was someone up there who wasn't speaking at all, that meant only three men 'guarding' him. He could take three men.

So he formed his plan, moving around some barrels and sacks until he was ready. Then, having stacked several of the barrels up as high as he could he pushed the tower over. They crashed to the stone floor with a clamor which he hoped would be heard above. Indeed the voices stopped talking for a moment. Then he heard the sounds of men moving along the floorboards towards the trap door.

Barami hid behind several other barrels, which he piled in such a way that he'd be able to peer through the cracks between them, and see what the men were doing.

One of the men shouted through the floor. "What are you doing down there?"

Barami didn't answer.

There were some softer murmurs he couldn't make out clearly then a pause, and someone was working with the bolt on the door.

Good.

They'd be expecting a hurt and dying man. He was still hurt, but now far from dying.

The door opened, and there came the stab of light from a lantern, which was thrust down into view.

"See anything?" one man said.

"Some barrels have been moved, some are broken. There was good mead in those ones!" He sounded upset. Good.

Barami groaned, hoping it sounded pathetic.

"He's still alive down there."

"Not for much longer I'd wager."

"Should we check on him?"

"If neither of you will go, I will. I don't want to lose any more good stock." A man, portly and short, stomped down the stairs into the cellar grumbling something about, "should have moved all this."

It seemed the other two wouldn't venture down, though. As the portly man began to look around, a second man, the one holding the lantern, did take a few steps down the stairs to get a better look.

"See him?" the one on the stairs asked.

"Nah," grumbled the portly one. "And some of this has been moved. What's he been doing down here?" That man was drawing closer to Barami's hiding spot.

He needed to time this just right.

He slipped to one side, hoping the portly man would go around the barrels he was behind in the other direction. He was in luck.

As the portly man looked around one side, Barami broke free and sprinted toward the man on the stairs.

This one was spry and quick. He jumped up and out of the cellar, but he dropped the lantern as he did. He was shouting, "Close the door!" to the other man still up above.

The door closed, but Barami had been fast enough. He reached the stairs as the door came down. With a burst of speed and strength, he rushed up the stairs and took the door with his shoulder. It lurched up. They hadn't had time to lock it. He also heard a satisfying grunt. It had hit someone.

He sprang up out of the hole and charged the man who had been holding the lantern. There was a fire starting in the room as the oil from the lantern burned and spread over the floorboards next to a wall.

Barami slammed into the man, his forearm across the man's upper chest. A quick punch to the throat and that one was down.

He turned to the other man, who was clutching one hand, rubbing it.

Good.

The portly one was also on the stairs coming up again.

He ran at the one on this level, slamming the trap door

down as he passed, rewarded with a pained, "Ow," from the man below.

The one up here tried to flee backward, but fell, hitting his head hard on the floor. He'd be a moment or two getting up.

And that fire was spreading.

Barami decided not to stay and finish these men. He barged through the only door in the room into... the cooking area of the tavern. There was a back door not far away, and he left through that.

He wasn't in great shape, but he ran as fast as he could out of the town, pausing once to catch his breath and turn back... to see the tavern in flames.

He couldn't say he was sorry.

JAIS HAD BEEN TRAVELLING A WHILE NOW. THE DAY WAS FADING, but he was fairly certain he'd found the place the krolls had taken his aunt. There was a long, high ridge running through the forest with a nearly vertical rock-face. In the side of that cliff was a cave, large enough for any kroll to come and go easily. This is where the tracks had led.

He used a little light rope, from his uncle's pack, to tie up the filly, leaving his uncle with the animal.

Then he approached the cave, carefully. A cave full of krolls was the last place he wanted to be, but his aunt might be in there, and he was determined to get to her, if she was still alive.

It was the 'if' that concerned him.

18

Caerwyn woke to a rather beautiful sunset.

"Alnia?" she called out.

"One moment," was the distant reply.

Uncertain if she was up for moving, Caerwyn gingerly tested her wound. It was painful, but more the sensitive sting of something healing, not a fresh wound. Between her natural healing and the healing goo, she hoped she would be done with it soon.

She tried sitting and found that easy enough, though still awkward, needing to lean and prop herself up to be anywhere near comfortable.

She could now see a pile of items had been gathered near her. It looked like blankets and some food. There was also a pile of wood, from tinder to logs. If this was Alnia's work the woman had been busy.

Alnia came into view, her white dress cut up and dirty as she carried an armload of wood. She dumped the new wood with the pile nearby and huffed. "Hello. Feeling better?"

"Yes, I think so. You gathered all this?"

Alnia nodded. "I wasn't certain whether I should move you, and it was getting dark, so I started gathering a few things from the house. Mostly stuff to help in case it was a cool night." After a moment she added, "That was a nasty wound, you certain you should be doing anything but resting?"

"We drahksani heal quickly. I'll be fine. I think." Caerwyn looked around at the other bodies not far away. "They all dead?" She really hadn't been certain about some of them. She also thought of something else. "How's your brother?"

"He'll live, but he doesn't heal quickly. He's sleeping. The rest of them but one are dead and that last one..." Alnia shrugged. "I think he'll be out for a while. I tried to clean him up as best I could."

Caerwyn adjusted her sitting position. The arm she was leaning on was getting tired. "I'm sorry you had to go against your own people... your own family."

Alnia looked away, perhaps at the sunset, perhaps at nothing. After a moment she said, "They made their choice, and I made mine. I think their choice was foolish, but they are still mostly decent people. I honestly don't really understand it."

"They are blinded by fear and hate. They cannot see us for what we are." Caerwyn didn't finish her thought: *you are blinded by love, my dear.*

"Others are going to come." It was an odd statement and came from nowhere. For a moment Caerwyn thought Alnia, who was still staring of into the hills, actually saw people coming. It took her a moment to realize it was a general statement.

"Yes. They'll be looking for these ones. They'll be looking

for Jais and myself. I should go. The longer I stay here, the more I put you, and myself, in danger."

Alnia lowered her gaze, but still seemed to be looking more through the earth than at it. "I think I need to come with you." She swallowed hard. This was something the other woman had probably been thinking a lot about, not an easy decision. "I don't know if I can stay here. Even though I've healed him, I don't know if Danz will forgive me for siding with Jais... and you. Others may feel the same, and honestly I don't know who I can count on to support me, if anyone."

It was sound logic, but Caerwyn didn't really want another companion. Jais leaving with her was fine, but... well if she was honest it was Alnia herself she didn't want tagging along. In her semiconscious state while resting she'd been thinking—rather selfishly—about Jais coming with her after all of this. If it were just the two of them... perhaps that would make it easier for them to...

But Caerwyn wouldn't turn Alnia away, that would just be wrong.

She sighed and nodded.

That decided, she needed to make one more decision: to try to leave now or wait until morning. She desperately wanted to go after Jais, help him, get him away from all this, but she knew her wound was still tentative at best. She needed rest, but wasn't sure she could afford the time.

And where was Barami?

She feared her longtime companion had finally picked a fight he couldn't win. There were far too many uncertainties for her liking.

"Do you need anything before we leave?" Caerwyn asked. Though she was fairly certain she knew the answer.

"I... I should find new clothes..." A long sigh. "But I dare not return to the village. I will have to make do with what I have."

Caerwyn nodded. They both would.

"How far is it to the woods, someplace to hide?"

Alnia looked around in the fading light of day. "About a couple hundred paces for me."

Caerwyn could make it that far. "I'm going to go grab my pack. I dropped it on the hill somewhere over there before the fight. Then I'll wander over to the woods, and we'll find a spot to rest. Go look for a relatively flat clear area a fair ways back from the edge. Then bring what you can from this pile."

Alnia nodded and walked away to do as instructed.

Caerwyn used Davlas to help her stand, though she was half doubled over to keep from stretching her wound too much. She hobbled around the battle scene until she found her pack, then knelt gingerly to pick it up. It had taken her a while, and it was nearly full dark now. By the time she returned to Alnia's pile of supplies, Alnia herself was returning.

"I found a spot. Hopefully it will do." She grabbed up an armful of blankets, a little food, and some other odds and ends. "Follow me."

Caerwyn grabbed a few other bits, careful in how much she carried, then limped along behind Alnia.

The spot the other woman had found indeed pleasant and well hidden. A large tree had fallen some time ago, uprooting itself. The great tangle of roots created a slightly cave-like area, providing some small cover from any inclement weather, but mostly hiding them from anyone searching around Jais' house. They dropped everything off, and Alnia went back for another load as Caerwyn started a fire with some bits of wood around the area, using her flint and steel. By the time Alnia return with some larger wood, it was burning well.

Caerwyn had been uncertain about starting a fire, but had reasoned that the great bowl of the tree would block the flame from any casual searchers, and since it was full night now, smoke would be hard to see against a night sky. As long as she kept it small she wasn't worried about people finding them because of it.

"I heard voices as I left," Alnia said setting down her armload. "People were headed up to find out what happened. We may want to keep the fire small for a bit and our voices low.

The girl had some sense.

Caerwyn nodded. "I'm due for more rest. Can you tend to all this?"

"Yes. Rest."

Caerwyn lay back on some blankets. The ground wasn't perfectly flat, but she was tired enough that it didn't matter. She was asleep quickly.

It was full dark when Alnia shook her awake. There was a terrified urgency in her voice as she leaned over Caerwyn and whispered, "Someone's out there!"

Jais crept through darkness.

In the cave, at night, there was no light at all, and yet he could still see. His vision wasn't great, but it was far better than being blind and stumbling around on this uneven ground. It was odd, as if everything was giving off some slight ambient light by which he could see, though it was quite basic, no color, just shapes, and certainly not for any significant distance. It was enough for him to move along slowly and carefully through the cave.

And it was a rather significant cave system. He was following the largest cavern as it wound down and into the earth, but there were many other small crevices and caves. He had even ducked into these a couple of times to avoid krolls. To his surprise there were many of the creatures here, coming and going, thumping and lumbering along, giving him lots of warning. They were not concerned about hiding themselves at all, which helped him evade them. But he was getting more and more worried about the sheer number of the things.

Both Caerwyn and Barami had expressed their confusion and concern about the number of krolls and how they were cooperating. They said it was odd, out of character. Well that meant this place was a significant confluence of oddity then, for as far as Jais could tell, this was their home, their 'base'. And he was starting to get the feeling there were far more here than he had expected, more than he could deal with.

His fear was growing, a gnawing, clawing sensation in his chest, when he became aware of a noise from up ahead and... light as well.

He could see more and more of what was ahead of him as light reflected off the walls from some well-lit place, and that made him warier.

When a smaller cave came into view, with light down its shaft as well, he ducked into there. No kroll should be able to fit in here. It was a tight squeeze for even his bulky frame, and he cut himself on a few sharp edges, fairly certain he'd reopened some of the cuts on his back. However it proved worth the pain as he found a slit through which he could see into a much larger cave.

Several large fires were burning, illuminating the vast cavern... that was crawling with krolls... and in the center of all those hideous shapes was something even larger.

The krolls Jais had seen stood between eight to twelve feet tall, varying heights and builds, like humans, and all were large and strong. This new one stood a full head, shoulders, and chest above most, and twice as tall as some of the smaller krolls. It was powerfully built as well with a form that was much less the hodgepodge of muscle and misshapen bone, and much more 'human'. Though to call this giant... thing human would still be a mistake. The general shape was right, but its chest and shoulders were overdeveloped and its arms too long, hands dangling at its knees. There was also something about it, something Jais couldn't place right away until it looked in his direction. Then Jais caught the glimmer in its eyes, the intelligence there. This one was not only bigger, but smarter as well.

It hit Jais suddenly in a wave of realization. This was their leader. This was the reason they were banding together. The next thing he saw confirmed that.

The thing spoke in some guttural, harsh language, and the krolls around it cheered, a horrid and bone-chilling noise. Then it lifted a hand which became engulfed in fire. It pointed that hand at a guttering fire in one corner of the cave and the fire leapt back to life, burning tall and strong... with no fuel that Jais could see.

...Magic...

Could this get worse?

It did.

His aunt was then carried in by a kroll, firmly holding her

squirming form. She was alive, but there was no way Jais could rescue her surrounded by dozens of krolls.

His heart sank, and he could only watch, tears forming in his eyes. This was not going to go well.

"I will be well, Jais. Do not worry for me."

Jais was so jammed into his spot he couldn't jump or turn, but the voice nearly stopped his heart, speaking so close, so quiet. He turned his head and saw beside and behind him the glowing form... of his aunt.

He turned to look in the large cave. She was still there. Checking behind him again proved she was there as well, at least some glowing image of her.

"Calm yourself. This is a spirit form. I haven't used it in many years, but it is one of my abilities."

Jais felt a wave of emotions wash over him. "I can't save you," he said softly, voice choked.

"I know, now listen for a moment, I have much to say."

A GLOWING BLUE FORM ENTERED THE SMALL CLEARING WHERE Caerwyn and Alnia hid.

"You!" Caerwyn said recognizing the form as Jais' aunt. "What is this?" Then as another thought occurred to her, she asked, "are you dead?"

"Not yet, no. But I fear I may be soon. There isn't much time so please listen. I know why the krolls have been so vigorous in this area, why there are so many. They have a leader, a krolloc, I believe by his size and intelligence. You must be very wary. There are dozens of krolls, yet still you must find a way to kill this being, for he will only incite more death and terror."

Caerwyn had questions, but kept her mouth shut as Sarelle continued.

"There is a cave deep in the woods, head east until you find a tall ridge, then follow that north and you'll find it. This is where the krolls are. Jais is here as well, but hidden for the moment. You must end this or these creatures will claim all these lands and kill everyone here."

The vision wavered for a moment.

"I am losing strength and my attentions are divided. I must go."

"Wait," Caerwyn said speaking quickly. "I'm wounded, can you heal me?"

The glowing form shook its head. "No, I spent too much earlier on your companion. Put some of my healing gel on it. That, along with your accelerated healing, should have you feeling well soon enough."

"We already have."

"Then you'll do well enough. Sorry I cannot do more."

Then the form faded away.

Only then did Caerwyn's keen ears pick up calls and shouts in the distance. One of them came through clearly. "I saw something. A light over there!"

She swore.

"We need to go. That mystical lightshow gave away our position. The others will find us soon."

Alnia nodded and acted without question. Their fire was already low, and there would be no need to cover it since someone already knew they were here. Alnia gathered up only a few things, what she could stuff into a satchel, as Caerwyn rose carefully, still leaning on Davlas for support.

Then they were off, moving slowly and carefully through the woods. Better to keep quiet now. Someone would find their site soon enough and know they were there, but in the dark of night, tracking them through the forest would be nearly impossible.

Caerwyn hoped.

THE IMAGE OF HIS AUNT WAVERED FOR A MOMENT. SHE LOOKED concerned and spoke quickly. "First off, I have visited your friends. The old southern warrior was badly wounded, but I was able to heal him and he has escaped. The woman was also wounded, but I spent too much of my energy on the man and could not help her. But Alnia is with her, and she seems to be recovering. I have visited them and told them where you are.

"Jais, this is important. That big one out there. That is a krolloc. They are larger and more intelligent than their counterparts, acting as leaders and organizers. He cannot be allowed to live. I cannot stress this enough. Even if it costs you your life, that thing must die. Once it's gone, these krolls will turn on each other and most will stop being a threat to the village."

"What do I care of the village? They turned on us as soon as they found out we were drahksani! They tried to kill me and would have done the same to you if you'd been home."

"Oh!" The expression on the image of his aunt showed her shock clear enough, but she shook it off quickly. "It doesn't matter. Hate us or love us, no one should be subjected to a plague of krolls such as this.

"My death is imminent, I know that, and my powers are strained at the moment. I will do what I can, but you still have a chance. Kill that thing and we save hundreds of lives!"

The image wavered again, and she seemed to shrink, looking faint. "I cannot keep this up for much longer, but I will be with you. My spirit is strong, and even after my death I may remain for a while. I love you, Jaistheric. Please do what you can, and I hope you live a long life after this."

He got the feeling she wanted to move closer to embrace him but she could not, and a moment later she was gone.

Jais looked back out to the krolloc and his followers. The form of his aunt was mostly limp now, she'd stopped struggling.

The krolloc held out a hand making a grasping motion and barked some command. The kroll holding Sarelle released her, but she didn't fall. Instead, she hovered there, still looking held. When the krolloc moved his hand closer to himself, she moved as well, drawing closer to him.

How was Jais to fight something with powers like that?

He tried to calm himself, rein in his racing heart and rapid breath. He tried to find some calm.

Then the krolloc began to speak, but this time it spoke the northern tongue.

Jais listened intently.

19

Barami woke to darkness... again.

Was he still trapped?

No.

His mind was fuzzy for a while as he tried to recall where he was, what had happened. It came to him slowly, the beating, the healing, and the escape from the cellar. He'd staggered as far as he could, then hid himself behind a shroud of bushes and retreated to unconsciousness.

Now, with his awareness returning, he took stock of his situation. He was hurt and tired, though having slept just now seemed to have helped him regain a little energy. His wounds from the mob were better after Jais' aunt's healing, but he was still sore all over, a radiating ache which seemed to drain his energy. He'd heard that some older people simply hurt all the time and had trouble moving. Well today he was feeling every inch of his more than forty years of age. But he could deal with that. There were more pressing problems, like his lack of weapons.

His Oken-adi had been taken from him, as had his shield.

He'd really liked that shield. It had been made in the Afgenni forges from the strongest, lightest steel they could make. He'd had it for years, and it had always served him well. But now he had no idea where it, or any of his other weapons, were. He couldn't risk going back into the village for them either. He could only move forward from here. That led him to his final dilemma, a lack of information. He didn't know where Caerwyn or Jais were or how they had fared. He needed more information as well as equipment. The only place he could think of to find that was up at Jais' cabin. That would be the best place to start.

So he grunted and groaned as he got himself up and began moving in that direction. The moon was setting, it was well into night, and it would still be quite dark when he got there. He hoped that would be a boon to him.

He crept across the hills toward the cabin. When he saw it he let out a long sigh. The cottage was burning in a giant fire. There were about a dozen men in a group off to one side, so he made a wide circle around behind them, coming at them from the forest, directly opposite to the fire. Hopefully their light-blind eyes wouldn't see him coming.

But he paused as he reached the forest's edge. There were voices off under the trees as well. When he peered into the inky blackness of the woods, he could see spots of light... torches. They were searching the forest for Jais or Caerwyn or both.

Barami paused and looked to gauge the turning of the stars. It would be several hours still before dawn. He was a decent tracker, but finding a trail at night would be virtually impossible. He doubted he could catch up to Caerwyn or Jais now. Come sunup he could catch their trail and find them, hopefully ahead of this horde.

But he could still use this situation.

He crept into the forest, toward one spot of light which seemed to be the farthest from any other. Moving carefully, he stalked the man, catching up to him in bits as he worked his way toward that torch. Once close enough, he took stock of his target. The man had an old sword and a beat-up shield. It wasn't much, but it was more than Barami had now.

Barami let the man get ahead of him again, out of earshot. His shirt was torn and ripped in several spots, he removed it entirely and expanded some of the tears until he had four oddly shaped strips. He put these together and wound them up to make them stronger, then he began stalking his target once more. He caught up again when the man stopped by a stream to take a drink. Barami crept up behind him and swung his makeshift rope around the man's neck. He pulled it tight, crossing his arms behind the man and planting his knee in the man's back to force him forward. The man had no chance to scream, and died gurgling.

Barami was no longer concerned with taking it easy on these men. They had shown they were willing to kill him, so his sympathy was lost. This was survival, and he'd do what he must.

He took the man's weapons and provisions, which wasn't much. He also stole the man's shirt, but it didn't fit him.

Now he just had to find a place to hide until morning, when he'd pick up the trail of his friends.

"Do you know how a kroll is made?" the krolloc asked Jais' aunt. Jais watched, trying to learn as much as he could before he would have to face that thing.

"I always thought you were the spawn of Holn," Sarelle said defiantly. Her body still looked limp and exhausted, but her spirit was still there in her voice.

"You are not too far off." Jais couldn't get over how well spoken the thing could be. He'd expected broken sentences and grunts. "Long ago, not long after drahksani were created, humans dabbled with forces beyond their control in an attempt to create their own equal to such power. They created krolls instead. We cannot reproduce naturally. We are truly unnatural. The only way we can create more of ourselves is to perform the ritual once again on a human. But that will only create another kroll. That is why we are so few. It takes four to perform the ritual, and most krolls would never band together for long enough to do so. Most of the krolls alive today are leftovers from times long past. Just as I am." He drew her closer still, making a pulling motion with the hand that he'd used to grip her with magic. She floated right up before his fanged visage, which wore a horrible grin. "Do you know how a krolloc is made?"

She said nothing, defiance in her eyes, if not in her body.

"The same ritual when performed on a drahksan creates a krolloc. So we are rarer still. Especially now that most of you drahksani have been killed off. There are so few chances left for us to create more leaders for our kind." He moved her away again, spinning her slowly in the air. "And we do so need leaders. Without me this rabble would tear themselves apart."

Jais knew where this was going now and began squirming out of his tight vantage point back the way he'd come. He needed to get to his aunt before the krolloc turned her into one of them. Even as he moved, the clear, booming voice of the krolloc followed him.

"It took me a hundred years to find three krolls to perform the ritual that first time. I've spent another century slowly building up my force to what you see today. I am nearly ready to attack the world in force, but I will need your help. You will start a new clan with those we transform from this village, and then there will be nothing in this world that can stop us! That is the way of our kind: dominate, transform, and destroy." There was a pause for a moment as Jais thought his aunt was saying something but he couldn't hear her. The response from the krolloc was laughter.

"Oh you will have little choice in the matter. The ritual cares not how willing you are. Would you like to see it?" A moment later the krolloc bellowed something in the other language.

Jais froze.

He was just reaching the main hallway which would take him into that cavern, and wanted to make sure there wouldn't be anyone there to discover him.

Then a woman started screaming, and he couldn't help but move. He ran out into the main 'hallway' toward the large cavern, but nearly ran into the back of a kroll as he emerged into the vast area. But what he saw both horrified him and relieved him. A woman he didn't know was being pulled from a pen he hadn't been able to see from his previous vantage point. A cage made of wooden bars and rough ropes contained a small group of people—it was the family from the farm that had been attacked by krolls not that long ago. As much as he was thankful that his aunt was being spared for the moment, the thought of any innocent person being turned into a kroll made him sick.

But there were a score or more of krolls between him and the woman, what could he do? Any one of these creatures would be a challenge for him, trying to fight through this many would be death. His aunt had tasked him with eliminating the krolloc, but looking at things now, he knew it would have to be through cunning and planning, not brute force.

So, with that woman's scream still ringing in his ears he once again retreated to a hiding spot. The main 'hallway' passed by the vast cavern so he moved to the far side and slipped into the shadows, watching from there.

The woman was dragged, probably quite painfully and unceremoniously to a metal rod which looked like it had been thrust down into some crack in the floor, then sharpened at the top. The kroll dragging her lifted her and pushed her down, back first, onto the spike such that it pierced her through the abdomen on one side. She wasn't dead, and wouldn't be for a moment or two, long enough for them to do what they planned, Jais guessed. The woman's screams intensified with pain and fear, turning to wails. Then the krolloc and three other krolls stood around her and began chanting. The chant sounded vaguely like the northern tongue, certainly not the guttural language of the krolls. Jais didn't understand any of the words, but it felt... odd. His skin tingled as his ears took in the noise.

Then he watched in horror as the woman grew. She burst the seams of her dress as her skin became lumpy and gray-green, her hair fell away, any features which made her a woman were dissolved into the lump of mutating flesh. She twitched and writhed now, no longer screaming, her body being bent and twisted by mounds of new muscle.

The ritual did not last that long, and Jais finally turned away as it finished, no longer morbidly caught up in the horror. The woman was a kroll now, with no vestige of her human heritage remaining.

"This is the fate that awaits you, drahksan."

Like Holn!

Jais strung his uncle's bow and had an arrow nocked within a few heartbeats. He'd been trained to shoot since he was ten. He could fell a deer at two hundred paces.

Aunt Sarelle was only about a hundred paces away...

But he hesitated, hands trembling, as he sighted her floating form down the shaft of the arrow.

He had to end this, before she was turned into an abomination. He had to end... her, but he couldn't. His hand wouldn't release.

His entire being was at war. He couldn't allow her to be made into a krolloc, but he couldn't kill her either. To take her life, the woman who had raised him, was absurd. She was essentially his mother.

"Jais, no."

The voice was next to him.

He looked to see that same glowing form of his aunt. "You don't need to do this. I would never ask that of you."

"But you can't mean to... I won't let you be turned into..." The words were too horrible to say.

"I won't. I have... other things in mind. You... need to go, before the krolls know you're here."

"Go where?" He looked back at the krolls, there were a couple nearest him who had heads raised, sniffing the air. Was that for him?

He moved farther down the rock tunnel, out of sight of the beasts. He returned the arrow to its quiver, the bow unstrung.

"Follow me." She floated away quickly down the passage away from the cavern, deeper into the caves.

Jais did as instructed, his heart tearing, knowing his aunt's life was measured in scant few heartbeats now.

"I deny you your prize!" his aunt's voice came to him clearly, if softly from behind him.

Shuddering, he wanted to ask what she would do, but couldn't, his curiosity outweighed by his concern.

Then there was a roar behind him and the thundering of heavy feet.

"Hurry! We're almost there," said the ghost form of his aunt, ahead of him.

The cave was narrowing, the walls here were smooth, and Jais noticed images on them as he passed. They were crude drawings of people and animals in a forest setting. He didn't have time to take a closer look as krolls were rushing in behind him. He picked up his pace, running as the tunnel narrowed down to a space only slightly larger and taller than he was. He slipped through that as the krolls neared.

The cave shuddered with the impact of the not-too-bright creatures into the confined space behind him. They were pushing at each other, reaching into the hole, trying to reach him, but none would fit.

He stood there for a half-heartbeat watching the chaos, then followed his aunt's form deeper still.

Finally, she stopped and said, "Rest here."

They were in an odd cave. Odd because it was so well defined. The stone was smooth, with a perfect arched ceiling above him, and even what seemed to be a stone bench cut out from an alcove carved into the wall. It was on that which he sat.

He wasn't exhausted, but he was winded enough to

appreciate the pause. That, and his emotions were all a tumble within him.

"Did you... Are you...?" Jais asked as he caught his breath. Again the words were too hard to say.

She floated over next to him and crouched next to where he sat, an ethereal hand on his knee. "Yes. It is done."

"Aunt Sarelle..." His voice was weaker now. "I've already lost so much." A lump grew in this throat, and it became hard to speak. He wanted to reach out to her, to touch her, hug her, but as he tried to put his hand on hers, it only passed through.

"I wish I could touch you," he managed to croak out.

"As do I."

"How... how are you still here, with me?"

She smiled sadly. "I told you earlier I would be with you for a short time after I died."

Again his morbid curiosity wanted him to ask how it had happened. He instead asked, "Was it... painful?" He wanted to think it had been quick and easy and painless.

The glowing from shared a sad smile. "No. As a healer and physical talent I have... had a fair control over my own being. I simply made it... stop. "

He felt hot tears on his cheeks, his lips pressed tight to hold back sobs as he nodded hastily.

She remained kneeling where she was as he wept for her, but as with his uncle he found his tears not lasting for long. He sniffed. "What do I do now?"

"You need to kill that krolloc."

"How?"

The shoulders of the ghost slumped. "That I do not know. The krolls, and probably the krolloc itself, likely have your scent now. They know you're here." She grimaced. "But while

I was in that larger cave I felt a breeze blowing in from the outside. If you could somehow get around to the far side of that cave you'd be up wind of them, they wouldn't know you were coming. That is all I can suggest." She glanced off down the tunnel they were in. "Perhaps this passageway continues around to the far side?" She shrugged.

It was worth a try. He didn't know how he was going to take down that massive beast all on his own, but he had to try, had to do something.

He nodded. "I will do what I must."

She nodded as well then reached out an ethereal arm to him, laying fingers on his cheek. He felt no touch, but a warmth there. "I can feel myself being drawn away. I am sorry I couldn't do... more." Her expression grew sorrowful. He was sure she'd be crying if she could. Her lips pressed together for a long moment.

Finally she said, "Be safe my darling."

He felt the warmth on his cheek intensify as the image of his aunt faded away to nothing.

"Goodbye, Aunt Sarelle. I love you."

From a distant place, or perhaps within him, a faint voice responded with: "I love you too. Goodbye... my son."

20

DESPITE HAVING RESTED FOR ONLY A SHORT TIME AND HAVING walked for the rest of the night, Caerwyn wasn't feeling that bad. Her wound felt better, but she hadn't risked removing the bandages to look at it. She didn't feel that comfortable yet. She was, however, at least able to stand straight without feeling like her insides were going to fall out. The pain was diminished as well, from a swath of intense burning and stinging to a line of stinging pain. Overall it was a vast improvement.

They had evaded the men sent into the woods to search for them. By virtue of needing to search, those men were moving slowly, ranging back and forth to cover large areas of the forest. Whereas Caerwyn and Alnia, who also had to move slowly to keep from making noise, could move directly away, and hence had quickly drawn out of range of anyone seeking them. Caerwyn led for the most part, as her vision was better. She whispered warnings when there were roots or dips, where branches would brush by them, and so on.

It was slow going, but after a while they had felt safe enough to stop once again and rest for a bit.

For some time now, Caerwyn had also been aware of something else. Something she'd forgotten about: she knew were Jais and his aunt were. She could sense them because they were drahksani and thus she knew exactly which direction to head.

Yet as she and Alnia rested, she stopped sensing one of the two. She didn't know which it was, and for a moment, panic rose within her that Jais might be lost, gone forever. Though after that thought, she felt guilty. His aunt was also a person to be mourned if lost. She was a great healer and powerful in other ways. She would be a great loss to their kind as well.

She didn't want to say anything to Alnia. The woman's state was fragile enough, tired and at her wits end. She'd wept, seemingly for no reason, several times as they'd moved through the dark forest. She'd kept the noise low, whimpering to herself, but Caerwyn was still well aware that the other woman was enduring her own trials this night.

"I don't think we're far away now," she said, hoping to cheer the other woman up. "A little farther then we'll come to where Jais and his aunt are."

Alnia's voice was full of a soured surprise when she responded. "You almost seem happy that we're headed toward a den of krolls, led by something even worse, if that's possible."

Caerwyn hadn't thought of that. "You don't have to go that far."

"Because I'm useless. I know. There will be little I can do to help you." The bitter tone seemed to deepen.

This wasn't going well. "You saved me. That's something."

Alnia sighed. "I know. I just... This is all so much. I'm not meant for this."

No she wasn't. "You're bearing it bravely."

"You're kind to say so, but I think you're lying."

So what could Caerwyn say to help this girl? Perhaps it was time to take a slightly harder approach. It had worked with her troops. "Things are only going to get harder from here." She kept her tone neutral, calm, but went on. "You've said you can't go back. Well even if we succeed in stopping these krolls, life won't be easy. Living out of a small pack, eating what we can hunt or forage, sleeping on the ground, in the cold or rain. That's my life, and your life now. You'll need to grow harder for such things."

Alnia gave a huff of a sardonic laugh. "You make it sound easy."

Caerwyn didn't think she'd made their life sound that easy at all.

"Just 'grow harder' like I could sprout a second skin of snake's scales. I am only starting to understand what you think of as a hard life. You can say all those words now, and trust me that sounds like the pits of Holn to me, but I get the feeling that living it will be so much worse. I'm not ready for any of this." Those last words were said amidst sobs.

So the hard approach hadn't worked. But Caerwyn had to agree, Alnia wasn't ready for any of this.

"You could still go back. See if you can find some joy in a normal life."

"Without Jais? With my family and friends always looking at me askance, like I'm some sort of traitor?"

"You'll be a comfortable traitor I suspect."

The sobs continued for a while without any response. Caerwyn waited.

"You don't know how good that sounds, but I can't," Alnia said once she was able.

"Why not?"

More sobs for a moment before she found her words. "Because even if they could forgive me for what I've done, I'm not sure I could ever forgive them!" The sobs were laced with anger now.

Caerwyn nodded to herself.

"Then you'll become hard like me. I'll teach you how to fight, defend yourself. You'll survive, and there will be good days, but as you say, things will probably be far worse than you expect for a while. It isn't easy to leave everything you know. Trust me, I've done it. But you get used to it."

Alnia sniffed. "You had to leave your family and everything else behind?" She sounded disbelieving.

"Twice. Both because I was drahksani."

"Twice?"

"Once when I was a child and my family was being slaughtered. I escaped, but I was only a child and had nothing. I had to learn to survive and live off the land, by my wits only. You think what's ahead of you is hard. Try doing it when you're barely old enough to know what's going on, and with no one to help you."

"That's horrible!"

"It was. But I endured, and so will you."

"I hate to ask about the other time."

Caerwyn laughed for a moment. It hadn't been a question, but she would answer. "That time was easier for many reasons, but still I had to leave behind everything I knew, family and friends, and I can never go back." Before Alnia could ask why, Caerwyn answered that too. "I was an adult, and I had a friend with me, but I was exposed as drahksani to my adopted family. It was only because I was held in high esteem, a person of great respect and privilege, that I wasn't killed outright. Instead I was banished. That was just over a year ago."

Alnia's tears seemed to be drying. "And here I thought you had always lived this way. I am sorry, Caerwyn. I can't imagine what you must have endured. Your life sounds like it's been far worse than mine."

"Perhaps, but there were many good moment as well. As you've had, I'm certain. Cherish those, hold them close. They will help to get you through what is to come. Just don't pine to return to those memories, down that road lies a dangerous path of regret and sorrow... even madness."

"Thank you."

"For what?"

"Telling me about your life. It helps."

Oh? Caerwyn hadn't thought of that approach, but apparently they'd gotten there in the end.

"Shall we move on then?" she asked.

Alnia drew a long breath and let it out, sounding determined in the darkness. "Yes."

21

JAIS CREPT TOWARD HIS DOOM.

He couldn't stop thinking of it in such terms. He saw no way he would get out of what he was about to do alive.

Even if he could get close to the krolloc without being seen—or scented—and maybe somehow surprise it, he was still fairly certain that it would take more than one blow to fell the thing. And more than one blow would mean more time. The longer he was there, the greater the chances that the krolloc would magic him in some foul way, or that another kroll would come along and help his master. It seemed like it'd take a miracle to kill the krolloc and escape with his life.

He crept down a narrow, jagged tunnel in complete darkness. He had followed the nice carved tunnel a little ways before it had turned back into the jagged rock above and below and to either side, which was more expected for such a deep cave. He could see in a limited manner, but made his way along partially by feel, his hands out on the walls. He knew he was turning, curving around to his right, and hoped that meant he was heading back toward the main cave. A little while ago he'd felt the air current's change. It hadn't been that noticeable, but he's started feeling a faint breeze blowing against his face in the darkness. So, if he was creeping toward the back end of that larger cave then he would be up wind of the krolls. They shouldn't be able to smell him.

That was something... if not a lot.

Light up ahead let him know he was getting closer to— what he assumed was—the large chamber. He moved more carefully. A wrong step could still announce his presence with an unwelcome noise.

Finding the end of the tunnel, he stayed within its shadows as he surveyed where he was, within the cavern of the krolls.

This was a good spot and a bad spot all at once. The cavern was long, and he was far from the end where most of the krolls were. That meant he was far from the great fires as well. There were many shadows and places he could hide as he made his way to the other end of the hall. He'd have lots of cover and time to work his way over to them. And yet, because it was so far away, that also meant he had farther to return once the deed was done. He was fairly certain they were faster than he, which meant they'd catch him before he could get back here. The ground was also quite uneven with many odd slopes and jagged edges. Again, good for moving slowly, not so good for running.

Yet he could not turn back from the task his aunt had given him. He truly knew very little about krollocs, but he could guess they were every bit as bad as she had made them out to be.

He left his bow and quiver here. They would do him no

good. As much as he could use the ranged advantage he doubted that such small projectiles would truly hurt that massive beast, even if he hit well with every arrow. No, his sword was his best chance to kill the thing, but that meant getting far closer than was comfortable.

As he snuck from his concealed spot to creep along the floor and around the stalagmites, he found an ironic grin on his face at the thought that he might die saving people who wanted to kill him. In truth, they got the best out of this deal no matter how it went. At least in their minds they would: either they got rid of a drahksan, or the krolls.

He tread with extreme care. There were small rocks and dust, covering this area of the cave, on which he might slip or that might crunch under his boots. He could make no noise, give no warning of his attack. It was painstaking, each step measured and scouted, every path well thought to keep him out of their sight.

To cross the couple hundred feet from the crevice to the place where he was closest to their light, and where he paused to make his final plans, seemed like an eternity. His heart raced, sweat slicked his forehead and dampened his clothes despite the rather chill air in these caves.

Jais had no idea if krolls slept or not, but gazing down on them now from his vantage point, hidden behind a thick column of stone, he learned that they did. He thanked any god that would listen for that. Not all of them were asleep, it seemed some, less than a dozen, just meandered around the cave, lumbering along, almost as if lost, no direction or goal apparent. Yet the rest were in various positions of repose, including the krolloc. The big beast was still another fifty feet away from Jais. There were two possible spots Jais might be able to hide along the way if any of the alert ones looked his way.

This was it. Probably his best chance was now.

He descended the hill of stone from which he had been watching the krolls, and padded along as silent as he could until he reached the first spot to hide. He'd been moving so quickly that he hit the jutted stone wall hard and it blew the air out of him in a huff. His heart thundered in his ears. His breath came so heavily, he was certain one of the krolls would hear it, but as he waited to see if there was any alarm raised, nothing happened. He glanced around the stalagmite and indeed nothing seemed amiss. It would be all uphill from here to another spot where the floor seemed to have shifted and broken, creating a four-foot wall he could hide behind. That stood less than ten paces from the krolloc.

He slipped around his current hiding spot, and rushed up the incline to the next, throwing himself down to hide there.

His heart was hammering, frantic. He'd seen the krolloc start to rouse as he'd reached this spot.

There was a roar. It was a feral and terrible sound which sent a shiver down his spine, turning his sweat cold and making his insides squirm.

He heard a great, hissing inhalation from somewhere above him, then... "Another drahksan!"

Gods! He was done for before he'd even reached the thing. He must have been too close, even being up wind, and the thing had scented him.

The krolloc bellowed more, but it was in the krollish tongue, and Jais couldn't understand it. He drew forth his sword, not caring if there was any noise. The rousing of the krolls was quite thunderous as it was.

He steeled himself, knowing that at any minute a giant

form was going to come looming above him. This would be his one and only chance to slay the beast. He'd cut the legs out from under a kroll before, perhaps he could do so again on this massive creature.

He drew in three quick, deep breaths, trying to steady his frayed nerves and steal his trembling limbs. Then, for better or worse, he shot to his feet and turned around, ready to face the monster coming for him...

Except it wasn't.

The krolloc was facing away from Jais, still bellowing orders to the other krolls and pointing back out toward the entrance of the cave.

But that meant...

Caerwyn.

She was here. She was the one the krolloc was sensing. This was perfect... for him. But it would prove most probably fatal for her, with that many krolls going after her. Still, he couldn't think about that now. He had a mission to accomplish, and this turn of events gave him his best shot.

He vaulted up onto the raised area he'd been hiding behind a moment before and charged the kroll. He was tempted to yell or bellow his own war cry, but kept himself silent, retaining his surprise.

Then he leapt, his powerful limbs throwing him high. He'd given up on his 'cut the legs out from under it' plan in hopes that one strike might end this. He hoped to decapitate it, but quickly realized he'd jumped too soon. The krolloc was so tall that only at the apex of his incredible jump could he have reached the neck of the thing, but he hit the peak too far away from it.

His mind worked out where he'd hit the thing, and he reversed his sword in his grip, plunging it into the beast's back with the full force of his charge. The sword shuddered as it sank in, jolted around by what Jais guessed were ribs. He retained hold of the hilt as he, too, slammed into the krolloc's back. He brought one foot up to try to lever himself off the beast hoping these things had hearts, and he'd struck that.

But it was fated not to be.

The krolloc screamed a savage roar of pain and surprise, flinging one of its long arms back around it at Jais.

Jais leapt away before he was hit, and nimbly landed on his feet.

But his sword was still ten feet above him, sunk to the hilt in the krolloc's back.

The krolloc spun and glared down at him, still bellowing a cry of rage.

Jais wished—for an eternal moment between heartbeats —that he could call the sword back to him as Caerwyn did with Davlas.

He could not.

He stood transfixed in terror for a long moment, expecting his death to come—torn limb from limb—but the krolloc apparently was too preoccupied with a blade stuck in his back, reaching around behind it, trying to pull the thing free.

It took Jais another stunned set of heartbeats to tell his feet to move.

Then he was running, hard and fast. He'd scouted the best path back to his cave on the way here and ran, leaping from rock to rock when necessary, with all haste. As he neared the crevice, he dared look back. There was no one following him. Perhaps the krolls were too confused by what had happened.

It was only then, standing at the mouth of his escape

tunnel, that he realized... he should have stayed. The krolloc had been distracted. He could have found a weapon and attacked it, punched it if needs be. But it was too late now. He'd been a coward, too terrified to even think of staying and trying to finish the thing.

He turned away, picking up his bow and quiver as he slunk into the shadowed crevice.

The bellows of the krolloc followed him... taunting him.

His own mind replayed his failure over and over.

He knew he'd had his chance... and he'd missed it.

22

ALNIA WAS TIRED AND SCARED. IT WAS AN ODD COMBINATION. She was alert for danger, but felt sluggish and slow.

She hadn't slept all night, even back before they'd been found in the forest. Caerwyn had fallen unconscious quickly... snoring. Alnia had remained awake and uncertain. She'd tried sleeping but her thoughts were a whirlwind and kept her mind spinning in directionless activity. Also she wasn't used to sleeping on the ground and couldn't get comfortable. So, by the time that strange apparition of Jais' aunt had appeared and she'd woken Caerwyn, she'd only grown more tired. The desperate flight through the forest throughout the rest of the night hadn't helped. She was exhausted.

And yet, they were nearing the place where there would be more krolls than she ever wanted to see together and her fear was piqued.

"This is it," Caerwyn said, crouching low, peering through some bushes. Alnia crouched, trembling with terror and fatigue. "The cave is just ahead, there in that ridge, do you see it?"

Everything was dark around them. Alnia had no idea how late it was, but was certain dawn had to be coming soon. This night had been far too long already. She yearned for some light or some rest. She wasn't sure which she wanted more at this point. She knew beyond any doubt that she wanted to be away from this place, but she hadn't known how to say that to Caerwyn, the seemingly fearless woman next to her.

"You can wait here if you want," Caerwyn said. "Or perhaps over there in the shadows of the ridge. It looks like there's a path up to the top. No better place to be than above these beasts. They probably wouldn't think to look there."

Alnia didn't answer right away. She wanted to help, but she knew she was too scared to be of any use here. She looked over at the 'path' Caerwyn had indicated, but she could hardly see anything other than the dark looming ridge.

Caerwyn must have taken her silence for reticence. "Either that or you can fight with me. I'll give you Davlas. You can call it back to you after you've thrown it. I—"

"No, I'll go. I can't see the path from here, but I'm sure I'll find it."

"I understand. Be..." The other woman stopped speaking as a distant rumbling reached their ears. "What's...?"

A new dread filled Alnia. So powerful she couldn't move for a moment. She wanted to curl up into a ball and hide here in these bushes. Her entire body shook with the intense fear.

"No." Caerwyn whispered the word, and it hung in the air for a moment as the rumbling grew louder. "No." This one was quieter, hardly heard over the new noise and shake of the earth beneath them.

Krolls poured out of the cave mouth. Alnia couldn't see

them, she'd pulled back from peering through the bush, but she knew they were there. She could hear their stomping feet and harsh, rasping breath.

"What are they doing?" Caerwyn's voice was the barest of whispers.

A new sound, a strange sort of sucking noise filled the forest.

"It looks like they're sniffing the air, but... oh, shades and shadows! They can smell us."

Alnia's pulse lurched. How did one hide from something that could catch your scent? Her mind settled on the ineffable conclusion quite quickly: you don't, not when you were this close and the air was still.

She heard a grunt, followed quickly by Caerwyn's urgent hiss, "They know we're here!"

Something happened to Alnia then, a sort of calm. All her terror and trembling, her fatigue and confusion, was pushed aside for a rather unnerving serenity. There was a certainty that swept over her.

She was going to die. That seemed inevitable now.

The only real choice she had left available to her was... would she make her death mean something.

She was surprise at the peace within her as she leaned forward and touched Caerwyn's shoulder. "You have a chance to actually do something useful. Use it." Then she turned toward the bushes which separated the two of them from the approaching krolls. "Let's see if they only hunt by scent or if a moving target will distract them." And she slipped through the bushes.

She heard a gasp behind her.

Before her were more krolls than she ever wanted to see, more than a dozen with more emerging from the cave as she watched.

The ones at the front had already seen her, but she wanted to get as many as possible to follow her to give Caerwyn a chance, so she yelled the first thing that came to mind. "You're all really ugly!"

Then she bolted away from Caerwyn's hiding spot.

She was filled with a wonderful exhilaration, a freedom like nothing she'd ever known. She nearly laughed with the feeling. These few moments, right now, being terrified and yet somehow overcoming it at the same time and knowing her death was imminent, were the most pure and full of her entire life.

Caerwyn had wanted to yell after Alnia, tell her to stop, pull her back... something! But the crazy woman had acted so fast and Caerwyn had been so surprised she'd not been able to do anything but gasp.

She heard Alnia's taunt and the ensuing charge and chase. She knew she needed to move, now, to make Alnia's sacrifice mean something, but she was planted here, listening with her so-keen hearing. Waiting for...

The scream...

Cut short so quickly...

A wet crunching sound...

Tears filled Caerwyn's eyes, but there was no time to mourn now. She rose carefully, not wanting to make a noise. A plan formed in her mind, and she began picking her way through the forest as quickly as she could.

Her heart was pounding, partly for fear of so many krolls

nearby, partly in shock at what Alnia had done. She hid behind a thick tree and peeked around it.

The krolls were still streaming out of the cave. By the gods there were so many! For the moment at least they seemed preoccupied with Alnia.

Caerwyn had to cross a small open space. She made a break for it, running as fast as she could. No alarm went up. She reached the path she'd seen earlier, which led up the ridge. The hillside was covered in moss and loose earth and rocks. Every grasp of her hand on a tuft of grasses simply pulled it away and threatened to topple her back down. It was steep, but at just an angle that she could almost walk up it. It was her haste that made her claw and crawl, trying to pull herself up faster. She scrambled up with as much speed as she could. She slipped a few times, sliding on her belly back down a few feet, which only made it harder to get a grip with her feet or hands to try again. The path grew narrow closer to the top, and she found more to grab, tree roots and exposed rocks.

She reached the top, breath rasping, filthy with dirt and sweat, hands scraped and bleeding. She crawled up from the steep path and simply rolled onto her back, chest heaving with heavy breaths. She was so tense and worn from the rapid flight that for that moment, as she lay there, she felt large hot tears leave her eyes, and she couldn't help but sob for a moment at Alnia's death.

What had the woman been thinking?

Move! Don't make her death be in vain. Her own voice in her head shouted at her, and she obeyed it. She rolled over to her hands and knees and crawled to the cliff's edge where she thought she'd be over top of the kroll cave. She was curious to see what the krolls were doing. If they knew of her where-abouts now?

She stayed low, pressed to the ground, earth and grasses crushed into her clothes and brushing by her face with a heady loamy scent.

She peered over the edge and saw the mass of krolls below. They were milling about now, some lumbering off in various directions, others returning to sniffing the air.

Caerwyn didn't know how their sense of smell worked. Would they find her up here?

She took a quick sniff herself and could smell only the dirt and grass around her.

None of the krolls below seemed to be alerted to her pres-ence so perhaps she'd managed to cover herself in enough dirt to fool them. She didn't know and wasn't going to stick around to test the theory.

She pushed back from the edge, scampering back until she was certain no one below would see her if she stood. She turned away from the cliff and took a moment to steady herself. She had hoped in coming up here to find a crevice, a way down into those caves. If the cave system was as large as she suspected it would range all through this part of the ridge. There should be a fissure she could use.

She sensed Jais below her and off somewhere ahead of her to her right. She moved carefully in that direction, eyes intent on the ground.

After a short while of searching, she stopped suddenly as a thought came to her... her wound.

With all the rush and commotion, the scrambling and flight, she hadn't even thought of it. She supposed that was a good thing. She could feel it, now that she was thinking of it, but it had not been in her awareness for a while now. She nodded to herself at that, she'd needed some good news. She considered it a boon and kept searching.

She found what she was searching for at the base of a thick, leaning tree. The tree's roots were already partially filling the gap, a dark void in the earth. She didn't know if this would lead anywhere, but she was at least mostly certain that if she got those roots out of the way, she would fit into the crevice.

Taking out her sword, she began hacking at the roots.

23

BARAMI WOKE WITH A START AND IMMEDIATELY CAUGHT himself from falling. He'd been sleeping in trees since he was a kid. You only had to know what to look for to find the right spot. He didn't have his net hammock with him—that had been taken with the rest of this things—but he still felt safer in a tree. So, after he'd taken that villager's weapons and gear, he'd found a tree nearby to wait for dawn, sleeping in the cradle where the trunk split into three main branches. It was far from as comfortable as any bed, but he'd learned when young to sleep anywhere while on the march, and it had never left him.

He looked around.

The sky was lighter, but not by much. Dawn was coming, but it still wouldn't be full light out, especially down under the forest canopy, for some time.

Still, he felt the need for haste. He should find his companions.

First he listened. He could hear nothing, no one searching the woods below and no calls or threats of people.

Then he scouted as best he could in all directions. He'd attacked the villager near a stream and could still see the body there. It hadn't even been found yet. These people were so very poorly organized. There was a wide gap in the foliage above the small watercourse and with the ever so slight increase in light, he thought he saw something down below in the mud of the stream-bank.

He climbed down from his perch and padded over to inspect his find. Crouching next to it he smiled. This was a bit of luck, which after the past few days, was a welcome relief. There in the mud of the bank was a large oddly shaped depression. Others might not know what to look for, but he recognized it as a kroll's footprint. What was even better was that within that large foot print was another print, a small horse's hoof-print. Now that he'd seen these, a quick inspection of the area revealed more prints. At least one kroll had passed through here, probably two. They'd been followed by a man and a horse. The man, Barami had a strong suspicion, was Jais. He'd noticed... however many days ago... that the young man's boots were ill-shod, and the pattern that these prints left in the mud was a fair match for Jais' soles, which needed replacing.

He rose looking ahead to where the tracks led.

Morning would be on him soon, but he had a direction now. He set off, urgency pulling him, hoping that Jais and Caerwyn weren't getting themselves into too much trouble.

Jais meandered back through the caves, the way he had come, until he found the carved tunnel and the bench he'd sat on when his aunt's spirit had left him. He hadn't noticed it before, but there was an opening not far away in the opposite wall. Within were more benches. He sat on one and—consumed with a morbid self-loathing—put his head in his hands, weeping bitter tears at his cowardice and fear.

He could not get the image of the krolloc, looming and flailing before him, out of his mind. Nor could he stop thinking about how he'd been so terrified in the moment he should have acted. He'd never have that chance again.

His aunt had trusted him to kill the thing, even if it meant his own death. But he and it were still alive, and his aunt must have been disgusted with him from where she watched up in Erival. He had no weapon left... well he had his arrows, but he maintained that if a long-sword shoved to the hilt into the krolloc had not killed it, then his arrows would do no good, except to annoy it perhaps. He had failed his aunt and put the village in jeopardy, even if they were all trying to kill him. More than that, this entire region was at risk because of him.

And Caerwyn.

The thing had scented her and had sent all those krolls out after her. Jais had no clue what might have become of her, but he couldn't see it being anything good. How she could defeat or escape that many krolls was beyond him.

And it was all his fault.

If he hadn't been so scared... perhaps... but what could he have done with no weapon... wrestle it?

He was no warrior. He knew that now. He was a boy who'd wanted to play at being a man. He'd wanted to swing a sword and fight battles and defeat monsters. He'd tried, true enough, even had some luck, which it must have been—not skill certainly. But even those first two krolls he'd faced, he'd needed Barami to rush in and save him.

No one would save him now.

He kicked a rock next to his foot, and it went clattering, echoing across the floor... much farther than he would have thought.

Jais blinked and took a look at where he was. He hadn't been all that observant upon his arrival, noticing only a couple rows of benches. He'd just wanted a place to sit and rest, but now that he looked around, he realized there was far more here. The floors were flat and carved in an intricate pattern. The bench he sat on was stone, but it was one of many which sat in rows with a central aisle cutting through them. Behind him stood a mostly smooth stone wall. It looked like the stone had been carved away and flattened out up to a height of about twelve feet. Beyond that was a rough and jagged stone wall arching up over him. There was the arched portal through which he'd entered within that same wall. The other walls... were similarly carved and smoothened. The other end of the large hall had a wide open area and... there were figures standing in the center of that plaza. They were large and carved of stone, two men and a woman.

It only occurred to Jais then that he was seeing far more detail than he was used to in these caves. He looked up to see a great round hole in the ceiling of this place. It was directly above the three statues, and through it he could see forest and the brightening sky of dawn.

He blinked away his tears, his defeat forgotten for a moment by an acute curiosity. He rose from his seat and approached the three stone figures, making out more details as he neared them.

The one man held a harp and a staff, depicted with long flowing hair and a lean, prime physique. The second man held up a cup with one hand and the other seemed weighed down with an orb, which, though cracked now, looked like it had been made of glass with a smoky interior, billowing clouds trapped within it. This man was less well defined of body, more rounded and a little taller in general. He had a bald head and a jovial, laughing face.

The woman... was a depiction of beauty. Both of her hands were raised above her head and her face turned upward, long hair cascading behind her as if she was worshiping the sun itself. The statue was portrayed in a loose gown which, though it covered the front of her torso and swayed in a skirt from the waist down, still somehow left little to the imagination. She was some artist's rendition of the perfect woman and even now, with pits in the stone and small chunks missing, she was still captivating.

Jais walked around the three of them, clustered together in the center of a ring on the floor which matched the hole in the top of this room. It looked like there was even a trough for run-off, if rain happened to fall through onto these stone beings.

Jais knew them now. It was fairly clear once he'd seen all the details and the fact that they were depicted together. They were the Ylsovan Gods, the three children of Ylvana and Sovana, the Virgin and the Matron, two of the three gods of creation.

The man with the harp was Thadros, god of music, inspiration, and healing. The one in the middle with the cup and orb would be Berem, god of celebration and revelry. The woman would be Asavi, goddess of beauty, love, and pleasure.

Now the open area at the front of the hall around the statues made sense. Jais had heard of such places as this, an

Ylsovan Festorium. A place for great revels that would put the celebrations of Klasten's Green to shame, if the myths were true. There would be a solemn time to pay homage to the gods, then a wild party of music, drinking, and passionate encounters. The myths said these celebrations sometimes lasted for days. It was perhaps where traditions such as Beremus had come from. But those stories were of the ancient peoples, who lived in the Age of Wonders, when the gods still strode the lands in physical form or rode dragons like men rode horses. If so then this cavern was... thousands of years old.

The gravity of that sank in slowly. He was in an ancient place and... he could feel it. More than just the knowing of its importance and age. There was another feeling here. Something that called to him in a way he couldn't describe. Perhaps there had been something about his drahksani nature which had pulled him to this place.

A smattering of pebbles cascaded down from above. Tumbling over the three statues.

"Jais?"

Was that Caerwyn's voice?

He looked up to find her looking down at him, standing next to the hole in the ceiling.

"Caerwyn? What ar—?"

"Oh, thank all the gods it's you!"

"How did you find me?"

"I can sense you. It's a drahksani thing. I knew you were somewhere under me, so I went looking for caves to climb down into. I found one, but it was too clogged with roots, so I kept looking and found... this." Before he could say anything, she turned away from the hole, and he heard her yelling, "Hold on I'm coming down!" A moment later a rope snaked down from the gap, though it ended still about fifteen feet from the floor.

Caerwyn appeared a moment later climbing down the rope.

"Your rope is too short," Jais called.

"I don't much care," Caerwyn huffed as she lowered herself. He supposed if she reach the end and stretched out she'd only have less than ten feet to drop... but before she could get there, the rope shifted up above, and another cascade of stones fell on her.

She coughed and... let go of the rope.

Jais stepped in to catch her. Luckily, she fell in the gap between two of the statues, otherwise it would have been much harder to reach her. She landed awkwardly in his arms, and he stumbled backward, managing to keep hold of her, going to his knees with a twist of his ankle.

"Hi," he said, blinking dust from his eyes, then coughing.

"Hi." Then she coughed at that same dust. "Just thought I'd drop in." She grinned, her dark eyes gazing at him with something he couldn't place. Her smile faded quickly. "Jais, I'm sorry, but Alnia is dead."

He almost dropped her then. His arms seemed to turn to water. Since he was already kneeling he simply put her on the floor. He felt as if he'd been punched in the gut.

He hoped he hadn't heard that right, but the words had been clear enough.

"What...? What happened?" He asked as Caerwyn rose to her feet. He couldn't look up; not into those dark and penetrating eyes which seemed to see his soul.

He heard Caerwyn's sigh and watched her feet as she stepped away a short distance. "I... don't really know what came over her, but she died saving me. She lured the krolls away from where we were hiding so I could escape."

"She... died for you?" That didn't sound right. Alnia was no warrior, not anyone who would ever run into a fight. "Shouldn't you have been the one to die to protect her?" The words were harsh, and a part of him knew it, but he still couldn't quite understand how he'd lost the woman he loved.

"I should have. Yes." The shame in her voice was clear.

That only made him feel guilty for his words and even more ashamed for his own cowardice. Alnia had died to help another, and yet he hadn't stayed to fight the krolloc. He might have died, but that was the sacrifice that heroes made. Alnia had never been a warrior, but she had been a hero. Somehow that made his disgrace so much worse.

He didn't have any words left, and once again, remembering his failure and fear, compiled with the grief of losing Alnia, he couldn't help but break into tears once again.

A moment later Caerwyn was kneeling next to him, arm around him. "I'm sorry," she breathed, her voice choked up.

And there he stayed, lost in his emotions, with the vague comfort of her next to him, for some time.

24

BARAMI WAS MOVING FASTER NOW THAT THE SUN WAS UP. IT was still dim in the forest, but that was enough for him to follow the path Jais and the krolls had left. He wasn't sure what the villagers had been looking for or where they had gone, but he didn't encounter them again.

Instead, he encountered krolls.

He could sense them before he heard them, their stomping tread evident to him as he remained still. He'd been crouching, looking at a set of tracks, and felt the vibration through the ground. It had to be something big. In this area, that seemed to be krolls, so he spared no extra time or thought and immediately climbed the nearest tree as high as he could. Then he waited, though it wasn't long.

He heard them, snorting and crashing through the forest. A moment later they came into view, a stream of them, all fanned out amidst the trees.

He'd never seen so many krolls in the same place, and they all seemed to be working as a unit.

Holn! He dared not breathe the word aloud. The name

used here for the god of darkness rolled off the tongue a lot easier than the southern name: Buro Hassi.

He held his breath, but still several stopped at the base of the tree in which he was hiding. They bent low and sniffed around.

Gods! They were scenting him!

And yet after a moment of grunting between them and searching the area around the base of the tree, they all moved on. Not one of them had looked up at him.

He almost laughed and thanked Hakan that the things were no smarter than dogs. They could smell 'human' but with their limited knowledge they could only think of humans being smaller than they were and ground-bound, not above them.

He waited a good while until he could neither hear nor see the krolls before risking the climb down.

That group of krolls caused him two points of concern. The first was, they had probably ruined the trail he was following, trampling all over it. But he could probably follow their trail back to where it started, and he suspected he'd get to the same place Jais had gone. The second concern was for the unsuspecting town of Klasten's Green. That many krolls would destroy the village and a good number of its inhabitants.

He felt a pang of worry for them, but it faded quickly. A part of him, the vindictive, self-serving part, said that they were getting what they deserved. Yet a deeper part said this would only ever confirm their suspicions about drahksani. The village already thought that Caer was controlling the krolls. This wave of the beasts would only seem like some form of retribution from the escaped drahksani.

He should try to stop it... but his life-bond had not been

made to that village, it had been made to Caerwyn. His life for hers, his repayment after she had saved his life so many times now. So, he would go onward and hope that wherever Jais was, that too was where he would find the woman he needed to protect.

~

Caerwyn held Jais, feeling uncomfortable the entire time.

She wasn't one who consoled others, she was a commander, not a confidant. She gave orders not sympathies. To compile her discomfort, she'd been the one who, in some ways, was responsible for the death of the woman he loved, hence responsible for his grief. She knew he shouldn't have to go through this alone, but had no clue what to say or do to make this any better for him. So she just waited for him to have his time.

Yet even as she waited, an urgency grew within her and started to itch at her. Jais' aunt had been clear that there was great danger here, that needed to be dealt with… quickly. Caerwyn knew of the existence of krollocs, but not much more than that. They were supposedly bigger and nastier than regular krolls, but there hadn't ever been many of them. So it was hard to separate the hearsay from the truth.

Jais sniffled a soft, "Thank you."

She wasn't sure the correct thing to say so went with a simple, "Whatever you need."

"I'm glad you were there. I'm glad she didn't die alone."

Well, in some ways Alnia had been alone, running frantically away from Caerwyn, but she wasn't going to tell Jais that. She had been with Alnia up until those final minutes.

"Where are we?" she asked. She'd had a little time to look around the large chamber they were in while Jais had his moment. "What is this place?"

He rose slowly. She relinquished her hold around him and stood as well. When he faced her his eyes were red and raw. His gaze moved past her to the statues next to them.

"It's a Festorium, I think."

The name seemed vaguely familiar. It had an old sound to it, like something her adopted father would have studied. "Oh?"

"See those three figures?"

She turned and looked at the statues. She'd noticed them before but not taken any lingering look.

"Those are the Ylsovan gods, Thadros, Berem, and Asavi. This was a place to celebrate life and create new life."

"Oh." It seemed like an odd concept. She'd never studied the gods much, though she knew them enough to curse the correct one if need be. Why would someone create a place to celebrate? Couldn't you do that anywhere?

"It's really old," Jais went on. "Perhaps thousands of years."

That was intriguing. This really was something her adopted father would have loved to study. "It's in remarkable shape."

"It is." She heard him making noises for a minute, like he was trying to say something but not finding words, "I think... I think magic was involved."

"Magic?"

"Can't you feel it?"

Feel...?

She took stock of herself. She was tired and sore and dirty. Her wound seemed to be doing well, but still she didn't want to risk removing the bandage just yet. Other than that... did she feel anything else?

There was something, an odd...

"Oh."

"Yeah. Hard to describe isn't it?"

It was. Something akin to mild gas pains, a bit of a 'discomfort' in the gut, but with a pull... a sensation that those statues were... calling to her?

"It's coming from the figures," she said softly.

"Huh."

She turned back to look at Jais behind her. "What?"

"You're right, but I hadn't made that connection. Oddly it does get stronger the closer to those things you get."

"I'm not sure if I want to get much closer." They were right next to them as it was.

His face contorted into a confused and admonishing look. "Really? You're afraid of magic? Isn't that a bit hypocritical? You are magic."

"I know but, well, even I didn't know I was magic until just a little while ago. I'm used to how I feel, and all my abilities are... sort of internal. I can't throw fireballs like the tales of wizards nor hinder people in their tracks like your aunt. Magic from other people is still a bit... odd."

Jais shook his head with an odd grimace. "I guess I can understand that." He crossed the couple of steps to the statues. She stood and watched from where she was.

"I feel better when I'm closer to them. Maybe... I don't know. Maybe there is something they can do for us if we... pray to them?"

"Pray?" She believed in the gods, sure enough, but only in a distant sort of way. She didn't really believe the priests that said the gods were looking down on them all the time and would return in physical form someday. No god had ever helped her. "You think that will do anything?"

Jais' shoulders slumped. His entire form, as broad and bulky as he was, seemed to collapse in on itself. He lost half of himself in just that simple act of dejection.

"Jais? What is it?"

"I could really use someone to pray to right now."

"Jais?"

He turned and sat on the raised stone circle around the figures. He put his head in his hands and shook it slowly. When he spoke there was a bottomless sadness in his voice. "I failed."

She was a little confused by all this. She sat next to him again. "Jais what happened?"

His words were now choked and interspersed with sniffles and tears. "I tried... My aunt told me I had to kill the krolloc and I tried. I got in a single blow... put my sword in its back... sunk to the hilt." He shook his head. "It wasn't enough. I could have kept going. It was distracted. I could have done more, but it turned, and I... I was so scared... I... I ran, and now everything is going to fall apart because I couldn't face that thing."

He'd tried to go up against a krolloc alone? And he was still here to talk about it? That seemed like a feat in and of itself. If any of the legends of krollocs were true, they took out kingdoms on their own, and were only slain by a score of knights or some band of legendary heroes. They weren't anything that a single man had ever defeated. Well, there probably was some mythic tale, but nothing she'd ever heard.

"Jais. You tried, and you're still alive. You can try again."

He sniffled. "I don't think it's going to let me get that close again. Krolls can smell us, and... last time I came from upwind and surprised it, but I don't think it's going to leave that part of the cave unguarded again." He looked up, cheeks wet. "That's why I thought, perhaps, if we prayed..."

"Ah. I see." Well certainly if the two of them were going to go up against a krolloc on their own, some divine assistance wouldn't be amiss. She didn't really believe it was possible, but there was no harm in trying. "Sure we can pray then." She was about to kneel when Jais got up, turning.

"I think I'll talk to them directly."

That was also something to try. She approached the three statues.

The depictions of the gods were in excellent shape for the age of this place, if it was as old as Jais thought. The stone was only chipped here and there, a few cracks and pits. The orb held by Berem was broken. It wasn't stone, however, but some form of smoke-filled glass. Yet even it was only split in two, almost cleanly as if the separate halves could be easily put back together.

Jais went to the goddess, Asavi, who was certainly depicted like no human woman Caerwyn had ever seen, a little too... perfect in her dimensions and features. If she was meant to inspire arousal for men, she'd probably done that quite well. Even Caerwyn found herself being a little swept up in the ecstasy on the statue's face. She forced herself to look away and back at the broken orb in Berem's hands.

"The orb of dreams," she whispered. She'd seen one of her adopted father's texts once with the god depicted with a sphere. It was said that was where all the dreams of all mankind were kept.

She reached out tentatively and touched one half.

Everything around her shifted.

She blinked, her hand pulling away reflexively...

She stood amidst a billowing mist, gray and thick. She knew she'd been in the hall with Jais just a moment ago, and should still be there now, but this place seemed too real. The mist was wet on her skin, smelling of pine and cedar. It began to fade and revealed a thick forest off to her right, but more than that, before her... was her home.

She swallowed hard, tears in her eyes. This wasn't the home she'd known in the south for so many years, this was the home which lingered only in distant foggy memories... the home of her childhood... the home of her true parents.

She trembled.

The last time she'd seen this place had been in a hasty backward glance as she'd fled the man killing her parents, a horrible memory, a horrible time. But here and now, all was peaceful.

The door to the small house opened, and Caerwyn flinched, her heart lurching in her chest.

From the doorway came... her mother, followed by her father, as they had looked when she'd been young, as she remembered them. She couldn't even run to them she was so overwhelmed with joy and relief and pain at the memory of their loss. It was too much, and she collapsed to her knees as they came to her.

Her mother looked so happy, overwhelmed with tears and a sad smile. "Ranin, look at her, how big and strong she's become. Can you believe this is our girl?" Her mother knelt and wrapped loving arms around her. They wept together in warmth and reunion.

Her father smiled proudly above her. "I always knew this is what she would become. A warrior maiden, tough as nails and brave. I'm so happy to see you again, Caeri."

Hearing her father's pet name for her, a name no one had

ever called her since, completely broke Caerwyn. Blinded by tears, she only felt him as he, too, knelt with her and enfolded her and his wife in a bear's embrace.

There they stayed for some time.

"We're so sorry," her mother said, muffled by the embrace. "No child should have to go through what you did. We both wish we could have been there for you."

Caerwyn found her voice. She had to speak. "You did everything you could. You gave your lives and gave me time to get away. There is no more a parent could do for their child." Then, with such a release of sorrow flowing out with her words she said, "I have missed you both so much!"

"We know and we've missed you too." This from her father. "Be in no hurry to be with us here in the everlasting peace. You have a long life ahead of you. We know you can face whatever the world throws at you."

"Thank you."

Caerwyn didn't know how any of this was possible but she was so very thankful for the opportunity. She recalled touching the orb... was this a dream? If so it was one she'd never dreamed before; one she'd never forget.

"You must return," her father said, though even he took another moment before releasing her. "I am so glad we had this chance to see each other again. There is so much I want to tell you, but we must return to our place and you to yours."

Her mother released her too and they all stood. Caerwyn still had tears blurring her vision. She smiled through the watery haze. "We'll have a long talk someday."

Her father smiled. "I look forward to it."

"Goodbye Caerwyn," her mother said and began to fade.

"Goodbye Caeri."

"Goodbye mama, papa. I love you both!"

The fog returned to surround her, then...

She blinked, her hand pulling away reflexively.

It was as if no time had passed at all.

But she was still crying, tears in her eyes. That's how she knew it had been real.

25

JAIS KNELT AT THE FEET OF ASAVI. SHE OF ALL THE THREE called to him at that moment. With the loss of Alnia still fresh on his mind and in his heart, the goddess of love and passion seemed appropriate to visit first.

Caerwyn was stepping up before the statue of Berem, reaching for the broken orb in his hand.

"Please," Jais whispered and reached out to touch the calf of the goddess depicted before him. He had more to say, but the words fled from him as soon as he touched the cold stone.

It was only cold stone for a moment, then it became warm flesh.

He looked up.

Standing before him was Alnia.

His heart raced, as did his mind. Confusion and joyful bewilderment coursed through him. Yet nothing else around him made sense. He was in a place of pure white, no walls nor roof visible.

"Alnia? You're alive?" He shot to his feet and embraced

her. She was very much warm and responsive in his arms, her arms wrapping around him tightly.

"No, Jais, I'm not." Her voice was low, a whisper near his ear.

He released her and stood back, keeping his hands on her shoulders, looking her over. She was dressed differently than when he'd last seen her, in what seemed to be a single piece of flowing white cloth, but other than that she seemed very much real and alive.

"You're having a vision," she said softly by way of explanation. "And given who you were praying to I seemed a reasonable person to convey the message."

"Message?" His mind still hadn't settled. He couldn't quite make sense of this, not yet. But her words and what he was seeing, the world of white, were sinking in. "Oh. So... you're not real?"

She shrugged. "I feel real. I did die, though thankfully I cannot recall those last moments. Then I was in a place of peace, and now I'm here with you."

"Where are we?"

"I don't know. Were you not here to begin with?" she asked.

"No, were you?"

She shook her head. "No."

"Where were you?"

"I cannot describe it. It was a place of joy and peace. That is all I know."

"Oh." He sighed heavily. "I can't believe you're gone."

She pulled him close again. "At least we were given this and... perhaps... it was for the best."

He pulled back a bit to see her eyes. They were calm, questioning. "How can you say that?"

She grimaced. "Jais, I gave up my life when I came to help you. I could never go back to that, and I don't really know if I could have lived a life in the wild. Here, I am at peace."

He felt moisture in his eyes, streams on his cheeks. He nodded. Her words made sense as much as he might not have liked it. "I'm sorry I got you involved in all this."

"Don't fool yourself, Jais. I got myself involved."

He sniffed back more tears. He didn't know what to say to her next. "I love you, Alnia."

"And I you, Jaistheric. Alas our time grows short, and I have a message for you, or more specifically a gift."

"A gift?"

She seemed to reach off into the whiteness, her hand vanished for a moment, and when it returned she was holding a sword. "This was your father's."

Jais couldn't quite make sense of those words. Perrick had never owned a sword that Jais had seen. He had a few long hunting knives which might almost be considered small swords, but nothing like this. The blade was sheathed, the scabbard was of heavy leather with runes traced down its length, it was exquisite work, and the sword itself was even more so. The cross-guard was thick steel. The sides were traced with gold and inlaid with blue and green gems. The grip was wrapped in soft leather and well worn, nearly smooth. The pommel looked like it was made of glass, but with a living fire, flickering within it. It was beautiful.

"My father's...?"

"Your birth father. You were taken from him as a babe to live with your aunt and uncle. He had always wanted to pass his blade down to you."

"My father." The words sounded strange on his tongue. A man he'd never known. A man his aunt had rarely spoken of.

All he'd really known of the man was that he'd married aunt Sarelle's sister and had been a knight. Other than that, very little had ever been said about him. He'd gotten the feeling that bringing up his parents was not easy for his aunt and uncle.

Alnia handed over the blade. Given the length and the heavy guard on it, he'd expected it to be much heavier, but it was quite light. Once again, he had no idea what to say about this. All he could think of was: "thank you."

"I must go now, Jais. I'm sorry, I love you." She leaned in and kissed him lightly. "Remember me, but do not pine for me. I want you to have love in your life. Do not let my memory hinder that."

He nodded. "I love you too, and thank you."

She smiled, her eyes gleaming, then she faded into the white around her.

He was once again kneeling on the floor next to the statue of Asavi.

With a sword lying next to him.

CAERWYN STEPPED BACK WITH A LONG RELEASE OF BREATH. Then drew another equally long breath to try to bring herself to a place of calm. She still wasn't sure what had happened, or perhaps more precisely, she wasn't sure how it had happened. She was certain she'd just had a conversation with her birth parents, dead nearly thirty years now. But how that was possible was a mystery.

She touched the broken orb again, but nothing happened this time.

She turned to Jais who was rising from where he had

knelt next to the statue of Asavi. He stumbled back a few steps, then his gaze met hers.

"I just spoke to my parents," she said softly.

He was holding a sheathed sword in his hands, which he hadn't had before.

The two of them blinked at each other.

"I..." He seemed uncertain of his own words now. "I just spoke with Alnia. She... gave me this." He held his hands out, the sword laid across them. "It belonged to my father."

Caerwyn blinked again. Experiencing her own mysterious event had been baffling enough. The fact that Jais had also experienced something similar was hard to comprehend for just a moment. As much as she'd sensed something special about these statues, she hadn't expected anything like this. And the coincidence of their 'moments' having happened nearly simultaneously was also a bit baffling.

"Oh," she said, as her mind slowly caught up with his previous words. "Jais. That's great! I'm glad you had a chance to see Alnia again."

He smiled, though there was a sad edge to it. "Me too." His hands fell to his sides, one still clinging to the sword. His gaze too fell to the floor. "It's a lot to take in though."

"Agreed."

His eyes returned to regarding her. "You said something about your parents?"

She smiled, then almost laughed as she realized her smile probably looked a lot like his, a little sad. "Yes. I was able to speak to them, even though they've been dead... a long time."

"It wasn't a memory?"

She shook her head. "No, my memories of them are so faint. This was far too vibrant and... it's hard to explain, but I know it was real." She looked at his sword. "I didn't come away with anything to prove it though, like you."

"I'm not sure I believe it's real." He lifted the sword and gazed at it for a long moment. Then he took the handle with his other hand and pulled it out from its sheath just a little. The steel gleamed in the dim light of the cavern.

Something about the pommel-stone caught her eye, and she drew closer. It was a ball of glass with a flickering fire within. She'd seen depictions of that before.

"Jais," she breathed. "That's... I think that's a dragon-forged blade!"

"A what?"

"At the least, that stone on the pommel. That's dragon-glass, with an inner fire that never burns out. And the blade is glowing. I'd be willing to bet it was at least enchanted by a drahksan, if not actually created in dragon fire."

"Oh?" He stared at it.

These were things of which he obviously knew nothing. She'd had her adopted father's entire library to look through as a child, and her favorite books had been about dragons. She was fairly certain of her assessment.

"Trust me."

"I will." He returned the blade to the sheath and looked up at her again. "How were your parents?"

An aching melancholy mixed with a relieved joy mingled within her at the thought. "Well enough. They are dead after all." She shook her head. "I must admit I never really believed in Erival, a peaceful place where people go after they die, but... maybe I was wrong. I just thought life ended and that was it. I was never one to put a lot of faith in the gods and their myths." She shrugged. "Now...?"

"I think we have some fairly solid evidence of the power of the gods."

She nodded. Her gaze slipping to the statue of Asavi. She stepped over to it with a whispered, "Perhaps..."

She touched the smooth stone of the goddess's arm.

She was in a forest.

Barami nearly ran into her. He stopped himself from his jogging, coming up short and blinked. "Caer?" His face fell suddenly. "Gods! You're dead aren't you? I'm too late!"

She cocked her head to one side. "Why would you think that?"

"Look at you. You're all glowing and... well..." He looked her over a bit more closely. "You're filthy actually. You're glowing blue and look like a shambles. I sort of figured you'd look a bit more... put together after you die."

"Possibly. But I'm not dead, so that's probably why I look like this. Where are you?"

He shrugged. "I don't know. I'm here. Where are you?"

She grimaced. "In a cave touching the statue of a goddess. The Goddess of..." Love, affection, passion. Perhaps she'd leave that part out. It did seem odd that she'd come to him... unless it was her affection for him which had drawn her here. He was a close friend. Her only friend. "I'm somewhere else. This is a bit confusing for me too."

"Ah." He looked her up and down. "You certain you're not dead and just confused?"

"Quite certain."

"Well then. How do I get to where you are?"

"That depends on where you are now." She did a bit of a turn, looking around her. The sun was rising... over there, which would be east. She thought of the cave and how she'd found it. As the words came to her for how to tell him how to get to her...

She was back in the cavern.

"No!" she cried in a clipped yelp as her hand fell away from the statue. She reached for it again. "Take me back. I need to tell him where we are!"

Jais voice behind her was a little odd when it said, "Tell Barami?"

"Yes."

"I think he knows. He's here."

She spun around. Barami was standing a few feet behind her not far from Jais.

"Oh!" She couldn't think of anything better to say. "How...?"

Jais shrugged at the same time Barami did. Both of them looked as surprised as she felt.

"I have a theory though," Jais said slowly.

26

Jais was talking, but Barami wasn't listening. His mind was still trying to catch up with everything around him. One moment he'd been running through the forest, then Caerwyn had appeared as some blue glowing form before him, and he'd thought she was dead. Then he was here, in this carved-out cavern with Caer and Jais and three statues who looked to be having a good time.

His body tingled. It was like having some shiver running down his spine, but it was all over, pinpricks of sensation which made all his hairs stand on end.

Something caught his eye, and he looked over at Jais' sword. Only that wasn't Jais' sword. This one was a master-work of craftsmanship and detail, inlaid with gems, including a dragon-glass pommel.

"Where'd you get that?" he asked.

Only when he spoke did he realize that they—the other two—had been speaking already, and he'd interrupted.

"What? Sorry?" Jais asked.

A little sheepish Barami kept on with his question. "That sword, where'd you get it?"

Jais shrugged. "It sort of arrived the same way you did. Haven't you been listening?"

Barami shook his head. "Sorry, no, too confused by all this. Where are we?"

Jais grimaced. "I supposed you did just arrive. Here's the quick recap. We're in a Festorium. It's ancient. These are statues of the Ylsovan Gods, and I think that when you touch one it grants you a sort of boon. But it only seems to do it once."

"Oh?"

Caerwyn laughed a little. "And you're a boon. My boon."

Barami smiled at that. "I am quite the boon." His mind still hadn't quite finished working its way around what Jais had said. "These are gods?"

"Statues of them yes."

"And they have power?"

Jais grinned. "Why don't you touch one and find out."

That sounded vaguely ominous. "Which one?"

"Any one you like, though neither Caerwyn nor myself have tried Thadros over there yet." Jais nodded to the one with the harp.

Barami wasn't about to experiment with that. He took a tentative step forward, looking at the other two statues, the large, rotund man and the rather well-endowed woman. Both looked like they were in the midst of having a very good time, one drinking, the other lost to rapture. He stepped toward the man. The most obvious place to touch was the extended hand with the broken glass orb. With a backward glance at his two companions, who nodded him onward, he moved in and touched the statue's arm.

It was suddenly cold. A biting wind cut through his loose and torn clothes chilling him to the bone.

This was a boon?

He was high in some mountain range and before him was a bubbling hot spring. A little ways beyond the steaming waters was a drop-off and a fantastic view of stark, sweeping mountains. It was beautiful.

But there was an eyeful of beauty within the warm waters as well. A woman with hair like blazing fire, lounged with only her head above the waters. Her eyes were closed, and for a moment Barami wondered if she too were a statue with skin as smooth and pale as porcelain. He took a step closer, his boots swishing through long grasses.

Her eyes flew open, glancing over at him.

She moved, faster than he anticipated. She lunged out of the pool, grasping an axe from a pile of things next to the waters and rolling over the earth, coming to her feet with amazing speed and grace. She held an easy fighting stance, ready, the axe held with both hands, gaze locked on him. She didn't seem to notice or care that she was quite naked. The cold perhaps didn't bother her yet as her skin was still quite red, probably from the heat of the pool. She had long, strong ropy muscles, bunching and twitching in both legs and arms. She was tall, taller than Caerwyn, taller than he was, her long, brilliant-red hair was wet and clinging to her face and body where it fell. Her eyes were a clear and dazzling green.

She said something he couldn't understand, but her tone was clear enough: accusing and cautious.

He had no weapon so he held up his hands. He tried the common tongue of the north. "Greetings."

She looked at him oddly. "Who be you?" Her use of the

northern tongue was a little rough and stilted. "I've not seen any man with skin like yours before."

He almost laughed. He was quite certain that his dark skin would be an anomaly where she was from, just as her paleness would be out of place where he was from.

"Where come you from?" she asked.

That would be hard to answer. He went with something vague, "The south."

"Why are you here?"

Also hard to explain. Especially if her question wasn't 'why are you here in the north' so much as 'why are you here spying on me bathing'?

Again an ingenious answer came to him just as he was running out of options. "The work of the gods."

She seemed to relax somewhat at that. Apparently it had been the right thing to say.

"You a god?" she asked, looking him over with newly appraising eyes.

"Me? No." So, what was he? "I'm... a... messenger?" He probably shouldn't have made that sound so much like a question. "I was sent by a god to this spot for some reason I'm not yet clear on."

"Send by the gods?"

"Yes."

She let her axe fall away to her side as she relaxed. "Join me?" She waved an arm behind her at the bubbling pool.

As much as that idea appealed to him given how cold he was, he wasn't sure what to say to her new hospitality. "Thank you, but no. You go back in. I don't know how long I can stay..." He sort of lingered on the 'y' of 'stay' as he realized he was back in the cavern with Jais and Caerwyn. Sometime around the "I don't know" of his sentence he'd returned. He caught himself and cleared his throat, stepping back from the statue.

"What did you see? Who did you see?" Caerwyn seemed eager to learn about his 'adventure'. Yet before he could speak she went on in a rush. "How long did it feel for you? We saw you walk up then step back. It was nearly instantaneous."

He cleared his throat again, then realized he'd already done that. "Ah, it wasn't long." Before she could ask who he saw again he pushed on. "Who did you see when you touched it?"

"My parents," Caerwyn answered, her demeanor changing from excited to somber. "My birth parents. They were just as I remembered them."

She hadn't talked much of her birth parents, and he'd never asked. All he'd ever gleaned was that she'd had a normal life, until some point when they had died and she'd gone on the run.

"I haven't tried that statue yet," Jais said. "But when I touched Asavi I saw Alnia and she gave me this sword, which was my father's apparently. As I was saying just after you arrived, I have my own theory on what is happening, but first, I'd like to know what you saw. Was it someone from your past, someone who died?"

"No. It was a person I'd never met before. I don't know if it was past, present, or future."

Jais grimaced. "That doesn't help much. My theory was that the statue of Asavi shows us someone we know well, a friend or loved one and... I think it grants us a gift, a boon. It gave me the sword and gave Caerwyn... you. But as for what the others do, I'm still uncertain."

Barami shrugged. "I could use a boon." He stepped over

to the statue of Asavi and touched one of her up-stretched arms.

Again he was transported. Only this time it was to the past... a day he would never forget.

He stood, tall and proud, washed and scented, on a dais raised high above a great crowd. He wore the native garb of his people: a soft leather skirt to the knees, no shirt, but a sash of bundled oil-cloth over one shoulder and tied off at the opposite hip. His dark skin gleamed in the southern sun and he knew, though he could not see it, his hair was thick and dark atop his head. This was before he'd begun shaving it, long before he'd needed to shave it.

But it wasn't himself he was focused on, but the woman before him: Caerwyn. He swallowed a lump at the sight of her. She was younger, though in truth that was hard to tell. It was mostly around the eyes that she'd aged. The woman before him made his heart thunder in his chest, her skin a beautiful—well-tanned—bronze and long black-brown hair, free from its usual braid, flowing down in waves to her shoulders. Her face was serene with a faint smile as she approached him. She spoke in Afgenni, the language of the south, criers in the crowd below echoed her words out farther and farther so the crowd could hear all that transpired.

"Barami of the Noa Oki Kigasi. You are here to swear an oath of servitude; an oath which shall bind you to me as guard and friend. Do you accept this service?"

"I do," he responded. He remembered at the time feeling less like he was swearing himself as her bodyguard and more like he was speaking the words of bonding to tie himself to her for life.

"Do you know the oath?"

"I do."

"Then speak it and forever be bound."

Only three days before this, Caerwyn—then a captain in her adopted father's armies—had been leading his unit out to deal with some raiders who'd been threatening cities in the east of Afgenni, but they'd been ambushed. Nearly his entire unit had perished dealing with the raiders. Caer had saved his life, killing one of the last raiders, who'd been attacking Barami from behind. He'd sworn there and then this same oath, but now would repeat it for all those assembled here in the capital today.

"I, Barami of the Noa Oki Kigasi, swear that my life shall, from this day forth, be bound to you, Caerwyn Afgenni, Captain of the Afgenni armies and daughter of Prince Ahslam Afgenni, Governor of Rahan Province. My sword is yours to command. My shield will always protect you. My life is yours to sacrifice as you will. I will gladly take any wound meant for you. As you live, I live and as you die, I die."

The words echoed out in the voices of the criers below among the crowd. A great cheer went up. As it did, Caerwyn leaned in with a mischievous grin and whispered. "I think I'll be saving you more often than not." Then shrugged and returned to her serene pose.

Once the noise from the crowd had died down she spoke again. "Then accept these gifts from the Empire and myself." An attendant handed her the items as she spoke of them. "A sword, as great as you are." Another cheer as he accepted his sword. The sword he would come to call Oken-adi, which meant a most stalwart friend. "And a shield of Mathran Steel, strong and light, to keep us safe." He took the shield as well.

Once again as the crowd cheered she whispered, "That's expensive, don't get it banged up too much." He had to work to keep from smiling, this was a serious occasion.

Finally she turned to the crowd and proclaimed. "See, my first and only Bond-guard. I thank him for his lifelong commitment!"

The vision faded, and Barami sighed as it did. That had been a proud moment in his life, one he'd not ever hoped to relive, and yet he had. He stepped back with a smile.

"I was right!" Jais said behind him.

His mind worked for a moment to think of what point the boy had been trying to prove. It had been something about...

...boons.

He only then realized the weight in his hands. His sword and shield. He knew them by feel, even without looking. When he did look down at them he smiled. They were the same as they had been those years ago, fresh and new, no scars or dents. He smiled wider.

"I think I like this place," he said with a nod.

27

JAIS FELT HIS SPIRITS LIFTING.

He was still far from what he might call happy or satisfied. His failure was too fresh and near in his memory, and he still badgered himself about his cowardice. But amidst the berating he was also feeling a small hope. Perhaps with his friends, with these new weapons and boons, they might have a chance to undo his mistake and kill the krolloc.

Yet before they did Jais was curious. As Barami and Caerwyn argued over who would touch the statue of Thadros first to see what he might grant them, Jais approached Berem and reached for the broken glass orb.

He found himself back at his house, but instead of being burned and destroyed, it was whole and undamaged. Inside he could hear his aunt singing a pleasant tune.

"Aunt Sarelle?" he called out as he entered.

She smiled up at him. "Hello, Jais."

He beamed, but almost instantly felt that pang of fear and regret. He had failed her, despite her direct command and her sacrifice. "I'm sorry, Aunt Sarelle. I failed you."

She swept out from behind their kitchen table and caught him up in a hug. "You were brave, my son. You hurt it dearly. Do not regret your choices. Had you stayed you may or may not have defeated it, but you would most certainly not be as hale and uninjured as you are now. Call it not cowardice, but prudence. You needed assistance and now you have it."

Her words soothed him.

She was not a large woman and with his broad shoulders he was easily able to fold his arms around her. "Thank you." He felt tears come to his eyes. "And I'm sorry."

She tisked. "I made my choice too."

"Yours was far braver than mine."

"That was only because I knew you were there. I had no chance against that thing. My best choice was to help you against it. I am no warrior, Jais." She sighed heavily. "And I have finally accepted you are far more your parent's child than mine, as much as I consider you my own son."

He felt more tears brewing at the edges of his eyes. He let her go and stepped back from the embrace. "I have my father's sword now..." He wasn't sure why he'd said that. It wasn't what he wanted to say. He finally asked what he'd wanted to ask for years. "What were they like?"

There were tears in her eyes as well. "You are so much like them. They were strong like you with the hearts of warriors. My sister was a better soul-weaver than I ever was and your father was a swordsman of incredible skill with abilities to channel energy through his blade. You look a lot like him, though, to be honest you're built more like my father, who was a great farmer with powers tied to the land."

Even this limited knowledge was more than his aunt had ever told him in life.

As if reading his thoughts she said, "I'm sorry I never spoke of them. It was always so hard."

He stepped in to embrace her again. "It's well, I understand."

This time it was her who broke away first. "Our time is limited, and there is so much I want to say. I hope I was like a mother to you. For you were the son I was never able to have."

He smiled sadly. "Yes, you were."

Tears were welling again as she waved slowly and vanished.

He stepped back from the statue in time to hear Barami laughing at something. He sniffed away his tears and looked over to where the tall, dark skinned man was stepping back from the statue of Thadros.

"You two are definitely going to want to try that." Barami couldn't seem to stop grinning.

"What happened?" Caerwyn asked stepping up beside Barami.

"No visions, nothing except a great feeling of relief and... It's hard to explain. I feel like I could take on anything at the moment.

"Seems worth a try," Caerwyn said stepping closer.

Jais was drawing near and watched as she touched the statue of the god of inspiration and music. She seemed to sigh out a great burden before drawing a great and easy breath. She stood taller, drawing herself up, and blinked; a look of awe on her face as she stepped back.

Before Jais could do anything Caerwyn was scrabbling at her shirt, lifting it to pull away a bandage around her midsection. There was a lot of red soaked into the pale cloth. It wasn't a wound she'd had when he'd seen her yesterday. So

Jais wondered if such a wound should have the bandage removed so soon. But when she pulled away the last of the bindings there was nothing but unblemished flesh underneath. Jais stepped in closer and could see a faint pale line, like an old scar across her belly.

"Even the stitches," she breathed. "Amazing!"

"Was it that bad?" Jais asked.

She laughed. "Bad enough, and it's gone."

Jais' thoughts turned to himself. His back was still raw from the wounds he'd taken yesterday morning fighting the krolls. In addition he'd taken any number of cuts and scrapes as he'd moved through the caves.

He turned away from Caerwyn saying, "My turn." He stepped up to the statue and touched the flank of the god of muses.

He felt all his cares and worries lifted from him: his failure, the deaths of his aunt and uncle, Alnia's passing, the inexplicable turning of the village against him. All of it was gone. The memories were still there and their mark on him had not vanished. There was pain, certainly, and it would return, but for now all of the heaviness which weighed him down was lifted. It felt like the weight of the world had been taken from him. Yes, he still had a task ahead of him and people depending on him, but he no longer felt that pressure. Then a wave washed over him, filling him with hope and encouragement. It was like he was breathing in the god's own divine breath. He felt his physical pains vanish and was left with only a sense of serenity and exaltation. It was a rush like nothing he'd ever felt before.

"Oh," he whispered as he stepped back.

The expressions of awe and joy he had seen on the faces of his companions suddenly made sense. "Oh," he said again.

He turned to the other two who were grinning at each other. He joined them in their silly expression.

"I shouldn't feel this happy that I'm about to go face a krolloc and his horde," Jais said.

"A krolloc!" Barami's expression stayed jovial but became a bit wild. "That's what we're up against? And a horde of krolls?" He laughed for a moment, then kept laughing as he said, "Why am I laughing?"

Caerwyn joined him. "Because we can do anything. That's how I feel. As crazy as our task may be, it certainly seems a lot more possible now."

Jais drew out his father's sword and looked at the gleaming blade.

I am with you, my son.

He nearly dropped the sword at the words. His surprise and amazement must have been visible to the others as Caerwyn asked, "What happened?"

He gazed for a moment longer at the sword, and nothing happened. "I don't really know. It's probably nothing, a side effect of all these visions we're having."

She shrugged and nodded.

Jais turned to the entrance to the temple. "I know where the krolloc is. Shall we go, before this inspiration wears off and we realize how bad an idea this really is."

"Lead the way," Barami said and Caerwyn nodded again.

Jais strode purposefully out of the Festorium and back into the dark caverns leading back to the cave where the krolloc had his lair.

One thing was certain in his mind this time. He would not run, he would not flee. Either the krolloc would fall or he would, and feeling as he did at the moment, there seemed like nothing that could stop him.

"Ah, friends?" Barami's tone was hesitant. Jais and Caerwyn turned back to him, already well into the cavern leading away from the Festorium. Barami was silhouetted by the light of the room behind him. He was just standing there. "You two remember I can't see in the dark right?"

28

TORCHLIGHT FLICKERED OVER THE FACES OF JAIS AND CAER. They'd found the torches just outside the strange temple area, and Barami had lit one. It seemed the other two didn't need light even in purest darkness.

"The krolloc will know we're coming," Jais said. "It can smell drahksani, so we won't be able to surprise it. At least Caerwyn and I won't."

Barami had a suspicion he knew what was about to come. "But I can, is that where you were going?" he asked Jais.

The other man nodded. It was odd that in the span of a few days he'd gone from thinking of Jais as a boy, to now thinking of him as a man.

Despite their task, no one looked concerned. Even Barami himself felt a sense of excitement and exhilaration. He was not a headlong, headstrong warrior. He didn't seek out fights, didn't rush into anything and he wouldn't now either, but still something of his caution had been tempered. He realized it was his fear. He wasn't afraid of what was to come, but his natural level-headedness remained.

Jais spoke again after the silence that hung between them. "Are you good with leaving us here and sneaking around to come in behind the krolloc?"

Barami sighed. He didn't want to leave either of them, especially Caerwyn. The desire was partially to protect her— as he'd devoted his life to do—and partially for his own safety. But he knew the benefits to splitting up. He'd be a wild card, able to surprise the krolls who would be ready for Jais and Caerwyn. It was a sound plan.

"Yes. Where do I go?"

Jais pointed toward a tunnel. "Follow that fissure as far as it will go. There are a few side tunnels, but they are all small, keep only to the main one, in which you should be able to keep upright, most of the time. The end of that will be at the far side of the kroll's cave. Put out your torch there and let your eyes become accustomed to the light in that cave. It shouldn't take you too long to get there. You should be able to creep through the back part of that cave with no one spotting you... unless my use of that route earlier alerted them to the entrance. So be ready for anything. The closer you can get to the main part of the cave the better, so you don't have as far to go when Caerwyn and I show up. Got all that?"

Barami nodded. "See you two in battle."

They both nodded to him and he left.

The caves were cool given how warm the days had been recently. Barami, in a light shirt, had been ill prepared for the chill and felt a shiver trace his spine then echo out through his arms and legs. His torch gave off a little heat, but not enough to warm him. He kept his sword and shield close— shield strapped to his arm and sword in that same hand, held in front of him—so they wouldn't be scarred by the stone walls. He wondered idly if these were his actual sword and shield. Certainly they looked newer, no nicks or scratches. Had these been created by the gods just for him, or had some miracle taken the existing items—confiscated by the villagers —and restored them somehow? It didn't matter truly. He had them now, and that was all he cared about.

He could have used some armor, but he'd do with what he had.

The flame on his torch flickered and danced, casting shifting shadows and illuminating the damp, harsh stone surfaces around him. Without the other two it felt like he was walking and walking without getting anywhere. He trusted Jais, but still had some faint doubts that the man knew exactly how to navigate these tunnels. Yet not long later he could see a different light up ahead. He extinguished his torch and let his eyes adjust to the near darkness for a moment. Then, moving carefully, he navigated his way to the end of the tunnel.

The larger cavern beyond was still mostly dark with only the far end lit, and that light was mostly blocked by the segmented nature of the large cave.

He scanned the area keenly, waiting. Jais had warned that krolls may have discerned his escape route. That was a signif-icant concern for Barami, but even as his eyes adjusted further and he scanned more of the room, he saw no forms. He doubted there would be many places something the size of a kroll could hide out there either.

So he began his careful path out into the cave and toward the lit half.

As much as he could not see any krolls, he could defi-nitely hear them. There were many guttural voices barking at each other as well as the heavy tread of their feet as they moved. Above it all was a single voice calling out orders in that same guttural language. Barami guessed that was the krolloc. When he was finally close enough to peer over a ridge to find out, he saw he was right.

There were twelve krolls, all in place now, widely spaced in two rough rows facing the other side of the cave, the other entrance. Behind them stood as large a beast as Barami had ever seen, near on twenty feet tall. Its back was to Barami and with one of the great fires in the room behind it Barami could see a line of dark... something... tracing down the thing's back. Jais had mentioned at one point he'd already hurt the thing, perhaps that was the wound and it was weeping... whatever these things had that passed for blood.

Barami shook his head as he ducked behind the ridge. This was impossible. Even with his renewed vigor and outlook from the statue of Thadros, he couldn't see a way to win this. Jais and Caerwyn would have to cut their way through a dozen krolls. That alone would be an epic feat if they could achieve it. Then they'd have to face the krolloc. Alternately, Barami himself could try to face the thing alone and that... just didn't seem like it would end well for him. He felt pumped and excited and fearless, but his level-headed nature just couldn't see a way he could win a one-on-one fight with the beast.

But he had to try.

He crept over the ridge and, moving very carefully now so as not to make any noise which might warn the big lug, he approached the krolloc.

CAERWYN FOLLOWED JAIS, HER EYES KEEN IN THE DARKNESS.

She had never been in such complete darkness before. Even out at night, under a cloudy sky there was always some light.

She kept her gaze alternating between Jais' back and the uneven floor, which was actually mostly level, but with rocks and dust and debris scattered all about. She assumed that long ago this had been kept clear and level for those who would come to the Festorium, but over the many years since its use, the hall had become strewn with bits of things.

A light grew up ahead.

Jais stopped and turned to her. "We're nearly there," he whispered. It was unnecessary, but she nodded anyway. His voice sounded sure, but tempered with a slight hesitation.

She expected him to keep moving forward, but he paused for a long moment. When finally he did something it was speak and his voice was soft, searching for words.

"Caerwyn, I..." He sighed. "I wanted to thank you."

Thank her? She was certain she'd ruined his nice peaceful life.

"For what?"

He shrugged with a look away, distracted. "For... everything. For keeping me alive, training me, for... being with Alnia and helping her."

"In truth she helped me more than I helped her."

"You know what I mean."

She did.

Jais sighed. "I just... I don't know what's going to happen in there and just in case one or both of us don't make it out. I wanted to say... thank you." He glanced at her and seemed about to say more, but then fidgeted and looked away again.

"Jais?" she prompted. It was clear he had something he wanted to share, just perhaps didn't have the words.

"I..." He gave a clipped, sardonic laugh. "If we do live

through this... I'll be honest, I don't know how I feel about... helping you... with your... child."

She blinked. She hadn't thought about that at all since the villagers had turned on them.

"Jais, don't worry about it." She grimaced. "Something tells me that if we do live through this we'll be travelling together for a while. There will be time for... other things... later. If you ever change your mind."

"Huh, I hadn't thought of that."

"What?"

"I can't go back can I?" It was a question, but she didn't answer. He'd need to answer that, and he did. "No, I can't." His gaze fell to her again. "Would that be well with you... if I joined you and Barami?"

"Barami will probably protest... for his own reasons, but yes. Jais we're... alike, you and me. You're welcome to travel with us."

He nodded, then a smile crept onto his face. "Then once again... thank you."

She slapped him on his meaty shoulder. "We need to stick together."

His smile turned to an easy grin. "Yeah." That look faded quickly though. "But first we need to survive this."

"Yeah."

He half turned, looking toward the light. After a long breath, he said, "Shall we go kick some krolloc arse?"

She moved up beside him. "I like the sound of that."

BARAMI SAW JAIS AND CAERWYN IMMERGE INTO THE WIDE opening on the far side of the cave, and the krolls near them bellowed war cries as the two of them charged.

Barami felt an idea come to him.

He too charged. He was close enough behind the krolloc that a last minute war cry of his own would give it little warning and give him the confidence he'd need.

He sliced at its leg as he passed, feeling his blade cut deep, encountering great resistance, the thing's hide and muscle were like wood, hard but not impenetrable.

The krolloc bellowed.

And that had just the effect Barami had hoped.

Hearing their leader cry out caused the krolls to turn or otherwise be distracted from the attack heading at them. So, for a moment at least, Jais and Caer would have easy targets.

However, this had also made Barami a target of the krolloc, and he knew it. He threw himself to the ground and rolled, feeling the great sweep of wind as the krolloc's massive hand had punched through where he had been. He came to his feet, shield ready.

The krolloc had been going to stomp on him, but seeing him standing kicked out instead. Barami spun to the side, his shield deflecting the thing's foot. Even with having mostly avoided the blow a shock rang up his shield arm so strong it went numb for a moment.

He paid little heed to that as he finished his spin and sliced down with his sword into the krolloc's leg. It bellowed again, this time reaching down for Barami.

He didn't have time to go anywhere so he did what came naturally, striking the hand that threatened to grab him. He severed two of its fingers, and the krolloc reared back.

A wild grin crossed Barami's face. He began to think that there was some chance he could do this; could defeat a krolloc on his own.

"Hold!" the beast bellowed, and Barami froze. He didn't stop moving because he'd wanted to, but because he couldn't. His body was stuck. He struggled against whatever it was that kept him from moving, but to no avail.

The krolloc's other hand wrapped around him, squeezing hard. He heard bones snap and felt the stinging shock of pain all over his body as he was lifted from the ground.

"You have caused me more pain than any human ever has," the krolloc spat out at him. "I don't know whether to turn you into a kroll or kill you now."

Barami didn't know what the thing was talking about: turn him into a kroll? Was that possible? It didn't much matter since he couldn't speak, but he sure knew which outcome he wanted. Death would be far preferable than anything that benefited this beast.

The krolloc squeezed harder, and Barami felt his body compress in ways it shouldn't. He would have screamed, have made a noise like none before in his life, but he could not.

"I'll decide later. I have more interesting prey at the moment."

The krolloc tossed him aside. He hit the uneven stone floor hard and, with the impact, felt even more pain spiking through him.

Tears came to his eyes, and a dark haze clouded his vision. This he could fight. He would remain conscious. He wasn't going to black out now. He wasn't sure what his body would be able to do once the magic hold on him abated, but he would try everything he could. He had to.

Even if that was all he could do with what remained of his life.

29

JAIS LEAPT, AND WITH A SINGLE SWING OF HIS FATHER'S SWORD, beheaded the kroll before him. He didn't expect it to die instantly. And it didn't. It flailed about at him, but it was less of a concern now, causing more chaos, hitting its allies. Jais slipped around it carefully and moved on to the next beast.

Never before had he felt anything like the union of mind and body as he did now. Whether it was some effect of his father's sword or the boons of the gods, he didn't know, but he was thankful for it. He wondered if this was what Caerwyn felt like all the time in battle; ready for anything, aware of every noise, sight, and smell. A noise behind him was no longer a distraction, but a warning. He knew how to react to it and exactly when to do so. Everyone around him seemed to be moving slowly. The reactions of his foes were far too late and clumsy. It was like he'd lost himself in the fight. He and his sword, moving as one, elevated beyond simply a person wading through the enemy.

A cut to a kroll's leg caused it to stumble into its neighbor and gave him a shot at the other leg, where he severed the foot at the ankle.

When the kroll righted itself, it could no longer stand correctly and it fell.

Jais was there to meet it, cutting one arm nearly all the way through, making it useless, then sinking his sword into the thing's chest, using its own falling momentum against it, then pushing it aside and off his sword, alive perhaps, but no longer any threat.

On to the next one.

He couldn't spare a glance for Caerwyn, but he knew where she was, how she fared. It was just a part of this battle-awareness. Just as he knew whether the grunt of a kroll meant pain or an imminent attack, he also knew her calls and cries were merely expressions of her prowess as she too cut through the horde around them. She was doing well enough for now. She didn't need him, nor did he need her.

Four krolls lay behind him, many more before him, but they moved aside, nearly as one, as something charged in from behind them.

The krolloc.

Yet the krolls didn't stop attacking, just allowed a new player to join the fray. Even as Jais blocked a blow from the kroll beside him, then whipped his sword around to sever the thing's hand, he kept his eyes on the krolloc barreling down on him.

It didn't stop, didn't pause, just roared and attacked him. One of its hands was spraying dark, thick blood from where several fingers had been removed, and there were cuts on its legs. Barami had wounded it. Yet even with Jais' battle-aware-ness, he hadn't seen what had happened to the southerner. Jais guessed it hadn't been pleasant.

Jais dodged the first hammer-fisted blow from the krolloc and came up almost underneath a kroll, cutting it high on the side of its leg then moving on before it could react. He was shielded from the krolloc now, behind the kroll, but the massive leader simply threw his minion out of the way. It hadn't been an idle throw either, but directed at Caerwyn, who ducked under the flying kroll as it passed.

Jais darted in with two quick slashes to add to a deep cut Barami had started on the thing's leg. A couple more cuts and he'd be able to sever it, but he wouldn't have that time now. He dropped and rolled to avoid a sideways bash from the krolloc, but felt the air move far too close with the great force of the swing. The krolloc tried to stomp on him before he could get up, so he rolled a little farther then rolled to a crouch and struck at the wounded leg again.

He felt bone this time, but his sword got stuck there for a moment too long. He released it and threw himself to the side just as a strike knocked him in the same direction. He survived with minimal injuries only because he'd already been moving in the direction of the attack. It knocked him several feet, and he rolled when he landed to try to reduce the impact. He felt muscles strain and bruise, skin cut and tear, but no bones seemed to break.

Pain was distant, an annoyance but not a distraction. He rose again as the krolloc moved in and raised its arm to smash him. He ducked and rolled toward it, hoping it hadn't expected that, and came up where he'd left his sword, still sticking out of the thing's leg, using his momentum to lever it out of the solid bone. Then he kept moving, ducking between the monster's legs with an off-handed slash behind him as he ran for better ground.

Another kroll moved to intercept him. Jais removed its

arm as it reached for him, then a leg as he passed by. It went down screaming, but he didn't have time to catch his breath. He could hear the heavy thuds of footfalls as the krolloc closed in behind him.

From the corner of his eye he saw Barami. The man looked like a mess, bloody and broken, but he was still alive, still moving. His gaze caught Jais' for a moment, and there was a steeled determination there. Jais gave a quick nod before turning to face his own problems.

The krolloc attacked. Jais ducked its first swing, raising his sword to block, but nearly lost the weapon for his efforts. He'd cut the thing's wrist but he didn't know how deep. Another hand was slamming down on him. He set his feet, braced himself and raised his sword to meet the hand. The momentum of the attack drove his sword to the hilt through the thing's hand and drove Jais to his knees. The krolloc bellowed and withdrew its hand. Then it made a grabbing motion with that same hand, and Jais felt... something wrap around him. It was like bands of iron, but invisible... made of air. It's what the thing must have done to his aunt.

He'd forgotten the thing's magic. It squeezed at him, but he resisted, flexing his bulk, trying to make sure his bones withstood the pressure. He cried out, more from his own effort to resist than any pain, as he was lifted from the ground.

"You have caused me enough trouble!" the krolloc bellowed and began a chant. In the distance Jais could hear other krolls echoing the guttural words.

Something flew by Jais' head and sank deep into the krolloc's eye. The krolloc shrieked and must have been distracted for a moment as the magic around Jais dissipated, and he fell, landing on his feet.

"Davlas!" He heard Caerwyn call out, and the spear returned to her. He spared her a glance and found that there were only a couple krolls remaining, and they were keeping to the side of this fight.

Caerwyn threw again, the spear blazing a path for the krolloc's other eye, but the krolloc's hand moved with amazing speed and caught the spear in mid-air.

Even as Caerwyn tried to call the spear back the krolloc snapped it in two like a twig.

"No!" Caerwyn shouted.

Jais, though beaten, bruised, and growing tired, knew he'd stood still long enough. He leapt at the krolloc, hoping to finish the thing off now that it was distracted.

It growled something unintelligible and batted him out of the air like a fly. He was tossed across the room and hit a wall hard before falling to the rocky floor. This time he was fairly certain bones had broken, one rib at least from the pain, most likely several in his legs as well, maybe an arm.

Darkness flooded over him, but he gritted his teeth to remain awake and aware. The pain was no longer a distant thing, it was immediate and intense. He couldn't move for a moment as simply breathing without blacking out took all his effort and concentration.

Caerwyn was stunned.

In a matter of just a few heartbeats she'd lost Davlas, and Jais had been thrown far from the fight.

Only she remained...

...Against the krolloc, wounded as it was, and two mostly unwounded krolls that had enough sense to stay at the fringes of the fight. They watched her warily. She kept one eye on them and the other on the krolloc.

It seemed to be flexing its considerable muscle for a moment, a look of intense concentration passing over it as it let out an extended grunt. She didn't know what it was doing until she saw several of the wounds on it closing and growing smaller.

It could heal itself, though with some considerable effort it seemed. And not completely, for some of the wounds remained, including the pierced eye. Perhaps it was growing weary. She could only hope so, as she was feeling the strain of this fight creep into her muscles and bones. That, along with the loss of Davlas, which had been like a third arm to her, and she was a little disoriented.

She switched her short sword to her right hand, realize that was the only weapon she had against the krolloc, and sighed. This was going to be a challenge.

"You will die like your friends if you defy me," the krolloc called out to her. "Or you can join me. Allow me to make you even stronger. Become like me and there is little this world can do to harm you. You drahksani are a dying breed and without you, we krollocs will dominate this world!"

She didn't need to consider the offer, but she wanted to give herself time to recover. She realized she was giving the krolloc the same time, but didn't care. "What's it like?" she asked with a bit of a shout to cover the distance between them.

The beast seemed a bit surprised at her response. Perhaps it hadn't expected her to be receptive to the offer.

"Take everything you are already and make it ten times as strong. You can convert humans to krolls to serve you without question. I have my own kingdom! You've seen how useless humans are against my minions. There will be little we could not conquer with a kroll army behind us."

"And would I be serving you too?" She couldn't help a little contempt slipping into her voice. She knew that, to make it seem real—as if she was actually considering this— she'd need to have some resistance and concerns. A large one would be her own autonomy.

"No. Krollocs cannot be controlled by other krollocs. Our minds are too strong. But you could control any krolls you find or create."

"And the krolls you already have. Could I control them?"

The beast laughed. "Perhaps, but it takes some time to master such things. I would not recommend trying to turn on me. Perhaps I might give you a couple, but mostly you would have to make your own krolls."

She began taking a few steps toward him, trying to make them look reluctant. "Who were you?" she asked. "Why did you do this?"

"I had little choice in the matter, and who I was before is long forgotten. I was weak before despite being a drahksan. Compared to this form, I was nothing. I was transformed against my will, but I quickly grew to like my new form. I've been like this for more than two hundred years! The power of the ritual sustains us. Krollocs can live as long as dragons!"

She drew closer. The krolloc was reveling in his own superiority, caught up in his own pitch. She wasn't sure if she'd convinced it she was interested, but it didn't seem concerned at her slow approach. Perhaps because of that sense of arrogance and power. Maybe it didn't see her as a threat at all.

She would be in a moment.

She scanned the thing's body looking for a weak point,

something she could exploit. The eye was the obvious one. If she could take out the other eye and blind it she might have a chance against it. Though if it had the same battle-senses as she did, just eliminating its eyes wouldn't hinder is as much as most people. The only weak spot was its left leg near the ankle. Several of the cuts had healed but it seemed Jais or Barami or both had cut it several times there, some deeply. Though with a short sword she'd have to get really close and might just break her sword in the process. It was a weak point, but one that would be harder for her to exploit.

She also searched for her friends. Jais had fallen behind a bunch of jagged rocks at the side of the room. She knew roughly where he was, but couldn't see him. As for Barami's location, she had no idea and after a quick glance of the area still couldn't find him. She worried for her friend, wondering what had happened to him.

She needed to keep the krolloc distracted as she got even closer. "This ritual, what does it involve?"

The krolloc laughed. "It isn't pleasant by any means, but the end result is worth it. You are plunged down on a stake in the ground. Your blood needs to flow freely. Then a group of at least four must surround you and chant the ancient words as you die. Then you stop being who you are and become something else, something incredible. It doesn't take too long, and once the transformation is done you'll be a force of nature."

No, that didn't sound that appealing. She'd definitely pass.

She was about to rush in and try to take out the krolloc's remaining eye, when she saw something in her periphery. She risked a glance.

Jais felt as if he was a beach and the tide was coming in. Only the tide wasn't water, but pain. Each wave washing over him was more intense than the last. He was grinding his teeth, eyes clamped shut and watering. He knew he'd most likely lose consciousness soon.

He dug deep within himself and there found the core of hope that the statue of Thadros had instilled. He latched onto that and remembered his aunt and her need of him. He thought of the parents he'd never known. A mother who had been a 'soul-weaver' of great strength and a father who could use this sword in ways like no other. That was what his aunt had told him.

I am with you.

That voice again, a deep resounding baritone. It was unfamiliar and yet...

"Father?"

A rumbling chuckle. *You can call me Dek if you like. It's short for Deklon.*

"How?" He heard his own voice, strained and squeaking.

Your mother was indeed powerful. Before I died she wove my spirit into this sword.

Jais felt the smoothed leather grip in his palm. His father's sword... his father's spirit. In the haze of pain that befuddled him he didn't question that he was speaking with his dead father's spirit through a sword. Somehow that made sense to him.

Your mother was also a great healer. You may have inherited some of her ability. Use it. Heal yourself. The voice was growing more urgent. Did it know something he didn't?

"How?" This time he barely got the word out, but the

voice speaking to him didn't seem to speak or hear the same as a living person.

I honestly don't know, son. healing was never something I could do. But you're dying. You need to try something.

Ah, so that's what his father knew that he didn't. Jais had still thought he could recover from this on his own, but apparently his injuries were more severe than that.

Which meant his only choice was to try to heal himself.

But how?

He tried to remember what aunt Sarelle had done. She'd used her goo, but that was just an aid. She'd explained it to him once, and he struggled—through his mind's ever increasing fog—to recall her words.

"I imbue the gel with a little healing energy when I create it. The gel itself will heal people quicker than any poultice or potion. But I can also use it in conjunction with my own healing if someone is severely sick or hurt. The gel then acts as a sort of conduit and increases my healing as I meditate over them. The gel is also less... directed in its effect. You can put it directly on a wound and that's fine, but if you have internal injuries or an illness it isn't as effective. That's when I need to concentrate on reading the body and directing my energy at the spot in question."

The words jumbled together for a moment, fading in and out of clarity for him.

Meditation... reading the body... directing energy.

He'd never been great at meditation. His mind always wandered, consumed with too many thoughts. Now... it was far worse, concentrating was nearly impossible through the pain.

He was having trouble breathing.

Unconsciousness, and with it probably death, tugged at

him. Maybe he'd skip over the meditating part and try reading his body.

He went back to that core of hope again. It was deep within him. If he had to place it physically it felt like it would be low in his chest, near his heart. From there he spread out his awareness. Things came to him slowly: a broken rib... no three broken ribs... and several other ribs fractured, the muscles around these were bruised and sore. Some of the broken bits of ribs were tearing into muscle or organs. Bleeding, internally and externally; he could feel the flow of blood and how it was all wrong, seeping in where it shouldn't and out like it definitely shouldn't. Outward from there he found his gut mostly intact, just bruised and jostled. His hip was fractured. His left arm broken, right arm sore, bruised and cut up. Left leg was broken through the lower portion and fractured through the thigh. Right leg was just sore and cut up. Feet were mostly fine, just tender from having been on them for days. His head was jostled, brain swollen, skin cut and bruised, a cut on his neck bleeding.

Now he understood how he was dying and how much time he had left. It was a terrifying realization, because it wasn't much time at all.

Now he knew what was wrong, but how to heal it? He needed to direct his energy at it.

What energy? His strength was fading fast, nearly gone.

Take some of mine.

How? He wasn't even able to speak the words anymore.

Touch my blade. I can channel energy through the blade itself.

He didn't respond. He just used his hand on the grip to pull the sword a little closer, inch by inch. Then stretched out a finger to find the blade.

He felt the cold steel.

And energy flowed into him.

It was a rush, almost too much, flowing in through his arm, and for a moment he didn't know what to do with it. Then he remembered his wounds and reconnected with them, directing the energy to the worst ones first. His brain shrank, and his mind cleared, that helped to use the energy his father was giving him more effectively: ribs and organs, internal bleeding and the worst of the external cuts, his neck and a few others. Bones moved back into position and re-fused from broken, fractures melted away and...

The energy was gone.

That's all I have for now, sorry, son.

It hadn't been enough. He was mostly healed, but far from what he'd call 'hale and healthy'. A few fractures remained, as well as most of his bruising and the sting from numerous cuts and scrapes. But he wasn't dying anymore and that was something. The rest he could heal on his own, given time.

He grunted and pulled himself up to a sitting position. His vision blurred for a moment, and he had to pause. He'd lost a lot of blood and was fatigued and worn, his strength and stamina seemed long used up. He wouldn't be much use in a fight. He needed an edge.

He shook his head to try to clear it and when he opened his eyes, he noticed something not far away.

The sword he'd used to stab the krolloc in the back, that first time.

It lay there... discarded, probably thrown away once it had been pulled out of the thing's back.

That was an edge... of sorts.

He thanked the gods and retrieved it. It took him a moment to stand, then another to find his balance. One of his legs was quite sore and weak. He'd be limping for a while.

He carefully climbed the jagged rocks shielding him from the rest of the room. As he did he became aware of voices, one clearly the krolloc and the other was... Caerwyn.

Caerwyn was saying: "...this ritual, what does it involve?"

The krolloc answered, describing what Jais had seen when the person had been turned into a kroll. He shuddered.

He reached the peak of the rocks and looked over.

Caerwyn's head shifted slightly, her gaze caught his. She gave a faint nod and smile before her attention returned to the krolloc.

"You're not doing a great job of selling this ritual," she said. She was quite close, and the krolloc seemed little aware of the danger so near, perhaps believing he was convincing her to join him.

Jais crept over the rocks and slipped as quietly as he could back toward the beast.

Caerwyn had to buy more time.

She'd been going to attack the krolloc before she'd seen Jais, but now, with him back in the fight, which she was incredibly thankful for, she needed to give him time to get into a better position. He was carrying two swords now and would have a far better chance of hurting this thing than she did with her little short sword.

She dropped her sword. It clattered to the stone floor.

"So, you will join me?" the krolloc said, even more surprised now. It laughed. "You'd be the first to willingly go into the ritual that I know of."

"I have always sought power." She was dangerously close to the beast now. She'd taken several steps from her dropped sword. However, half of Davlas lay nearby, the end with the point. She wasn't sure how it would fly in such shape, but was relieved that there was at least some weapon within reach.

"How many krolls do you control?" She glanced back at those dead or dying behind her. "I haven't taken them all from you, have I?"

"Hardly," it said and laughed. "There are more out there raiding the village as we speak."

The village?

If the krolls were freely running through Klasten's Green, there wouldn't be much left of the town now. Caerwyn felt a pang of sympathy for the town's folk. Many of them were innocent, decent people. Some... were less so, but still didn't deserve such a fate.

Jais was still a little ways off, clambering over some of the more uneven rocks around the edge of the room.

The krolloc grunted, and she realized she hadn't said anything in the last few moments. She was practically at its feet, weaponless. She had no clue what to say next, and Jais was still too far away.

The krolloc began to turn.

Her mind flashed with the memory that the beast could smell drahksani. It might know Jais was coming. She needed to distract it further.

She put a hand on its leg. "Tell me about your life."

The words seemed odd, even to her, and the krolloc looked down at her with a skeptical expression. Then it laughed, and it wasn't a pleasant sound.

"You think you'll keep me from noticing your friend?"

She swore in her mind.

She dove to the side just as it kicked out at her. She grabbed the half of Davlas nearby, then rolled and came up ready. She threw as the krolloc turned toward her, raising a hand to shield its face. The spear sank into the hand and that was it. Her hope of taking out its other eye was gone. It made a grasping motion in the air. She'd seen it doing this to Jais. It was magic of some sort. She expected to feel something, but nothing happened.

The krolloc looked a little confused at her lack of reaction as well. It lifted its hand and looked more confused. Caerwyn shrugged and took that moment to get farther away from it, sprinting up and over a low rise of rocks, heading toward Jais. She landed on the other side and was surprised to find Barami there. He didn't look well at all.

He groaned at her. His puffy, bruised face looked incapable of speech.

Gods, he looked like he'd been trampled.

Jais rushed toward her, no longer concerned with hiding himself. "Caerwyn, it's coming!"

She reached down and grabbed Barami's long-bladed sword. She wasn't as familiar with this particular weapon, but she knew it well enough to fight with it.

Jais arrived in a rush as the krolloc drew close behind her, its shadow covering them. "If you can keep it away, I might be able to help Barami!" Jais whispered and offered one of his swords. She shook her head at his offer of the blade, she'd do better to put all her strength behind this one larger blade. She didn't know how he could help Barami, but now wasn't the time to question it.

She spun and lashed out at the krolloc's foot, cutting deep into the ankle, unfortunately it wasn't the already weak ankle, and it didn't seem to notice. She danced away from its kick at her, hoping to draw it farther from Jais and Barami, but it didn't take the bait. He reached out toward Jais and picked him up with its magical grasp.

"Stop or I'll crush him!" it called out. She couldn't stop, and she knew it. She charged back in and swung at the same leg she'd hit just a moment ago, it tried to avoid the blow, but it was moving slowly, perhaps distracted by its magic. She nicked the bone with her cut, and it did back up a step this time.

She heard Jais' cry of pain, but could not pay any attention to it. They had one mission, to kill this thing, and she hoped Jais could handle himself and survive this.

She pressed her attack, her body and mind working as one as she felt the calm familiarity of battle envelope her. She deflected its attempts to grasp at her physically with its other hand, the one missing fingers already, while working at weakening its legs.

Then it was swatting at her with its other hand, and she hoped that meant it had given up on Jais as opposed to the other option. She pressed harder, cutting hands or legs, whichever got closer to her. The krolloc was backing up. It bellowed to the other krolls still in the room to help it.

Caerwyn smiled. She knew it would never have done that if it wasn't weakening.

She had it.

Jais landed on his feet, barely, as air returned to his lungs with gulping breaths. He didn't know how much longer he could have withstood the krolloc's magical grasp and was thankful it had released him when it did.

Caerwyn had the beast retreating and Jais took a moment to lay down his swords and kneel next to Barami. He still didn't really know how to heal, but he placed his hands on the dying man and simply tried to push energy into him.

Barami gasped, as Jais felt his own pitiful reserves of vitality drain once again. The exchange didn't take long, and when it ended, Jais felt as weak as a puppy.

"Thank you," the other man croaked, his voice hoarse. He wasn't dying, but he still looked rough. Jais himself probably didn't look that much better.

"Stay here, we can take care of this," Jais said then retrieved his two swords. He stood, wobbled, then took a moment to balance himself. He was exhausted, like he'd spent the whole day chopping wood. His arms were like water, and the swords in his hands felt far too heavy. But he had to help Caerwyn, and he found enough strength to walk over to where she' had taken the fight.

Two krolls were closing in behind her. Perhaps he'd target them first.

He let out a war cry, mostly to distract those other krolls, partly to see if it might give him a little more energy. The two of them looked his way, but kept going after Caerwyn.

He grimaced. Did he really look like nothing to worry about?

He found some energy to jog over to them.

He brought his swords in on each side of a leg as he reached one, but the blades practically bounced off the hard flesh. He really was drained.

Point this sword at it.

Jais obeyed his father's suggestion. A beam of iridescent... something... shot out of the blade and hit the kroll square in the back... then proceeded through it, up and away, hitting the ceiling of the rock chamber.

The kroll fell in a heap.

Oh, wow. This could work.

Can you do that again?

Once, perhaps. I have little energy left.

Jais smiled. That was all he needed.

He leveled his father's sword at the remaining kroll.

Now.

The light glistened around the chamber as the last kroll fell.

"The big one's all yours," Jais said and fell to one knee. He was spent and huffing hard. He hoped Caerwyn could finish off the krolloc as he certainly had nothing left in him.

Caerwyn heard Jais' comment and nodded. She didn't really know what Jais had done, but her senses told her there were no more krolls trudging up behind her, and there had been two bright streams of light. She would ask him about it later, for now her attention was solely on the krolloc.

Her previous attempts at talking to the krolloc, distracting it, had allowed her time to recoup some energy. She could feel that vigor slipping away now though, fighting this thing required a lot of movement and effort. She needed to finish it off quickly.

With two hands on Barami's sword she kept the krolloc moving by swinging the long blade and dancing around its attempts to crush her. Several more times it reached out and made a grabbing motion at the air, but nothing happened to her. She wasn't going to question it, not while in battle, but she was thankful that whatever the krolloc was trying to do wasn't working.

Around the room they moved. She cut chunks out of it, while it grew weaker and weaker. It landed one solid blow on her. A fist slammed down on her, and she didn't have time to move out of the way, she blocked with her sword and hoped her muscles would hold. The sword bit deep into the thing's fist, and the force of its strike slammed her down to her knees. She had to use two hands, one on the blade of the sword to keep the blade from chopping down on her as well. Still the blade had come down at her. She'd had to lean back to avoid it splitting her head. Instead it bit into her chest, scoring a line of pain, but that was where the force of the blow dissipated, and she was able to throw the fist off after that and scramble to her feet again. Her one hand was bleeding now from a deep gash, as was the long cut across the top of her chest. But still she charged in at the krolloc, unrelenting. Her energy was waning. This needed to end... now.

Both of its ankles were chewed up. She kept working on them, hoping to bring the big thing off its feet.

She saw her chance and took it. The krolloc had stepped forward with its left foot and wavered slightly, she dove in, rolling and came up with a swing of all her might to that ankle.

For a heart-rending moment the sword stuck, unmoving.

Then the krolloc's own fist slammed into her once again. The force of its own hit drove her sword through its ankle.

It bellowed as she rolled away from its crushing blow.

She'd been knocked to one side of it and for a moment she couldn't breathe. Her vision blurred. Her back and right side were awash in pain, sharp and stinging, broad and throbbing, it was nearly too much. But her mind registered the sight before her, the krolloc fell to its knees, its head turned back, mouth open in a bellow of pain, though she didn't really register the noise.

But it wasn't dead.

She grimaced as she tried to rise, but pain lanced through her and darkness danced around her vision, threatening a blackout. She couldn't risk it.

Desperate she called for Davlas, but the spear did not come. She had no other ranged weapon... except...

She dug into a pouch and pulled out her sling and a smooth stone.

She still had one good arm, so she propped herself up to a sitting position and loaded the sling, quickly getting it up to speed. She wasn't as accurate with her left hand, but she prayed to Davul, the god who had guided her spear so many times, and let the stone fly.

It sank into the krolloc's good eye as the beast was regaining itself. It was a small thing, nearly insignificant against a creature so large, but yet again the krolloc wailed in pain, covering its eye.

But it still hadn't been enough.

"Caer, my sword!"

She knew that voice.

Without really knowing where he was, other than off to her right, she slid the sword along the rocky ground to where Barami must have made his way over to her. Rolling her head to one side she caught sight of him. He looked worse than she felt. But he picked up his sword slowly and for a moment seemed to glance from it to the krolloc, as if gathering the courage to do... something.

Then he cried a wordless yell of desperation and determination and ran an awkward hobbling charge toward the beast, raising his sword high and holding it with both hands, blade out before him in a reversed grip. He jumped so he could catch the thing in the chest and caught it unaware. The sword drove deep into the thing's chest. It toppled backwards with a useless swing in Barami's direction.

Despite the pain, Caerwyn lifted her head to watch the

beast fall. Then she saw something which made her smile, teeth still clenched from the soreness radiating through her.

JAIS HAD BEEN ON HIS HANDS AND KNEES, TRYING TO FIND SOME semblance of strength or at least catch his breath to help Caerwyn. But all he felt like doing was collapsing into a long sleep.

He too heard Barami's cry and lifted his head to see what the man was doing. In his condition, any sort of attack would be crazy.

What Jais saw was more than he expected.

The krolloc, on its knees, loomed close. When had it gotten here? Had he been so distracted he hadn't noticed it? He scrambled to pick up his swords from where he'd laid them on the ground. But it was facing away from him and wasn't a threat... yet

But then Barami hit the thing in the chest sinking his large sword so deep the tip of it, just an inch or so, pricked out of the thing's back. Then the krolloc fell backward... toward Jais.

He raised his swords, blades crossed above him, in a desperate block. His father's sword blazed to life with light as the krolloc's neck caught the two blades. Jais couldn't take the impact and was pushed flat...

But not before he'd seen his swords sever the head of the krolloc. It bounced once, then rolled away.

Jais lay, semi-pinned by the heavy body of the beast, its viscous black blood leaking onto him, but he didn't much care.

It was dead.

And by some miracle all three of them were still alive... he hoped.

Where was Caerwyn?

He didn't have the strength to get up, but he rolled his head around and caught sight of her, half-propped up, looking beaten and battered, but smiling grimly at him.

He smiled back... then he blacked out.

Two weeks later, thanks to the increased healing of a drahksan, they were close to well again. Barami was a different story.

Caerwyn had been the only one able to do anything of consequence after the battle. Knowing that the krolloc might have called some krolls back to the cave, she'd dragged the other two, both unconscious, to a smaller cave. Then she too had collapsed and rested.

But she needn't have bothered moving them. There was no sign that anyone had been back to the larger cave when they checked later.

Once they were feeling strong enough, Jais and Caerwyn had carried Barami back to the statue of Thadros for him to touch it and be healed. For whatever reason, it hadn't done much. There was some minor effect, but nothing as strong as the first time. So even with Jais' healing during the battle, the aged human would need a lot of time to recover.

Jais had said that suited him well as he couldn't leave just yet.

They left Barami to heal, and Caerwyn went with Jais as he tended to what he referred to as 'his duties'. First they found the body of his uncle and buried the man. A grave in the forest would have suited the huntsmen well enough. They found a quiet glade with a spot of sun, dug up a sapling growing in the spot then Jais had replanted the tree over his uncle's body.

As he stood there over the man's grave he told her, "Uncle Perrick taught me to take only what was needed from the forest." He'd sniffed away some tears and with a sad smile said, "Even in death my uncle will give back to the forest. His body will help feed this tree, make it strong. I think Perrick's spirit would appreciate that."

They had searched for Alnia's body, but found nothing.

Then Jais had returned to his home. It was a shambles and mostly burned down, but he dug through what remained for the better part of a day, coming out with some not-as-charred clothes and a jar of his aunt's healing gel he'd found rolling on the floor. He'd brought out a few other items as well, personal things, and stuffed it all into a pack.

Caerwyn watched him, his face grim. He knew he wouldn't be coming back here for a while... perhaps ever. She sighed for his loss. He'd lost so much: his aunt and uncle, his love, his home, his village.

She couldn't understand it, but he'd insisted on going to see Klasten's Green as well. So, they had made their way to a hill overlooking the village and there they lay watching the activity below.

There seemed like precious few people.

But they were rebuilding.

"Where did the krolls go?" Jais asked shaking his head in confusion.

Caerwyn shrugged. "My best guess is that they went their own way once the krolloc was dead. It was his influence over them which was making them act as a unit. It must have been. It's the only explanation for why they would have acted as they did, fighting together, helping each other. When the krolloc died they would have gone back to their own ways and probably began fighting amongst themselves as much as anyone else. You saved your village, Jais."

Though she wasn't sure how much of a consolation that was, given what the village had done.

After they had lain there for some time, Jais finally sighed a heavy breath and said, "Let's go."

So it was that Caerwyn took this boy from the only home he'd ever known.

In the back of her mind her initial reason for coming here... coming to him, niggled at her. She wouldn't bring it up now. It wasn't the time. Perhaps she never would. How could she ask more of this young man who'd given everything he had?

Three weeks later, with Barami mostly recovered, they'd moved on.

Then, one afternoon a few days after that, as they travelled a rough wagon-way, with a peaceful river on one side and a sparse forest on the other, Jais spoke.

"Caer?"

It was odd to hear him call her by the shortened name which only Barami had ever used. It was the first time he had. Perhaps he felt familiar enough with her now to do so. She searched her feelings about this closeness and found she liked him using the nickname.

"Yes?"

He let out a bit of a laugh, it wasn't much and it wasn't

really mirthful, but it was the most hopeful emotion he'd shown since leaving. "You came here to find me, right? To... mate with me?"

It felt suddenly awkward to have him saying those words. She was thankful Barami was up ahead, scouting the trail.

She swallowed a lump in her throat. She could get over this awkwardness. She'd been a general for the gods' sakes. "Yes."

"Do you still want that?"

Did she?

They walked in silence for a while as she considered. The truth was that despite everything that had happened she still wanted a child. Whether it was with him or not...? She wasn't sure.

"I still want to have a child, a drahksan child, yes, but I don't feel I have any right to ask such a thing of you. I'm sure we'll find other drahksani, eventually."

He nodded. "Good. You're a friend. I've been through too much with you for you not to be. I..." He hesitated for a long moment. "I don't know if I'm ready to have a child... yet. But I think that, perhaps, if you still wanted one when I am ready, I might be... I could be the man you... have it with."

She nodded. "Then I'll wait."

He smiled over at her, a genuine, kind smile, and it warmed her heart.

But perhaps she wouldn't have to use Jais in that way. Already she was sensing another drahksani somewhere ahead. The pull wasn't as strong as Jais' had been, but it was something.

So, they walked together, side by side, but still... distant as their shadows stretched long on the road before them.

And a new thought began to bud within Caerwyn's mind.

Perhaps in addition to a child she had a new quest: to find other drahksani and help restore her race to glory once more.

To learn more about R. Michael's books and to sign up for his newsletter to receive exclusive announcements and new release notifications visit: www.rmichaelcard.com

OTHER BOOKS BY R. MICHAEL CARD

BLOOD OF DRAGONS

Book 1: Soul Seeking

The King's Outlaw

GUARDIANS OF LIGHT

Book 1: The Last Scion

Book 2: Scion Rising

Book 3: Scion's Sacrifice

TALES OF THE SEVEN KINGDOMS

The Goblin King

The Swordmaster's Apprentice

ABOUT R. MICHAEL CARD

R. Michael Card has loved fantasy since he read his first Dragon Lance book so many years ago. He has been writing for twenty years but has only recently decided to start sharing his work with the world. He has always enjoyed the lighter side of epic fantasy, the grand adventure, and has infused that love into his works.

He lives near Toronto, Ontario with his beloved wife and their cat. He has had a plethora of careers, working in software, insurance, trades, and education, with jobs ranging from washing cars to career counseling.